WHO

"Smart, sophisticated, [...] cal mystery is captiva[...] and compelling from its irresistible beginning to its unpredictable end."

—Hank Phillippi Ryan, author of the
award-winning Charlotte McNally Mysteries

"Didn't need my crystal ball to see into the future of this wonderful debut. A sexy, funny, and engaging whodunit set in Tinseltown. *Who Do, Voodoo?* is a winner."

—Lesley Kagen, national bestselling author of *Good Graces*

"A spellbinding blend of voodoo and tarot traditions. *Who Do, Voodoo?* is a superlative supernatural mystery."

—Cleo Coyle, author of the national bestselling
Haunted Bookshop and Coffeehouse mysteries

"A fresh and entertaining premise for a new series that is cleverly plotted and executed."   —*RT Book Reviews*

"Fans will enjoy accompanying the charming lead pair as they explore the supernatural."   —*The Mystery Gazette*

Berkley Prime Crime titles by Rochelle Staab

WHO DO, VOODOO?
BRUJA BROUHAHA

BRUJA BROUHAHA

ROCHELLE STAAB

BERKLEY PRIME CRIME, NEW YORK

THE BERKLEY PUBLISHING GROUP
Published by the Penguin Group
Penguin Group (USA) Inc.
375 Hudson Street, New York, New York 10014, USA

Penguin Group (Canada), 90 Eglinton Avenue East, Suite 700, Toronto, Ontario M4P 2Y3, Canada
(a division of Pearson Penguin Canada Inc.) • Penguin Books Ltd., 80 Strand, London WC2R 0RL,
England • Penguin Group Ireland, 25 St. Stephen's Green, Dublin 2, Ireland (a division of Penguin
Books Ltd.) • Penguin Group (Australia), 250 Camberwell Road, Camberwell, Victoria 3124, Australia
(a division of Pearson Australia Group Pty. Ltd.) • Penguin Books India Pvt. Ltd., 11 Community
Centre, Panchsheel Park, New Delhi—110 017, India • Penguin Group (NZ), 67 Apollo Drive,
Rosedale, Auckland 0632, New Zealand (a division of Pearson New Zealand Ltd.) • Penguin Books
(South Africa) (Pty.) Ltd., 24 Sturdee Avenue, Rosebank, Johannesburg 2196, South Africa

Penguin Books Ltd., Registered Offices: 80 Strand, London WC2R 0RL, England

This is a work of fiction. Names, characters, places, and incidents either are the product of the author's
imagination or are used fictitiously, and any resemblance to actual persons, living or dead, business
establishments, events, or locales is entirely coincidental. The publisher does not have any control over
and does not assume any responsibility for author or third-party websites or their content.

BRUJA BROUHAHA

A Berkley Prime Crime Book / published by arrangement with the author

PUBLISHING HISTORY
Berkley Prime Crime mass-market edition / August 2012

Copyright © 2012 by Rochelle Staab.
Cover illustration by Blake Morrow.
Cover design by Diane Kolsky.
Interior text design by Laura K. Corless.

ISBN: 978-0-425-25149-2

BERKLEY® PRIME CRIME
Berkley Prime Crime Books are published by The Berkley Publishing Group,
a division of Penguin Group (USA) Inc.,
375 Hudson Street, New York, New York 10014.
BERKLEY® PRIME CRIME and the PRIME CRIME logo are trademarks of Penguin Group
(USA) Inc.

PRINTED IN THE UNITED STATES OF AMERICA

10 9 8 7 6 5 4 3 2 1

ALWAYS LEARNING   **PEARSON**

For Flo and Romie

ACKNOWLEDGMENTS

My warmest gratitude goes out to the friends and pros who generously lent me their time and expertise along the way: Viva Barkowski, Lynn Sheene, Pat Sadowski, Adilia Cordero, Holly Adams, Charlie Springer, Sylvia Tchakerian, Diane Fuller, Pat Sabatini, Carole Bloom, Lara Nance, Steve Shrager, Greg Reid, JoAn Brown, Doreen Klee/Jewish Family Service of Los Angeles, Officer Paul Ricchiazzi/LAPD, Officer Michael Lewis/LAPD, and Alfred and Max from the Los Angeles Gang Tour. And a very special thank-you to my wonderful editor, Michelle Vega. Group hug.

Chapter One

Nick Garfield, my boyfriend and college professor of mainstream, arcane, and bizarre forms of religion, took four chunks of unshelled coconut from the Santeria altar and set them in my hand. "Your turn to ask a question, Liz. Obi cannot lie."

Nick's interest in the supernatural was academic; my interest in the supernatural was zero. But I didn't want to insult our elderly hosts, Paco and Lucia Rojas, both devout Santeria practitioners. And after six months of dating him, Nick's playful, gold-flecked brown eyes could get me to do pretty much anything. What harm could a little Saturday-night fortune-telling game among good friends be?

We were gathered for a triple celebration dinner in the Rojases' apartment above their botanica near MacArthur Park. Celebration Number One: Paco and Lucia's sixtieth wedding anniversary.

The Rojases' living room, aged with use and seasoned by six decades of marriage, felt as comfortable as a grandmother's hug. An old television Paco called his "front seat for Dodger games" sat on a metal cart in the corner behind two rose jacquard armchairs. The scent from the fresh gardenias on the mahogany dining table circled around worn furniture, over the candlelit altar in front of the window, and across to the mahogany desk where a yellowing photo of a slender, handsome Paco in a black suit with the ravishing young Lucia in a tight-waist, satin wedding dress was prominently displayed.

The other two guests—the midsixties, vibrant, and brilliant Dr. Carmen Perez; and her business partner, the dignified, white-haired Dr. Victor Morales—had performed the coconut shell ritual with Nick while I prepped dinner with Lucia in the kitchen. Celebration Number Two: Lucia taught nondomestic me how to make homemade tamales. We were gathered to feast on the results.

I juggled the coconut between my palms. "Some background on this Obi person? Just so I know what to ask him?"

It was like I handed Nick a microphone. He squared his shoulders and pulled at the cuffs of his tweed sport coat. "Obi is the mouthpiece of the orishas who manifest Olodumare, the omniscient high-being in Santeria and other Yoruba religions. The shells are the voice Obi employs to foretell the future. A divination tool."

He lost me after the second *O* deity but I got the gist. I said, "Let's see how tactful Obi is. Will my first lesson at cooking tamales be a culinary success?" I tossed the coconut onto the white lace coverlet on the altar. The four shells fell brown skin up.

Carmen arched a brow. Nick shifted his stance. Victor pressed his lips together, looking as clueless as I felt.

Paco, whose robust girth was a testament to Lucia's excellent cooking, swept up the coconut with a rough hand and dropped the pieces into the bowl of water on the altar. "You didn't teach Liz the incantation. The answer means nothing. Obi is teasing her."

Before I could ask why Obi teased me, petite Lucia scurried out of the kitchen and set a salad bowl the size of a bicycle tire on the dining table. Her dyed strawberry red hair was rolled into a bun at the nape of her neck; wisps of white roots haloed her hairline. "Liz, bring out your tamales. Paco, open the wine. Everyone else, sit down. It's time to eat."

I pulled Nick into the kitchen with me and took a bright yellow platter from the cupboard. As I stacked the tamales onto the plate I said, "Okay, Professor, explain. What did the four brown sides up mean?"

"Nothing. Not relevant. You didn't ask the right question."

"Liar. You didn't say anything about right or wrong questions," I said.

He put his arm around my shoulder. "Sorry. There are only four answers and none of them have to do with food."

"You egged me on to ask a question. Now I want to know the answer," I said.

"You rolled Oyekun. Death."

"Death? For dinner?" I laughed. "I know my cooking isn't *that* bad."

3

* * *

We sat at the round dining table set with silver, crystal wineglasses, and green, blue, white, and yellow Talavera dinnerware. The scent of garlic and onions drifted off the steaming plate of tamales in the middle. A romantic Mexican ballad played from the turntable in the corner.

Paco filled our wineglasses from a bottle of Monte Xanic Cabernet Sauvignon, and then raised his glass in a toast. His wide, toothy smile lifted his wiry silver mustache and crinkled his dark brown eyes. "To Liz and my Lucia for this wonderful dinner."

"To Liz and Lucia." We clinked our glasses together and drank.

Victor said, "To Paco and Lucia. Happy sixtieth anniversary."

"To Paco and Lucia," we echoed.

"You know how to stay happy with a woman for sixty years, Nick?" Paco said.

Nick scratched his chin. "Don't get married?"

I glanced sideways at my bachelor boyfriend.

"No," Paco said. "You listen to her. Let her know you'll be there for her."

"He's right." Carmen pointed at herself. "I was happily married for forty years."

I chuckled. "To four different husbands: Uncle Bill, Uncle Jim, Uncle—"

"They weren't your uncles, sweetie, and I *was* happy with each and every one of them. Happy to be with them and happy to divorce them," Carmen said.

Carmen and I weren't related by blood but she was family. In the sixties she and my mother became best friends as members of the Cherry Twists—six go-go dancers on *Hollywood Hop*, a Los Angeles TV dance show. All of the Cherries were at the hospital the day I was born, and they were a constant presence in my parents' home as my older brother, Dave, and I grew up.

Hollywood Hop helped pay Carmen's way through medical school. She dedicated her general practice to Latino community, and ten years ago she founded Park Clinic, a small multicultural outpatient clinic she and Victor ran across the street from Botanica Rojas.

The Cherries provided our reason for Celebration Number Three: in ten days my mother and her friends would host a gala to raise money for Park Clinic's plumbing upgrade, including the installation of public-access showers for the homeless in the area.

I raised my glass. "I'd like to offer a toast to Carmen, Victor, and Park Clinic. May your fund-raiser be a huge success."

"To hot showers," Carmen said.

"And copper plumbing," Victor added as we drank.

We passed the plate of homemade tamales and the bowl of Lucia's tangerine and jicama salad around the table. I unwrapped a corn husk and took a bite of its steaming contents, savoring the taste of sweet cornmeal and tender meats seasoned with onions, garlic, and a kick of chile. Another quick bite, then I dared to check the faces of my victims, er, fellow diners. Nick and Victor chewed with nods of happy approval. Paco gave me a thumbs-up.

Carmen let out a moan, her eyes closed. "Divine."

"All the credit goes to Lucia, my excellent teacher." I smiled across the table. Lucia beamed back with pride.

Victor finished two tamales, asked for a third, and then said, "What happened to the lock in the hall downstairs, Paco? Why the slide bolt?"

"Damn, smart-ass, punk gang members broke the lock a few nights ago," Paco said. "Locksmith won't have the replacement parts until Monday. The slide bolt works good."

"Except you have to run up and down the steps to lock and unlock it every time someone comes or goes," Lucia said, reaching for another tamale.

"What do you want me to do, *mi belleza*? I won't leave the door open."

"How do you know the vandals were gang members?" Nick said.

Paco stabbed his fork into his salad. "Who else?"

"We have an alarm on the botanica door loud enough to summon Santa Muerte," Lucia said.

"If we remember to set it," Paco said.

Nick wiped his mouth with a napkin. "How is business, Paco?"

"We cut back the hours." Paco relaxed in his chair. "I don't want Lucia working so hard anymore. She likes to keep the shop open for the neighbors, but we do most of our trade selling herbs in bulk to the other botanicas in town. I get a lot of offers from real estate agents who want us to sell the building, but we won't." He pointed at Lucia. "She won't allow it."

"And neither will you," Lucia said. "This is our home. Those people would tear our building down like they tore down the rest of the buildings on this block. You want to move away and leave our customers to shop with the gangsters at Oscar Estevez's botanica?"

"I don't want to talk about Oscar at the dinner table. I handle gangsters like him my own way," Paco said.

Victor arched his brows. "Does that mean you decided to run for neighborhood council, Paco? People would listen to you."

"At my age?" Paco's laugh shook his shoulders. "Never. I like being the loudmouthed codger at council meetings. If the councilmen want to shut me up, they can move the gangs out of Westlake. Throw them in jail where they belong. And take Oscar Estevez, too."

"I wish they would." Lucia gazed wistfully toward the windows behind the altar. The pink glare of streetlights shone through the white lace curtains. "Westlake was safe and so beautiful when Paco and I met. We could sit outside on the stoop at night. Nobody locked their doors. When the gangs took over and brought in the prostitutes and drug dealers, people got scared and stayed inside. Our sidewalks are deserted at night now. Tourists stopped visiting the park."

"The city works hard to make the streets and MacArthur Park safe," Carmen said. "Victor and I wouldn't be renovating the clinic if we didn't believe in this neighborhood. The Metro station brought some of the tourists back." She turned to me. "Liz, you're getting to know some of the local women in your sessions at the clinic. What do you think of them so far, sweetie?"

My Saturday Wellness Group—weekly group therapy sessions to counsel women through stress—was Carmen's brainchild. She approached me in March to start the group and I agreed without hesitation, enthused to expand my practice into community service and work with her.

"The women are wonderful. Lively. Interesting. We had three more sign-ups last week. The group dynamic has good energy," I said.

"You bring good energy with you," Victor said.

I grinned at Victor, my prediction to become Carmen's hubby number five. An easy guess on my part: at my mother's holiday party in December, the two longtime friends kissed, not so platonically, under the mistletoe where Nick and I spent most of the evening.

Paco passed me the platter of tamales. "Liz, are you going to Mexico with Nick this summer to visit my friends in the mountains? The guesthouse is next to their ceremonial fire pit. I hope the late-night moaning doesn't keep you up."

"We eventually fall asleep." Nick winked at me.

"Mexico?" I said, cheeks burning with embarrassment.

"Paco put me in touch with a group of *brujos*—Mexican witches—in Catemaco in the Tuxtlas mountain region. I thought you might like to take a research trip there with me in July. It was going to be a surprise." Nick grinned. "Surprise."

"How romantic," Carmen said. "A getaway in the tropics hosted by witches. Oh." She suppressed a belch. "Excuse me."

"Your stomach?" Victor touched her arm.

I stopped chewing and winced. Damn, those coconut shells better not be right.

Carmen waved Victor away then turned to me. "Not the food, sweetie. My gallbladder is acting up. Your delicious

tamales were worth a little agitation. I'll just take an ant-
acid."

"You promised to get an ultrasound at the hospital on
Monday," Victor said.

"Yes, Doctor. I'll be there. Thank you for reminding me
and announcing it to our friends, Doctor," Carmen said with
sarcasm.

Victor mimicked her. "And I'm going with you, Doctor."

Carmen touched her finger to his lips. "Shush. Enough
about my health. Tonight we dance. Paco promised to teach
Liz the salsa."

We cleared the table and moved the furniture against the
wall, creating a small dance floor. Lucia selected a vinyl
album from her collection beneath the turntable, put the
black disc in place, and dropped the needle on a raucous
Mexican number. Paco and Lucia demonstrated the salsa
cheek to cheek, breaking apart only to twirl under each
other's arms. Carmen swayed to the beat with Victor. When
the next song began, Paco pulled me onto the floor.

"Wiggle your hips, Liz. The salsa comes from here."
Paco pounded his heart. "And from there." He smacked my
behind. "Follow me. Quick-quick-slow, and five-six-seven,
and . . ." He gripped my right hand and guided me across
the floor. His forehead glistened under wisps of white hair
as we moved together.

Nick and Lucia clapped to the rhythm, calling out,
"Salsa!"

I loosened my body to fall into the beat, laughing as Paco
guided me back and forth and then turned me under his arm.
In the middle of the song, a buzzer sounded near the door.

Paco bowed then passed my hand to Nick. He went to the intercom and pressed the button. "*Hola.*"

A hearty female voice sounded through the speaker. "Paco, it's Teresa. I'm outside. Will you unlatch the door?"

"Coming down," Paco said.

As he left the apartment, Lucia called behind him, "Tell Teresa we saved tamales for her dinner."

Nick slipped his hand around my waist and pulled me close while the music played. He touched his forehead to mine. We swayed, our bodies pressed together. He whispered in my ear, "Do you know how sexy you are?"

The sound of a distant gun blast outside echoed through the doorway.

Then a scream.

Chapter Two

The scream cut through the music. I pulled at Nick as he started toward the door. "That sounded like gunfire, Nick. You can't—"

"Paco's out there. Stay inside. Call the police." He flew into the hall with Victor behind him.

I darted for my purse and phone. Dialing 911, I dashed behind Carmen and Lucia into the bedroom. As we looked out the window overlooking the street, my stomach clenched. Nick and Victor knelt on the sidewalk beside Paco, his pale yellow shirt steeped in blood, and the still body of a dark-haired youth.

My heart hammering, I related the details to the emergency operator. "I heard one gunshot but I see two victims on the ground." I gave her the address then rushed through the apartment, out to the corridor, and into the stairwell leading to the vestibule and the street.

Carmen preceded me down the stairs and she ran out the door faster than I believed a woman in her sixties could move. Lucia took the steps slowly, clutching the rail. Below us, a woman in a black sweater, yellow uniform pants, and sneakers cowered in the vestibule.

"Teresa, what happened?" Lucia said.

Teresa's chest heaved as she gulped for air. Her words came in sobs: "A drive-by. They shot Paco and José."

We hastened past Teresa and went outside. Lucia clawed Victor out of the way and crumpled to her knees next to Paco. Her keen anguish sliced through my heart like a razor.

Sirens wailed. Within seconds an ambulance and fire truck stopped at the curb. EMTs and firemen filled the sidewalk. Two LAPD patrol cars pulled up, blocking traffic. A small crowd gathered across the street. Carmen pulled Lucia away from Paco and cradled her as the EMTs set to work.

Medical technicians checked the wounds, pulse, and airways of both men. Paco's eyes were open and rolled back. José's chest was a massive open wound.

The EMT with Paco said to his partner, "Jesus. I think this is a shotgun wound. Brutal."

Teresa hovered beside me, fixated on the technicians bent over Paco and José. I touched her shoulder. She didn't budge.

"Your friend. José? Is there someone we can call to be with him?" I said.

"I only met him a few days ago." A tear rolled down her check. "He's just a kid. A nice kid."

"Do you know his last name?" I said.

"Saldivar. His name is José Saldivar. He ate at the

12

Chicken Shack the last few nights, came in right before closing. He told me he worked nearby."

"Where?" I said, hoping we could locate family or a friend. Paco had us. José was alone. I couldn't stand that he was alone.

Teresa shrugged ignorance. "All I know is that he takes the train to Boyle Heights. He walked me home on his way to the MTA station." She pointed toward the station, two blocks west.

"Did he tell you *anything* about his family? Who he lives with?" I said.

"The Chicken Shack is a couple blocks from here." She thumbed to the east. "We talked about nothing. The weather, the Lakers. He's just a kid . . ."

As the EMTs worked over Paco, I hoped against logic to see him sit up, move, or speak. Their frantic efforts seemed to move in surrealistic slow motion with only Lucia's muffled sobs cutting through the rapt silence. Agonizing moments later, Paco and José were pronounced dead at the scene. Lucia let out an agonizing wail. Carmen and Victor folded her into a protective embrace. I watched, stunned, as blue tarps were placed over the bodies.

Teresa backed up against the window of Botanica Rojas. Nick came to my side and we held each other tight until a young LAPD officer approached the three of us.

"Did any of you witness the shooting?"

"I did," Teresa said, her eyes focused on the covered bodies a few feet away.

He took her name. "Tell me what happened."

"José and I were talking on the sidewalk," she said, looking up. "Paco came out and started to say something to us. A car came around that corner." Teresa pointed up the block. "I saw a shotgun barrel come out the back window. I heard a shot. Paco and José fell. I thought they were gonna shoot me, too. I screamed and ran inside."

"What was the make and color of the car?" the policeman said.

She hesitated.

"Ma'am?"

"The car was black," Teresa said. "One of those big black SUVs. The windows were tinted black."

"Follow me," he said. "I need you to wait over there for a detective."

Carmen and I took Lucia upstairs to the apartment. She knelt at the Santeria altar under the window, rocking back and forth with her hands folded to her forehead. Nick followed and turned off the salsa music still playing on the turntable. Carmen fell into an armchair with her arms wrapped around her stomach, watching Lucia. Victor, his hands and shirt bloody, came in and went straight into the kitchen.

We sat or wandered around the room in shocked silence. I kept my eyes on Lucia. As a psychologist, I was trained in emotional trauma and knew there was nothing immediate I could do or say to erase her pain. All I could do was be there for her.

The door buzzer jolted the stillness. Nick answered the intercom and waited until a tall, fortyish detective in a rumpled gray sport coat appeared at the apartment door.

"I'm Detective Matt Bailey, LAPD," he said, showing his badge. "Can I come in? I'd like to talk to Mrs. Rojas."

Carmen rose from the armchair. "She's in shock, Detective."

"I understand. I won't take long," he said.

Bailey, lanky with dirty blond hair, approached Lucia with a gentle and apologetic manner. He crouched at her side. "Mrs. Rojas, I'm very sorry for your loss."

Lucia didn't move. "Leave me alone. Go talk to my husband. He's outside with Teresa."

"Mrs. Rojas, I—" Bailey said.

Victor came out of the kitchen and set his hands on Lucia's shoulders. "I'm Mrs. Rojas's physician, Detective. Do you have to do this now? It's not a good time."

"I understand. I'm sorry, Mrs. Rojas." Bailey straightened. "Where can the rest of us talk?"

We filed into the dimly lit corridor. Victor leaned against the doorjamb with an eye on Lucia inside.

Bailey jotted our names in his notebook. "I know how difficult this is, but I need statements from you while your memory is fresh. My partner took Teresa Suarez to the station to go through photographs. I'd like your account of what happened tonight, and some background. Where were you when the shooting took place?"

Nick summarized the evening up to the point the buzzer rang, then said, "Paco went downstairs to unbolt the door for Teresa."

"After Paco left, we heard the shot," I said.

"And Teresa's scream," Carmen said.

"Teresa. Are you talking about Teresa Suarez, the witness?" Bailey said.

"Yes. She lives in the apartment at the end of the hall," Carmen said.

Bailey glanced down the corridor. "There's only one other door down there. How many tenants occupy the building?"

"There are only two apartments," Carmen said. "Mr. and Mrs. Rojas live in front. Teresa lives alone in the back."

"Teresa doesn't have a key to the door downstairs?" Bailey said.

"The lock was broken a few days ago," Victor said. "Paco installed a temporary slide bolt."

"Who broke the lock?" Bailey said, writing in his notebook.

"Vandals." Victor folded his arms.

Bailey lifted his eyes. "Was the break-in reported to the police?"

"No."

"Did Mr. Rojas have any enemies?" Bailey said.

"Of course not. Paco was an old man," Victor said through clenched teeth. "Why the hell would anyone shoot him? Why are you asking us this? Obviously they were after the kid. Who was he? What do you know about him?"

Bailey flipped through his notes. "José Saldivar. Did any of you know him?"

Nick and I shook our heads.

"I don't—didn't," Carmen said.

"No," Victor said. "I've never seen him before. And I know most of the boys from this neighborhood."

"What about Teresa Suarez?" Bailey said. "What can you tell me about her?"

"She waitresses at the Chicken Shack during the week and works part-time for Dr. Morales and me at Park

Clinic on Saturdays," Carmen said. "She's a good girl. Does her job. Efficient. Doesn't complain. Always on time."

"Does Mrs. Suarez have any gang affiliations?" Bailey said.

Carmen and Victor exchanged glances.

"Teresa's husband is in jail," Victor said.

Bailey stopped writing. "For what?"

"Murder," Carmen said, glancing at Victor again. "He was sentenced for fifteen years to life for knifing a man in a bar fight five years ago."

"You mentioned vandalism on the door lock," Bailey said. "Did Mr. Rojas suspect anyone?"

Victor narrowed his eyes. "The gangs, of course. They intimidate everyone."

"I assure you, the gang unit will do a full investigation, Dr. Morales." Bailey closed his notepad. "I'll be back to talk to Mrs. Rojas in the morning. If any of you think of anything that could help, call me. I'm sorry for your loss." He gave each of us a card.

As Bailey turned to leave, I stopped him. "Why do you think they were shot, Detective?"

"I don't like to comment before I have facts," he said.

"I come from a family of police detectives. I know you have an initial theory or a guess."

Bailey shook his head. "You know as much as I do right now. The obvious theory would be the shooter was after either José Saldivar or Teresa Suarez or both, and Mr. Rojas got in the way. I need more information to sort out the details, so if you'll excuse me?"

Nick followed Bailey downstairs. I went inside and headed for the kitchen to make coffee. I needed to do something normal. Coffee was normal. As I filled the pot with tap water, Lucia walked in.

"My mind. How could we forget dessert, Liz?" She reached to the overhead cabinet and took out a platter. Then she went to the refrigerator and removed a metal mold. She took off the cover and flipped a flan onto the platter.

I turned off the faucet, stunned. Carmen had followed her in. We gaped as Lucia pulled a knife from the drawer.

"Don't just stand there with your mouths open, ladies. Take some plates and forks out to the table. Tell Paco to come in here and help me," Lucia said. "Where is that man?"

I gently took the knife out of her hand. "I'm sorry." I pressed my lips together, knowing I couldn't avoid the truth, even to ease her pain. "Paco's gone."

Lucia shook her head. "He's downstairs. He'll be back."

Carmen slipped an arm around her. "Paco's not coming back, sweetie. Leave the flan. Come. I want you to lie down." As she guided Lucia out of the kitchen, she turned to me. "Liz, there's a prescription bottle in my purse. Get it, will you? I want to give her a sedative to help her rest."

I brought the pills and a glass of water into the bedroom. Lucia lay on the bed, propped up by pillows, with Carmen at her side. Across the room, Paco's old burgundy sweater hung over the back of a chair. His slippers waited under the nightstand. My eyes roamed to each small reminder that Paco wouldn't be coming home. I pulled down the window shade. Below on the street, the police and EMTs waited for the coroner to arrive to take the covered bodies to the morgue.

"How is Lucia?" Nick said when I returned to the living room.

"Resting," I said. The word felt inadequate. Devastated came to mind. Shocked, hurt, and numb magnified beyond comprehension. I had no personal reference for what Lucia was going through. I studied the Kubler-Ross Five Stages of Grief in school, along with follow-up workshops with colleagues. But my shock over Paco's death and the resulting emotional toll on Lucia and the rest of his friends felt raw and unnerving.

I sat down at the dining table. "We can't leave Lucia here alone. Certainly not this week, and probably a lot longer."

Victor paced the room. "I'll stay with her. I know she needs us. Grief takes time to work through the body and, at her age, the shock and stress could be debilitating. I have her medical power of attorney. I promised Paco I would take care of her if anything should ever happen to him. I didn't think . . ." He rubbed his forehead. "I'll talk to her about hiring a live-in, someone to stay here with her."

Carmen came out of the bedroom. "She's asleep."

The four of us organized a schedule to stay with Lucia in shifts until Victor interviewed and hired a satisfactory live-in caretaker. Victor would sleep in the guest bedroom. Carmen would come mornings. Nick and I agreed to alternate afternoons.

Victor made a list of what needed to be done for Paco's funeral. The rest of us put the apartment back in order. Carmen washed the dishes. Nick moved the furniture back into place. I finished straightening the living room, and stopped in front of the Santeria altar. The four pieces of coconut were in the dish of water where Paco tossed them.

Obi cannot lie.

Chapter Three

When Nick and I left the apartment, a lone squad car was parked in front. Someone had left two hurricane candles burning on the bloodstained sidewalk. We climbed into Nick's SUV, drove west, and then north and onto the 101 Freeway toward our homes in the San Fernando Valley. Nick kept one hand on the steering wheel and held mine with the other. Exhausted, neither one of us spoke until we passed the Hollywood Boulevard exit.

Nick pounded his fist on the wheel. "I don't get it. There were three people on that sidewalk. Who was the target? José? Teresa? Paco? All three of them? From what Teresa said, Paco and José didn't know each other."

"Neither did Teresa and José, really."

"I want to know all about José Saldivar. I'm calling Dave in the morning," Nick said, referring to my brother Dave, a detective in RHD, the elite LAPD Robbery-Homicide Divi-

20

sion. They became best friends over twenty years ago as roommates at the University of Illinois.

I followed two years behind them at school, too young and too smitten with Jarret Cooper, the star pitcher on the U of I baseball team, to notice what a catch Nick was back then. Nick disappeared off my radar after he graduated. Two years later, I married my baseball star and spent over a decade moving from town to town, following his pro-baseball career while I studied for my PhD. My travels and marriage ended soon after Jarret was traded to the L.A. Dodgers four years ago.

By then Nick had moved to Los Angeles. He took a position teaching Religious Philosophy at NoHo Community College. I saw Nick occasionally when Dave dragged him to one of Mom's give-me-a-reason-to-throw-a-party soirées. We were friendly acquaintances until a psycho used voodoo to intimidate my friend Robin last year, and I asked Nick, an occult specialist, to help her. Together, Nick and I caught the psycho and fell in love. Like. Infatuation. To be confirmed.

Nick eased his car into the far right lane and took the Ventura Boulevard exit into Studio City. Pale lavender peeked at the base of the eastern horizon. He parked in front of my leased town house on Carpenter Avenue and walked me up the small flight of steps to my front door. "Get some sleep, Liz. It's going to be a long, rough week."

"None of it seems real, Nick. I'm devastated about Paco. My heart is breaking for Lucia. She doesn't have family to turn to."

"She has Victor and Carmen. And us. We'll take care of her. We'll get Lucia through this." Nick kissed me lightly.

"I'm sorry the weekend turned out this way. Would you like to spend next weekend together at my house?"

"I'd like that," I said. My kitten, Erzulie, mewed from behind the door. Her tiny radar ears could hear Nick from miles away. "Your little taupe friend with the whiskers will like it, too."

Late Monday morning, traffic zipped by on 7th Street as I rang the buzzer to Lucia's apartment. The two hurricane candles left on the sidewalk the night of the shooting were surrounded by flowers, more candles, and photographs of Paco, forming a makeshift memorial.

Carmen came downstairs and unlocked the door for me. She almost knocked the bag out of my hand as she enveloped me in a fierce hug. "I'm so glad you came early, sweetie. I promised Victor I wouldn't miss my ultrasound appointment at the hospital."

"How is your stomach?" I said.

"Let's not talk about it. I'm sure it's the stress."

I followed the familiar aroma of Carmen's vanilla-scented perfume upstairs. "How is Lucia?"

Carmen paused before we walked into the apartment. "Honestly? Hard to say."

Lucia tilted her up face from her chair beside the altar. Her skin was drawn, and her hair was tied in an unkempt knot. Dark circles framed her eyes. Her vacant stare broke my heart all over again. The fire was gone.

I held up the bag. "I brought you raspberries from the farmer's market. Your favorite, right?"

As if raspberries would help.

"Paco's favorite. Put them in the refrigerator. Thank you." She turned to his photo on the altar. "Raspberries for dessert tonight."

I opened the refrigerator, smiling at the stacks of aluminum-covered casserole dishes that lined the shelves.

"The neighbors were here in a steady stream yesterday," Carmen said from behind me. "Even Father Nuncio from Our Lady of the Wayside stopped for a visit." She lowered her voice. "Lucia won't talk about what happened yet. She told everyone Paco was downstairs with Teresa but she won't say anything else."

"Denial is the first stage of grief—a normal reaction." I tucked the berries into a bottom drawer and closed the fridge.

"To a point. Not appropriate for more than a few days," Carmen said. "We'll see. If she doesn't open up, maybe I should find a psychiatrist for her."

Her rush to judgment surprised me. "I think it is still a bit premature for a psychiatrist. I'm glad the neighbors came by. Contact with familiar people will help Lucia a lot more than drug therapy. Did Teresa visit?"

"No. Maybe she doesn't know what to say," Carmen said. "Is she home now?"

"She left for her shift at the Chicken Shack an hour ago. I tried to talk to her. She apologized, saying she was too late for work to talk." Carmen glanced at her watch. "Speaking of . . ."

"Go. I'm here as long as Lucia needs me. What's the word from Victor on the caretaker search?" I said.

"He just called. Tony found a referral from Father Nuncio. Victor is interviewing the woman this afternoon, and

23

if she's suitable, Lucia can meet her tomorrow," Carmen said.

Dr. Tony Torrico was Carmen and Victor's associate at Park Clinic. I nodded, impressed. "You can't ask for a better character reference than a local priest. What about the funeral? Do you and Victor need help with the arrangements?"

"We handled everything this morning. The funeral parlor will pick up Paco's body from the morgue and cremate him tomorrow. Fidencio offered his restaurant on Alvarado for the wake on Wednesday afternoon. Nick is hiring a town car to drive us to the funeral parlor, then to the wake. I'm having the memorial cards printed," Carmen said. "By the way, sweetie, don't wear black to the wake."

"Why?" I said, confused.

"Santeria followers believe black stirs negative energy. The wake is a celebration. Wear something colorful."

After Carmen left, I warmed up one of casseroles for lunch and tried to coax Lucia to eat. She didn't want to talk; I didn't force conversation. When the locksmith arrived to replace the downstairs lock, Lucia went to her room and closed the door.

The phone on the desk rang. I answered, "Rojas residence, this is Dr. Cooper."

"Mrs. Rojas?" The voice was young, female, and chirpy.

"No, I'm a family friend. Who's calling?"

"This is Marjorie from C&C Commercial Properties and Investments? I'm calling to confirm Mr. Rojas's appointment this afternoon?" Every sentence was a question with the girl. I wondered if she was a *Jeopardy* fan.

"I'm sorry." I waited a beat, hating what had to be said. "Mr. Rojas passed away this weekend."

"Oh. I'm sorry. Well, um, will Mrs. Rojas keep the appointment then? Mr. Cansino can see her at four thirty?" Marjorie said.

"No," I said, disgusted by her callous indifference. "Mrs. Rojas is in mourning. What company is this again?"

"C&C? I can squeeze Mrs. Rojas in for a meeting with Mr. Cansino next week? How about Monday at three?"

I clenched my teeth. "Mrs. Rojas isn't scheduling appointments. Call back another time." I hung up.

Lucia wandered out of the bedroom, rubbing her eyes. "Teresa. There you are. Finally. I saved tamales for you in the freezer. Where's Paco?"

"I'm Liz." I took her hand. "Teresa's not here."

She studied my face. "Liz? I'm sorry. Paco teases me about my forgetfulness. Is Teresa still with him?"

"No, Lucia. She's not. Paco's not coming back. Can we talk about what happened Saturday night?"

Lucia dropped my hand and went back into the bedroom. She didn't come out until Victor arrived at five thirty.

The Chicken Shack was on the corner of 7th and Burlington Avenue, two blocks east of the Rojases' building. Because I'm a native Angeleno, I drove. Because it was rush hour it took ten minutes to get there.

I entered the small restaurant, wrinkling my nose at the heavy smell of grease. Glass-tented steam tables filled with pans of chicken and side dishes lined two of the walls. A solo male diner followed me with his eyes from a booth at the window. The rest of the six tables were empty.

A "CASH ONLY" sign was taped on the cash register where Teresa waited on a customer. She wore her dark brown hair off her face, secured with a hair clip. Her heavy eyeliner and eye shadow failed to mask her puffy eyes.

She handed the man a bag of food and change, closed the register, then said to me, "Do you want to order something?"

"I'm Liz Cooper. Do you remember me from Saturday night?"

"I remember." She wiped the counter with a rag, emotionless. "What do you want?"

"I came to see how you're doing," I said, smiling to engage her. Everyone deals with pain differently and Teresa seemed to be using the ignore-it-and-it-will-go-away method. "How do you feel? I'm surprised you're back at work."

"I feel like crap but I can't afford to miss a day's work. I need the money. Surprise—they don't pay me to stay home and feel sorry for myself," she said.

"Lucia is having a hard time, too," I said. "Teresa, she thinks Paco is with you."

A sad smile flickered across Teresa's face, and for a moment, I saw how much she cared about the old man.

"I know if you visit Lucia you could help her."

She put her hands on her hips. "What am I supposed to say? I'm sorry? I'm sorry I wasn't shot instead?"

"No. If she wants to, you could talk about Paco with her. Help her get through this. She asks for you, Teresa."

"I thought I recognized you the other night. I know who

you are now. You're the new shrink at the clinic. You run the Wellness Group on Saturdays. What are you doing, recruiting me?"

I shook my head. "Not my intention at all. I came here for Lucia's sake. She's hurting. But the Wellness Group does help women work through stress. If you're interested in venting, everything said in group is confidential."

Teresa's eyes flashed. "Nothing in this neighborhood is confidential."

"Your call. But will you please go see Lucia?"

"I'll think about it." She bit her thumbnail.

Chapter Four

Honoring Paco's instructions and his wishes to be near her for eternity, Lucia shirked tradition, refused a conventional funeral, and had Paco cremated. Wednesday afternoon Victor and Carmen took Lucia to the mortuary, picked up Paco's ashes, and brought them to his wake.

As promised, Fidencio closed his Alvarado Street restaurant for the group of friends and neighbors gathered to celebrate Paco's life. I wore my brightest red party dress, setting my sadness aside to appreciate the kick Paco would have gotten from the high-spirited celebration in his honor.

Nick was with someone he knew at the bar. I stayed close to Lucia's table near the foot of the stage. Onstage behind me, silver-studded, black-suited mariachis accompanied by violins and trumpets serenaded the crowd. Little boys in stiff shirts and tiny girls in tutu dresses dashed through the dining area, hiding under the tablecloths. Adults with plates of enchiladas, tortillas, and beans from the banquet tables were stuffing their emotions with Fidencio's excellent food. The white-jacketed waiters hustled to keep pitchers of sangria flowing as the crowd toasted to Paco and to life.

Teresa waltzed through the crowd in a body-hugging royal blue sheath. She sashayed toward the stage, saw me, and then hung a sharp right toward the bar. It wasn't the first time someone had avoided me at a funeral. Rough to disguise feelings with a shrink at hand.

Seven water-filled goblets, candles, coins, cigars, bottles of tequila, and piles of fresh fruit surrounded the brass urn containing Paco's cremated ashes. Lucia, in a long white lace dress and mantilla, sat beside the urn with Carmen and Victor. Miguel, Park Clinic's security guard, knelt before Lucia swiping tears off his mustached face.

Victor appeared pallid and drained in his maroon sport coat and gray slacks. Carmen was striking in a splashy, low-cut, red and green print dress with her raven hair pulled behind her ears in jeweled clips.

I whispered to Carmen, "Why don't you and Victor take a break and get something to eat? I'm happy to sit with Lucia."

"You're a treasure, sweetie. Thank you." She leaned in. "She's been calm. Victor gave her a mild sedative before we went to the mortuary."

Carmen urged Victor away, leaving a vacant chair beside Lucia for me.

An elderly gent kissed Lucia's hand, and then removed a cigar from the pocket of his salmon guayabera—an island shirt with embroidered panels. Inhaling the aroma of the tobacco, he set the cigar at the foot of Paco's urn. "Smoke this slow, old man. Make it last until I join you."

The next in Lucia's stream of visitors was a man in his early fifties with groomed black hair and a strong forehead. His blue suit, tie, and white shirt were so crisply tailored I could almost smell the starch in his collar. He bent toward her with a smile that missed his eyes. "How are you, Lucia? You doing okay? If you need *anything*, you know you can call me."

Lucia squinted at him, unsure. "Do I know you?"

"It's Ray. Ray Cansino. Paco and I were good, good friends. We're going to get you through this, Lucia. Whatever you need, wherever you want to go, you let me know. We'll talk." Ray tucked a business card into her hand and left.

I stroked Lucia's back. She turned to me. "Do I know you?"

"Yes, Lucia, I'm your friend, Liz."

"Liz?" She stared at me until recognition lit her eyes. "Liz. I'm sorry. There are so many people I haven't seen for so long. My mind is playing tricks on me. Of course I know you." She cupped my face. "When are you and Nick getting married?"

I squirmed. "I don't know that we are."

"Nick is a good man. Don't waste a day you can be together. Where is he? Where is Nick? Did he come to the party with you?"

Party?

"Yes. He was just here a few minutes ago. Do you feel okay? Can I get you something to eat or drink?" I said.

"Not yet. Fidencio's is our favorite restaurant, you know. We came to the opening in nineteen sixty and we eat here every Sunday night. Fidencio even named a dish after Paco.

Those men in the band?" She pointed to the musicians, her eyes glistening. "Paco and I fed them candy when they were children. Everybody loves Paco. But he gave his heart only to me."

"I know. I'm so sorry, Lucia," I said.

"Sorry about what?"

"I'm sorry about Paco. The police are doing everything they can." I glanced at Detective Bailey across the room.

The reports Bailey gave us in the last few days were grim: a code of silence in the neighborhood hampered the investigation. After four days, the police still didn't know much about José Saldivar. Even my resourceful brother Dave came up short on information when Nick asked him about Saldivar's past.

"The police are useless," Lucia said. "My orishas tell me what to do."

I nodded, vaguely understanding her reference to the deities Santeria practitioners call on for help. Nick taught me the term when I asked him to explain the Santeria belief system. My utter confusion about the complex religion cleared when Nick likened the orishas to the pantheon of Greek and Roman gods.

A paunchy, baby-faced, middle-aged priest in black shirt and a white roman collar sat down at Lucia's side. "Mrs. Rojas, I bring condolences from the congregation at Our Lady of the Wayside. I'm offering a Mass in Paco's honor at ten on Sunday morning. Will you come?"

"I'll be home with Paco, Father Nuncio," Lucia said.

"If you change your mind I can have one of the parish council members pick you up and drive you to church."

Lucia stiffened. "I'm not going to change my mind. Your

parish council wants Paco and me to close Botanica Rojas. Tell your self-righteous, intolerant prudes to keep their distance unless they want to buy a Santeria spell from me."

I flinched. Father Nuncio didn't.

"Now Lucia," he said. "They don't feel that way. You know that you're very welcome at our parish."

I felt a tap on my shoulder and turned. Cruz DeSoto, the reed-thin, brunette caretaker Victor hired, stood by my side. Her thin lips, close-set eyes, and skinny nose were off-center on her square face, giving her a lopsided appearance. According to Victor, Cruz came to the job with extensive caretaking experience and solid references.

"I'll sit with Lucia if you want to get something to eat," Cruz said. "Carmen and Victor are close by. Don't worry. I'll watch her."

"Thank you. I won't be long." Smiling, I gave her my chair then scanned the crowd for Nick.

He wasn't hard to spot. Six feet, sandy haired, tan, and wearing a burnt rust guayabera, Nick towered over the man with him at the bar. The short fellow with a beer gut and a black pompadour left before I reached them.

"Who's your friend?" I said to Nick.

"My friend? Ah, that was the infamous Oscar Estevez, here to pay his respects."

"The Oscar Estevez that Lucia and Paco didn't like?"

"Didn't like is being generous. But yes, one and the same," Nick said.

"How do you know him?"

"His botanica caters to a certain Mexican cult I researched a few years ago. We're not friends, but we talk." Nick peered over my shoulder. "Who's with Lucia?"

"Father Nuncio and Cruz."

"I have to give Cruz credit for starting her new job the day of Paco's wake." Nick stepped back, giving me an admiring once-over. "Did I tell you today how beautiful you are?"

I tugged my scooped neckline to cover my peeking cleavage. "You did. But thank you again. I still feel like a tramp wearing a red party dress to a wake."

"Paco would approve. I certainly do," he said. "Sangria?"

"It's a little early. Are you trying to loosen me up?"

"Yes."

"Not going to happen." I cocked my head at the buffet. "I haven't eaten since breakfast. How about some food?"

"How about both? I'll get the drinks, you get the food, and I'll meet you at a table."

"Deal."

I sidetracked to the long buffet line near a middle-aged couple engaged in conversation. The two appeared as out of place at Paco's wake as country fans at a midnight rave. She wore a conservative black suit and pumps, and her brown hair was teased into a bubble. His heavy lids, flat nose, and droopy jowls reminded me of a bullmastiff.

"Must you eat, Bernie?" the woman said, turning her back to me. "Can't we give our condolences and leave? I feel like I'm sinning in this room of heathens. This whole affair is a sacrilege. You'd think Paco Rojas was a saint with the way these people are making offerings to his ashes."

"Zip it up, Erica. I was this close." He pinched his forefinger to his thumb. "I almost had Rojas warmed up to sell his building. I want Mrs. Rojas to know I paid my respects if—"

"You are not that crass," Erica said.

"I'm not stupid, woman. I'm not here to make a sales pitch. But I'm not the only Realtor here. Raymon Cansino just left."

My mind whirred, the pieces clicking into place. Raymon Cansino was the man who was just with Lucia. Mr. Cansino, as in the phone call I took on Monday. *Paco's good friend?* Curious.

"Selling that building won't mean anything if your soul ends up burning in hell," Erica said.

"You don't mind burning through my dough while we're still alive. Go and ask your Padre over there if you're sinning. He's not ashamed to be here."

"Father Nuncio is here? Where?" Erica craned her neck toward the guests. She gasped. "I don't believe it. Teresa Suarez has a lot of nerve to show up here."

"Who?" Bernie said.

"Over there." She pointed across the room at Teresa. "The woman in the blue dress."

"Nice rack," Bernie said. "What's the problem?"

"Paco Rojas is dead because of her loose morals. She was cheating on her gangster husband in broad daylight. Paco was outside with her and her lover that night. The second bullet hit him instead of Teresa. No wonder she's laughing. She tricked the devil."

"Her husband shot them?" Bernie said.

She tossed her hand. "His deputies or whatever they call them. Her husband ordered the hit from jail."

"Geez, how do you know all this?"

"My manicurist told me."

Bernie snorted. "The case is solved. Call the police and collect your reward."

I held back a grin. When waiters brought the line to a halt to exchange empty chafers for fresh servings of food from the kitchen, I stepped out of line to say hello to Detective Bailey at a nearby table.

"Nice of you to pay your respects, Detective. Or is this official business?"

"Maybe a little of both," he said, cocking his head.

"Do you think Paco's killer is here today?" I glanced through the room.

"Could be," he said. "Some gang members run the street from behind so-called legitimate businesses. I was across the river at the Saldivar funeral yesterday, same type of crowd, different territory. I'm curious if any of the same faces are here."

"And?" I said.

He cracked a smile. "And nothing. How is Mrs. Rojas?"

"She has moments when she accepts what happened, but she's still in shock. Dr. Morales has her on medication. Any updates on the investigation?"

"Nothing I can or want to talk about, Liz. Still looks like Paco was collateral damage in a revenge kill, and Mr. Saldivar and/or Mrs. Suarez was the intended victim." He tilted his head at Teresa, swaying in front of the band with a drink in her hand. "Although Mrs. Suarez doesn't seem too worried right now."

"Why shouldn't she dance? People work through their emotions however they can, Bailey."

"I stand corrected," he said.

"Is there anything Nick or I can do to help?"

"Call me if you or Mrs. Rojas remembers something salient." Bailey leaned in. "But don't let your law enforcement genes or curiosity steer you into unnecessary trouble. This is a rough neighborhood."

"Believe me, investigating murder is not on my mind. But I hope someday Lucia can have closure."

"I want that, too," Bailey said.

Nick slipped between us. "I left a pitcher of sangria on the table next to Lucia's. Would you like to eat with us, Bailey?"

"No, thanks," Bailey said. "I'm leaving in a minute."

Nick and I got back in line and filled two plates. We took our food to the table and sat with Carmen and Victor.

Victor crossed his arms and glowered at his partner. "She made a mistake."

"No, Victor." Carmen flushed. "I'm telling you she did not recognize me. And she asked Fidencio if he saw Paco."

"She was confused by all the people around her. Let it go. Lucia is tough."

A voice from behind us said, "I don't agree, Victor. In my opinion, Lucia should be placed in a nursing home."

Chapter Five

I turned to the sophisticated, olive-skinned man in his early fifties behind us. Dr. Anthony Torrico's dark, curly hair was slicked back from his square sculpted face. He smelled like amber and spice, and in his tailored gray suit, white shirt, and blue tie, he exuded arrogant sexiness.

"You obviously don't know Lucia," Nick said.

"Obviously?" Tony scoffed. "You obviously don't know me."

"Gentlemen, please," Victor said. "We all care about Lucia. Tony, meet Nick Garfield. Nick, this is Dr. Tony Torrico, our physician associate at Park Clinic. Please, let's sit down and talk about this. We all share concern for Lucia."

Tony turned away from Nick's salutary nod and sat next to Carmen.

"Lucia is much better off at home," I said to Tony. "Coping with violent death is a huge challenge to the system, and a move now, on top of the shock and her grief, could impact both her mental and physical health. We all know she shouldn't be alone. That's why Victor hired Cruz."

"Cruz is a caretaker, a stranger to her," Tony said. "Lucia doesn't have close family for emotional support. She would be better off in a home, surrounded by professionals."

Nick snorted under his breath.

"Lucia won't leave her home," Victor said. "And I won't force her. She has her friends. She has us. I'll watch to see how Cruz and Lucia get along."

"Liz made an interesting point, Victor. Shock affects state of mind, especially for the elderly. Is Lucia capable of running her business and making decisions?" Tony said.

"I'll be available to advise her," Victor said. "Before Paco died, he and Lucia asked me to assume power of attorney over their affairs, medical *and* legal. They wanted assurance they could live out their years in their own home. I'm committed to follow their wishes. As soon as Lucia and I complete the paperwork, I'll have full authority. If her health deteriorates, I'll replace Cruz with a licensed professional nurse—at home."

Tony cocked his head. "And Lucia is of sound mind to sign the documents?"

"Definitely," Victor said.

"I didn't realize you're taking over both capacities," Carmen said. "You'll be her legal guardian and remain her doctor?"

"Just legal. I'll consult on her health care, of course, but splitting the medical and legal responsibilities seems more ethical to me," Victor said.

Victor's consummate professionalism ended our table

debate. Carmen and I exchanged reassured smiles. I'd picked up my fork to tuck into the plate of enchiladas, rice, and beans in front of me when a screech of microphone feedback jolted my attention toward the stage. The band stopped.

Lucia stood on the small dance floor in front of the band, tapping the head of the mike. "Is this on?"

The crowd went silent. A waiter darted to her side and blew on the mike. "Testing."

Lucia waved him aside then said, "Thank you all for coming to our anniversary party. Paco? Where are you? You're being rude to our friends. Come up here and dance with me."

I started to get up, but Carmen held me back. "Let Victor handle this."

"There you are." Lucia came toward our table, reaching for Victor's hand. "Come, Paco, dance with me, my love."

"No, Lucia." Victor rose. "I'm not Paco. I'm Victor. Give me the microphone. Please, sit down. You're confused."

Lucia stepped back, blinking. She glanced back at Paco's urn on the table behind her. Slowly first, and then with increasing momentum, she began to shake her head as if the realization of Paco's death had slapped her in the face. Victor put his hand on her shoulder. She wrenched away.

"Leave me alone. I have something to say." Lucia clenched the microphone, addressing the room full of people. "You think you're our friends? You came to tell me you're sorry? It's your fault Paco is gone."

Carmen, Nick, and I got out of our chairs. Lucia pushed each of us aside. "I want my say."

"Lucia, please, everyone here loved Paco," I said.

"Loved him?" She elbowed me away, turning to the

39

crowd again. "You killed him. All of you. You murdered Paco the second you let the gangs run our streets. I'll have my vengeance on you, starting now."

Lucia circled the restaurant with one hand on the microphone, the other to her throat. "A hex. A *brujeria tie* on you, on the neighborhood. That's you. And you. And you." She jabbed her finger at a woman, a man, then another man. Startled adults hustled children toward the door. She continued, "All of you, your shops, your homes, your children, and your ancestors. I curse your destiny." She went to the base of the stage and said to the mariachi, "Start the music so Paco and I can dance to their doom."

Carmen waved *no* at the musicians. Victor, Nick, and I blocked Lucia from the remaining crowd. She teetered, dropped the microphone, and then crumpled into Victor's arms. He cradled her until Nick brought a chair.

"Should I call an ambulance?" I said as Victor knelt by her side.

"No. I can take care of her," he said with a clipped tone. "She needs to go home. Where is Cruz?"

"I'm here, Dr. Morales," Cruz said.

He glared at her. "Who gave her a microphone? Weren't you watching her?"

"I . . ." Cruz shook her head. "I didn't know what she was going to do."

"Well wake up," Victor said. "Help me get Lucia out to the car."

Victor and Cruz guided Lucia out of the restaurant. Nick picked up the urn with Paco's ashes. Carmen and I followed them out.

"Victor should be alone with Lucia so he can calm her

down," Carmen said. "I don't have my car, and Tony had to go back to the clinic. Can you and Nick drive me home?"

"Of course," I said.

When we reached the parking lot, Victor settled Lucia into the backseat of the hired town car. Cruz took the urn from Nick and then got in next to Lucia.

Before Victor got into the front seat, Carmen stopped him. "Maybe you should stay with Lucia again tonight. Take tomorrow morning off. Tony and I can handle the clinic patients."

"No. Your stomach. The doctor warned you to take it easy," Victor said.

"Well, bull. I'm a doctor. I know how I feel. You don't need to be fawning over me. Lucia needs you more. I can take care of myself. Tony can certainly handle the patients," she said. "Go. We'll talk later tomorrow, after you get some rest."

"All right. Just take care of yourself, Carmen," Victor said, getting into the car.

Lucia waved through the car window as they sped away.

Carmen climbed into the front seat of Nick's red SUV. "Still has the new car smell."

"Because he babies the thing," I said.

"Good. He takes care of things. He'll make a good father," Carmen said.

I got into the backseat and tried to breathe. Either there was no air or I couldn't take in the thought of Nick and me as parents. Or married. Hell, we hadn't reached the *I love you* stage yet.

Nick inched the car into the heavy traffic and steered north, past the merchants lining both sides of Alvarado. We passed 7th Street, and the fountain shooting water in the center of MacArthur Park Lake. Trees lush with bright green leaves and flowerbeds vibrant with April blooms lined the sidewalk along the park.

Carmen's shoulders jerked. "Oooh." She bent forward, holding her side and gulping air.

"Are you all right?" I said.

"I shouldn't have had the enchiladas," she said. "I think they were too rich for my stomach. I'll be fine in a minute."

I sat back. Something Lucia had said earlier confused me. "What did Lucia mean, Nick? What is a broojer-something tie?"

Nick enunciated: "Broo-hay-REE-a. *Brujeria* is Spanish for witchcraft. In sections of Central and South America, including regions where Lucia and Paco traveled to buy herbs, *brujeria* refers to black magic. A *tie* is an obscure form of a hex. When Lucia held her throat as she made the threat, her gesture was symbolic. A *tie* creates a blockage to bind the subject with negative energy and thoughts, creating paranoia."

"A violent threat," Carmen said. "I've known Lucia a long time. I never knew her to invoke black magic."

"Lucia has a sophisticated knowledge of the variants of religion and the occult from south of the border," Nick said. "Santeria may be her practice of choice, but in our conversations Lucia gave *me* lessons in obscure rituals of nontraditional belief systems. The hex she invoked this afternoon is irreversible. The locals who understand black magic will be threatened, and will probably scare the hell out of those who don't. It's a mind game—like voodoo."

42

"They can't take the hex seriously. Her friends must know Lucia was crazed with grief," I said.

"They take her very seriously, sweetie," Carmen said. "No one doubts her power to control minds."

"Bewitch an entire neighborhood?" I snickered. "Hexes escape reason. Only naïve people believe in the supernatural." I caught Nick's eye in the rearview mirror. "No offense."

"None taken." He glanced at Carmen. "Liz likes a logical explanation for everything."

"I understand the comforting draw of symbolism. But I prefer to use logic to solve my problems," I said. "Do you agree, Carmen?"

"Intellectually, yes," Carmen said. "But when I was a girl my parents and grandparents prayed to their Santeria statues on one side of our living room, and to Catholic saints on the other side. Childhood beliefs are hard to unlearn no matter how logic contradicts them. My family taught me to believe in a power beyond. I'm surprised, Liz. I thought you understood Lucia and Paco's beliefs. Your mother believes in the supernatural."

"I respect the reverence Paco and Lucia have for Santeria and the influence it had on their lives," I said. "On the other hand, I was raised by a mother who wouldn't buy mechanical toys for us if Mercury was retrograde."

"Poor Liz." Nick turned left on Wilshire Boulevard, through MacArthur Park. "What did you miss? Barbie's convertible?"

How did he know I wanted that damn pink car for my eighth birthday? "Say what you want, wise guy. Mom's supernatural baloney drove me to the rational side. I hope

43

local compassion for Lucia overwhelms the fear of a hex. She needs her friends right now."

"She's lucky to have a friend as compassionate as Victor," Nick said.

"He's a saint, isn't he?" Carmen said.

"Confess," I said leaning between the seats. "Is he going to be husband number five?"

Carmen laughed. "If he's lucky. No, if I'm lucky. Victor is the most principled man I know. He truly cares about all the people in his life."

"You're both saints if you can tolerate someone like Tony Torrico," Nick said.

"Don't let Tony's arrogance put you off," Carmen said. "He's a good doctor. He works extra hours when Victor and I need him. Tony is an asset to the clinic and the whole neighborhood. You have to get to know him."

"I don't have to, but if he gets involved with Lucia's care, I will." Nick turned right off Wilshire Boulevard onto Bronson Avenue and parked the car in front of Carmen's two-story English country house in Hancock Park.

Before she got out, Carmen turned to me. "Sweetie, don't forget you have a physical and TB shot tomorrow. I know we've been distracted, but the exam and the immunizations are a staff requirement."

"I'll be there, Carmen. I'm sorry I put it off so long. Nick is driving to the clinic with me. We'll check in on Lucia afterward."

"Good. I'll see you both tomorrow, then," Carmen said.

As we pulled away, I said to Nick, "You're sure you don't mind waiting for me at the clinic?"

"I waited twenty years for you. An hour is a snap."

I ignored his tease about his college crush on me. He hid his feelings for me back then, while I batted gaga eyes at Jarret, my future ex-husband. "Thanks. I hate getting shots."

"I'll buy you a post-shot cookie. We can bring a bag of them to Lucia to cheer her up," he said.

"I get *one* cookie?"

Nick steered through Laurel Canyon into Studio City and turned right onto Sunshine Terrace, a shortcut bypassing traffic on Ventura Boulevard. He curved past the bungalows and houses that bordered Carpenter School and dropped me off at my front door on Carpenter Avenue.

My kitten, Erzulie, meowed from inside while I collected my mail. I adopted Erzulie the same week Nick and I began our . . . affair? Dating? Relationship? Nick was Erzulie's superhero. She wove between his legs and sat at his side whenever he visited. She howled at the door when he left. No doubt her current cries were because her radar ears recognized his exiting car rather than heralding my return home. If Erzulie had thumbs, she'd pack her food dish and move in with him. Our occasional weekends at Nick's were a kitty karnival for her. She rummaged in the crawlspace beneath his house, hid in his cabinets, and followed him everywhere. Me? I'm just her meal ticket.

I dropped my mail on the coffee table and followed Erzulie upstairs to my comfy, girly bedroom. I loved the whole town house, but the bedroom was my haven. After years of renting houses in different cities during Jarret's career, I created my post-divorce environment to suit my personal taste—all white, plush, and soft. No dirty cleats or sweaty uniforms in sight. I hung up my dress, slipped into sweats and sneakers, swooped my hair into a loose ponytail, and went back downstairs.

Erzulie led the way again, stopping every few steps to be sure I followed her to the kitchen. When we got to the pantry cupboard, I took out a yellow can of Deep Sea Delite, one of Erzulie's favorites.

She jumped on the kitchen counter. I opened the can while she watched with the focus of a brain surgeon. I knew her plan. Erzulie aspired to learn to open the cans herself and eliminate me, the middleman. I couldn't blame her. Independence was a gift.

As Erzulie inhaled her dinner out of the dish on the floor, I poured a half glass of white wine and sat on the sofa to go through the mail. The phone rang.

"Oh good, you're home. It's Mom. I just got off the phone with Carmen. I heard you had quite the afternoon. When you get to the clinic tomorrow, remind them I'm bringing over cases of socks and underwear for the homeless on Friday. In fact, why don't you delay your appointment and come with me to the clinic then?"

"Sorry, I have to go tomorrow," I said.

"You can still come back with me on Friday and help me carry the boxes."

"What about Dad? I have clients on Friday."

"Your father has an LAPD retiree luncheon. You only have clients in the morning, right?" Mom knew my schedule as well as she knew her hairdresser's days off. "We'll go in the afternoon. Carmen told me about the hex at the wake today. Chilling. I hope you weren't anywhere near Lucia Rojas. Do you think it will affect our fund-raiser?"

"No, Mom. Lucia was angry and upset. The hex means nothing." I began to open my mail.

Conversations with Vivian Gordon were low maintenance on the reply end, but I had to give Mom at least half of my attention. She was known to slip in little bombshells, committing me to things I didn't want to do. She rattled on about Nick conjuring a hex-breaker and what she thought I should wear to the fund-raiser. The flyers, coupons, and bills in my mail required little attention until I came to a white envelope, hand addressed to me in unfamiliar penmanship. I slid open the flap and took out the letter inside.

"Carmen told me the hex cleared the room," Mom said. "This won't do at all. The Cherries solicited local merchants for donations. I don't want our guests to cancel out of fear of leaving their houses. We promised Carmen and Victor . . ."

Her words faded out as I read the letter in my hand:

Dear Dr. Cooper,

> *Your three-year lease at 3915 Carpenter Avenue, Unit B, expires at the end of May. We hereby inform you the lease will not be renewed due to planned ownership occupancy. Your full security deposit will be refunded pending inspection. It has been a pleasure having you as a tenant. We wish you the best of luck in the future.*

The letter was signed by the lease company and dated two days ago.

I was getting evicted in six weeks.

Chapter Six

I leaned back into the sofa cushions with the phone to my
ear. Everything in my living room was the same—the
calming milk white walls and furniture, the brick fireplace
I burned in autumn and winter, the towering orchid in the
center of the pine coffee table, and Erzulie curled at my side.
But I felt different, a stranger.

Mom stopped chattering. "Liz? Did you hear me? Elizabeth, what is wrong?"

"I'm losing the town house, Mom. I have to move. The
lease company sent me a letter. The owners are moving back
in at the end of May." Saying the words out loud made the
reality worse. This wasn't my home anymore.

"I told you not to lease that place. If you'd just tried
to work things out with Jarret, you could still be living in
that nice big house in Royal Oaks right now."

"We did work things out. We got divorced." I couldn't

stop myself from snapping at her. Mom ignored the opposing directions Jarret and I took toward the end of our marriage: I focused on my career; he dallied with flings and booze.

"You're upset, dear. I meant you could have kept the house but you insisted on leaving," Mom said.

"I hated that house. I like where I am now."

"So buy your own house. You have the money."

For once, Mom made sense. Fifteen years of marriage to a major league baseball pitcher left me with a generous divorce settlement. My leased town house was supposed to be a temporary stopover until I decided where I wanted to live. Temporary turned into almost four years in Studio City, a charming community of upscale professionals, artisans, and studio workers centralized to Hollywood and the San Fernando Valley. I liked the convenience and the people. I had even considered making an offer to buy my town house.

"I'll call Dilly Silva tonight and tell her to pull some listings," Mom said, referring to her fellow Cherry Twist, a Realtor. "She'll find you a nice place to buy."

"Dilly sells real estate in Encino. No offense, Mom, but I don't want to live in Encino."

"She has contacts all over the city. She rented the Mayfair Hotel ballroom downtown at half the rate for the fund-raiser. Tell Dilly where you want to live and she'll find you a deal. I'll help her search."

Mom house shopping for me? Double shudders. "Please wait. I don't know what I want to do yet."

"No time to wait, dear. This is a big deal. We'll start—" Mom gasped. "It just dawned on me. You were hexed. Were you standing in Lucia's way today?"

Logic only lasted so long in Vivian Gordon's world.

* * *

At twelve thirty on Thursday I said good-bye to my last client, freshened my red lipstick, and drove from my courtyard office on Ventura Boulevard to meet Nick at my town house. I found him parked in front, fresh from his last class at NoHo Community College and looking professorial in a navy sport coat and Ivy League blue button-down shirt.

His smile made me smile. I hopped into his SUV. "Were your students smart enough for you this morning, Professor?"

"Never. But they try. Were your clients crazy enough for you?"

I smoothed the skirt of my beige linen dress and buckled my seat belt. "Not crazy. A little neurotic, maybe. Distressed. But nothing fatal."

Nick drove down the hill toward Ventura Boulevard and CBS Studio Center. My phone rang.

"The hex struck again," Mom said. "Carmen is in the hospital."

"What? What happened? Is she all right?" I put my smartphone on speaker.

"She woke up in the middle of the night with horrible stomach pain and drove herself to the hospital," Mom said. "Her doctor did emergency gallbladder surgery on her at ten this morning. I'm at Good Samaritan now, waiting for her to come out of the recovery room."

"Is Victor with you? He must be wild with worry."

"He doesn't know yet. Carmen didn't want to upset him."

"You have to call and tell him, Viv," Nick said.

"Carmen asked me to wait until she got back to her room, so she could tell him herself."

"But Carmen told Victor not to go to work today. What about her clinic patients? We're on our way there now. What if he decided to go in?" I said.

"I'm sure she contacted someone at the clinic before she went into surgery. You know Carmen—Park Clinic comes first. Don't say anything when you get there. And don't call Victor. Let Carmen do this her way. Promise, dear?"

I wasn't happy about it but I promised. "When Carmen wakes up, tell her Nick and I are thinking about her." I hung up the phone and turned to Nick. "What else could happen?"

"I wouldn't ask, Liz. When I do, fate makes a point of showing me." He squeezed my hand. "At least we're okay."

"You are. Me? Not so much. Yesterday I received a letter telling me I have to move in six weeks. The owners want my town house back."

"What are you going to do?"

"I don't know."

He turned left onto Vineland Avenue, passed the Beverly Garland hotel, and made another left onto the 101 Freeway toward downtown. We sped through North Hollywood and past the Hollywood Bowl in silence.

As we neared the Sunset Boulevard overpass, Nick said, "Move in with me."

My jaw dropped. My heart did a happy flip then caution smacked it midair. *Was he serious?* I was tempted. Nick made me happy. He made me laugh. He was easy to be with. The sex was great. And he was so good to curl up with in bed. But I relished my freedom, too. I came and went as I pleased, didn't answer to anyone, had control of my remote and my refrigerator. Could roam around makeup-free in sweats if I felt like it. Leave the TV on all night if I wanted to. Eat all the chocolate in the house by myself.

I opened the car window a crack. Too noisy. Closed it again and said, "No. I mean, no thank you."

His face slackened. "No?"

"Living together is a big commitment. It's too soon."

"Move in until you find a place. Stay as long as you like. I want to make your life easy and I'd love to have you there. Take some time, and think about it."

"I will." I couldn't argue with sweet and irresistible, but Nick had to know that if I moved in with him temporarily, leaving would be difficult. "I have six weeks to worry. Between Paco's murder, Lucia's state of mind, Carmen's surgery, and the fund-raiser, I don't want to think about moving anywhere right now. I'm concerned for Lucia. She's all alone."

"She's not alone. Cruz is there. Teresa is down the hall. Victor will make certain Lucia is safe in her building," he said. "And she has us."

"Yes. She does have us. Nick, didn't Paco tell us they would never sell the building?"

"Right. Victor confirmed at the wake that Paco and Lucia were committed to staying in the neighborhood." Nick cracked a curious smile. "Why do you ask? Are you thinking about buying it?"

"No, I wouldn't displace Lucia. I asked because there were two real estate agents at the wake. I overheard one tell his wife he was warming up Paco to sell before he died."

"I wouldn't believe him. Paco mentioned a few brokers

tried, and he turned them down cold. The building has been in Paco's family since the nineteen thirties."

Nick's car phone rang as he eased into the right lane toward the Alvarado Street exit. He pressed a button on his steering wheel to answer. My brother's voice boomed through the speaker.

"Hey, it's me. Busy?" Dave said.

"On our way downtown," Nick said. "Any word on José Saldivar's background yet?"

"Some. Saldivar was a twenty-year-old Boyle Heights gang member who spent some time in juvie for B&E. The coroner's report listed a knife and five hundred in cash in his pocket—a lot of money for a kid to carry on the streets. He might have been dealing."

Nick frowned. "What the hell would a Boyle Heights drug dealer be doing in Westlake with the wife of a rival gang member?"

"Find the answer to that, and we'd have motive."

"Any other witnesses on the car or the shooter?"

"No one on the street will talk. Typical. Forensics confirmed the bullets came from a shotgun, probably at the bottom of MacArthur Park Lake by now. That's all I know," Dave said.

"It's more information than we got from Bailey. I wish you were involved in the investigation."

"Sorry. I know Rojas was a friend, but unless the shooting blows up into a high-profile murder investigation and RHD gets involved, I can't interfere. It's Bailey's case. If he asks for my help, I'll do whatever I can."

"Thanks, pal," Nick said. "I hoped I could give the widow some kind of news. She's in pretty bad shape."

"Yeah, I heard she snapped and did a hex at the wake. Scared the hell out of everyone. But that's not why I called. Did you hear the news? Lizzie was kicked out of her town house. Lock your doors. She needs a place to live."

Oh great. Mom was already working the phone. I rolled my eyes. "I'm right here, Dave. Didn't they teach you about speakerphones in detective school?"

"Geez, Nick. Nice going," Dave said. "You could have warned me."

"I told you we were on *our* way downtown. I don't have any secrets from Liz." Nick winked at me.

"I do," Dave said.

"Like what?" I said. "Please, share. I can't be the only news on the Gordon family hotline today. Do you have a date for the fund-raiser yet?"

"None of your business."

I grinned. "So that's a no."

"Whatever," Dave said. "Where are you exactly? Out buying monogrammed towels?"

"Yeah—F.U.," Nick said. "We're heading south on Alvarado toward Park Clinic on 7th."

"Iffy neighborhood. Don't park your new car on the street."

"Great part of town. The art deco architecture and old buildings are magnificent," Nick said.

"With drug dealers, addicts, pimps, gangs, and prostitutes in the doorways."

"Old friends, Dave?" I said.

"Some of them."

Chapter Seven

Getting out of Nick's red SUV without flashing the crowded Park Clinic lot was a challenge. No problem when I wore slacks or jeans. Big problem in my short sundress and heels. Nick lent me a hand before the guys loitering near the sidewalk caught a show.

We strolled between the rows of cars in the L-shaped mini-mall. A Chinese-Mexican-American deli, a convenience store, and a cell phone outlet occupied the south end, off the street. The green opaque windows of the clinic spanned the entire west end.

Nick held open the front door with the "PARK CLINIC" logo stenciled in white. I walked inside to the scent of pine and rubbing alcohol. Ivory walls trimmed in sage green displayed declarations from associations lauding the dedication of Carmen and/or Victor, Tony Torrico, and the staff of Park Clinic. Spotless gray and white linoleum flooring covered the reception area and the hall leading to the offices and exam rooms in back.

Miguel the security guard greeted me by name with a polite smile. Nick dropped into a plastic chair by the window, a polite distance from a young Latina mother nursing her newborn. I stopped at the reception desk laden with photos of teenagers in graduation gowns, each with the same round face and broad nose of the full-figured woman in violet, smiling up at me over her nameplate: Tonia Letitia Jackson, Receptionist.

"Hi, Jackson," I said. "I have an appointment for my staff physical and a TB shot."

The corners of her mauve lips drooped as she tapped her neon yellow nails on her keyboard, clicked the computer mouse, and squinted at the screen. "Uh-uh. Huh. Uh-huh." She looked up at me. "Dr. Morales and Dr. Perez aren't here. Does it have to be today, hon?"

"I promised Dr. Perez I would. What about Dr. Torrico? You know how Carmen is about rules."

"Don't I." Jackson clicked her mouse and scanned her computer screen. "Sit tight. I'll try to squeeze you in to see Dr. Torrico between patients."

She dialed her phone. "Liz Cooper is here for her physical and TB shot. Can you fit her in?" After a long string of "uh-huhs," she hung up and handed me a clipboard. "Fill this out and bring it back to me."

I crossed the waiting room and dropped into the chair beside Nick. "Victor isn't here. I wonder if he heard from Carmen and went to the hospital."

"Or he doesn't know about Carmen and he's still with

56

Lucia or home asleep. He was up for four nights in a row with her. I hope she's better today," Nick said.

"You can wait for me at Lucia's if you want. I'll meet you there after I see Dr. Torrico."

"I'll wait." Nick folded his arms and stretched out his legs while I filled out three pages of standard medical history.

When I returned the clipboard, Jackson peeked over my shoulder. "That your husband?"

I glanced at Nick, slouching in his chair, and said, "My boyfriend. Cute, right?"

"Not bad for a skinny white man," she said. "He good to you?"

I grinned. "He's a keeper."

Helen Leonard, the clinic's efficient head nurse, came into the waiting room. "We're ready for you, Liz." I followed her into the hallway past the children's playroom, turning left at the open Dutch door to the dispensary, then to the row of exam rooms and offices. She put me inside the last exam room and said, "Everything off except for your panties. Gown opens in front."

Every examination room in every doctor's office looked the same to me: beige walls and cabinets, steel instruments, cupboards, exam table, stool, hook to hang my clothes and purse, and magazines so ancient that Brad was still with Jen. The temperature inside was as cold as the steel wastebasket.

I took off my dress and bra and put on the patient shamer, an open-in-the-front blue paper gown. Sitting at the edge of the exam table with my bare legs dangling, I waited for the dreaded shot, feeling nothing close to demure, comfortable, or stylish in my paper frock.

Helen came back in, took my blood pressure, did a finger prick blood test, and then weighed me.

"Deduct two pounds for the gown," I said. I earned the extra grace on my weight—I wasn't counting on a blood test, even if it was just a small pinch.

Her eyes darted up from the clipboard, and she was still chuckling while she prepared the TB shot. After a stinging jab in my arm, I pulled my paper gown closer and tightened the plastic drawstring.

"Dr. Torrico will be right in," Helen said.

"Helen, did you talk to Dr. Morales today?" I said. Vague enough to keep my promise to Mom but still digging for info—just a little.

"No. I didn't." She avoided my eyes and scurried out.

I flipped through magazines until I heard voices outside. The door opened and Tony Torrico entered.

Even if I wasn't hungry, a good menu was fun to read, and Tony Torrico was a good menu. Elegant in his white doctor's coat, his eyes sparkled with charm, his demeanor light and easy. A gust of chilly air swept in as the door closed behind him. I crossed my arms over my frock, cold and embarrassed.

He put out a manicured hand, flashing a very white smile. "Carmen told me you'd be in today, Liz. It's good to see you again. Yesterday was a rough day for everyone. You heard the news about Carmen, yes?"

I unwrapped an arm from my waist to return his warm handshake. "Yes, I heard on my way here. Does Victor know?"

"I assume so, though we haven't talked. Helen got an e-mail last night saying he wouldn't be in. I've been too busy with patients to call him." Tony glanced at the clipboard in his hand. "You haven't had your employment physical yet?"

"Sorry. I hate shots." I withered in my stunning paper outfit like a self-conscious teenager.

"Well, Carmen and Victor are adamant about their rules." He put his stethoscope around his neck. "The exam won't take long, then we can go in my office and chat. Just lie back."

I doubted if Dr. Could've-Been-A-Model needed the stethoscope. My self-conscious heart pounded. I had to show up for a physical the day both my elderly doctor friends were away.

"How's your health?" Tony said.

"Excellent."

"Any recent problems? Colds? Flu?" He set the stethoscope on my bare chest.

I flinched from the icy metal. "Nothing."

"Do you exercise?"

"I run a few times a week and try to stay active." I counted gymnastics in bed with Nick as active.

"Where did you get your PhD?"

"University of Georgia," I said, his neutral chitchat calming my nerves and taking my mind off his hand on my shivering body.

"Are you from Atlanta?"

"No, I was born here and my family lives here. I got my undergraduate degree at UI-Champaign, then earned my PhD in Atlanta when my ex-husband was pitching for the Braves."

"Sit up." He moved behind me and tapped my back with a steel instrument. "You must have been a good student to jump from school to school and complete a doctorate."

"I was determined," I said.

Tony tucked the stethoscope in his pocket and picked up the clipboard. "You can get dressed, Liz. I'll meet you in my office."

Happy to discard the paper robe and be in my own clothes again, I walked to Tony's office next to Carmen's and Victor's offices at the top of the hall. I waited in a chair across from his desk, gazing at the photos behind him while he finished a phone call. Tony on the golf course; Tony and Victor on a dais at the Beverly Hilton Hotel; Tony with a famous actor turned politician; Tony accepting an award. Beneath the photos, two golf trophies from the Bellevue Country Club bookended stacks of paper on a credenza. Tony and more Tony. No distinguishable family or children. If he was married, he kept his personal life very personal.

He hung up the phone. "We won't get the blood test results until tomorrow, but you appear to be in excellent health, Liz. Congratulations. Keep up the good work. I'll let Carmen and Victor know you completed the physical. I didn't realize how close you were to them or that you knew the Rojases until I saw you at the wake."

"We're very close. Nick and I became friends with Paco and Lucia because of Carmen and Victor," I said. "Carmen and my mother are both members of the group sponsoring next week's fund-raiser."

"I hope Carmen recovers from her surgery by then. I'd hate . . ." He stopped himself and held up a hand.

"Don't worry. Carmen is one of the most determined

women I know," I said. "She'll have Victor carry her in if she has to."

"Please tell your mother how grateful we are for the time and effort her group put into helping the clinic. The showers will add some dignity to the homeless in the neighborhood. Assure her I will donate my own time to work with the Cherries on details if needed." He closed my file to signal the end of our meeting.

"One more question, if you don't mind?" I said.

"I don't mind if it's a short one, Liz. I have patients waiting."

"Lucia Rojas?"

Tony nodded, his face grave. "Yes. What about her?"

"Her behavior yesterday at the wake. I thought about what you said. I still believe she's safer at home, but agitation and failure to recognize familiar faces are symptoms of dementia. What do you think?"

"You should discuss this with Victor. Lucia is his patient," Tony said.

"I don't want to approach Victor without a second opinion to validate my suspicions. And you had a definite opinion yesterday." I sat forward. "I'm curious what led you to the conclusion that Lucia belongs in a nursing home."

Tony leaned back. "Victor and I discussed Lucia briefly when he asked for my help to hire a caretaker. Paco's death was a severe shock to her nervous system. Yesterday I noticed Lucia veered between fantasy and reality. The hex on the neighborhood was, in my opinion, the act of a troubled and hurt woman. I see your concern about dementia. Her age makes her a strong candidate."

"I wish I knew more about her medical background.

Lucia's personality changed dramatically after the shooting. I care about her. I want to help her," I said.

"In your professional opinion, does Lucia's mental state make her a danger to herself or others? If so, there are legal measures you can initiate."

"I can't take legal measures. I'm not her psychologist. I'm asking as a friend," I said.

"Oh." Tony straightened in his chair. "I assumed by your questions that you were acting as her psychologist."

I shook my head. "I'm sorry if I was misleading."

"My fault for misinterpreting. We'll keep this discussion between us, and leave it at that." Tony stood. "Call Helen tomorrow for your blood test results. My best to Carmen if you see her."

I left his office and walked into a commotion in the reception area. Two little boys I remembered from Paco's wake pulled at each other and at the skirt of the wild-eyed young mother trying to soothe the screaming baby in her arms. A blood-soaked towel covered the baby's arm; a red bump swelled on his forehead.

Helen brushed past me to the mother. "Mrs. Lopez, what happened?"

"His arm. He fell down the steps. His arm." She kissed the baby's head. "Senora Rojas hexed him. The *bruja* broke my baby's arm."

Chapter Eight

Helen spotted the bloody towel on the baby's arm and said, "Jackson, get someone to take the other children to the playroom. I have to get the baby into an exam room right now."

The boys, bursting with the raucous energy of four-year-olds, broke loose and darted across the room to a braided little girl on the chair next to Nick. Mrs. Lopez hesitated. The baby shrieked in her arms.

"Take the baby and go with Helen," I said. "I'll watch your children."

Mrs. Lopez whispered *gracias* and followed the nurse into the hall to the exam rooms. The boys stood side by side on a chair, fighting to push each other off. Before I could reach them, one jumped down and made a break for the front door.

"Whoa." I caught him by the scruff of his T-shirt. "I bet there are games in the playroom for boys just like you. Does that sound like fun?"

He nodded his brown curly head and then pointed at the little girl. "Is Maria allowed, too? She's six."

"Yes, but here's the deal. The gamekeeper only lets quiet children in the playroom. Think you and your brother can be quiet for a little bit? Good games. I saw them."

Both boys agreed with enthusiasm. This childcare thing was easier than I thought. I sat next to Maria and let the boys crawl onto my lap. But the boys didn't just sit. In an endless succession of motion they squiggled for comfort, picked at each other, and toyed with my hands and arms with sticky fingers.

Maria, in pink from her T-shirt down to the laces on her sneakers, had Nick engaged. "And then the witch put a hex on us because I know because I heard her and there were lots of sirens last night then today my baby brother fell down the stairs and my mother said we can't go outside to play anymore until the hex is gone or the witch is dead."

"Don't worry, Maria," I said. "There are no such things as hexes."

Maria glared at me. "Are too. The hex pushed my baby brother down the steps. My mother said so."

Nick, in a voice serious enough to hush a courtroom, said to Maria, "Scary stuff. I think your situation requires an *antidoto*. Do you believe in magic?"

She nodded slowly.

"Fairy godmothers and good spells?" He leaned in, as if to share a secret.

Another nod from Maria. The boys slid off my lap and huddled at Nick's knees.

"You're in luck," Nick said. "I happen to carry magic

64

hex-breaking pills. If I give each of you one to break the hex, will you promise to behave and obey your mother?"

The children bobbed their heads. Nick rose, turning his back to us. I heard a small rattle as he slipped something out of his pocket.

He faced us. "Open your hands."

Three small palms stretched in front of him.

Nick put an oval white mint into each hand. "Put this on your tongue. Don't chew. When the magic pill dissolves, the hex will be gone."

The boys shoved the mints in their mouths.

Maria studied the mint, doubtful. "This is a Tic Tac."

"Are you sure?" Nick said. "Sometimes magic comes in disguise."

Maria turned to me. "Do you believe in magic pills?"

Her big brown eyes shone up at me, waiting, as I mulled a way to translate my skepticism into child-speak. "I believe in the power of little girls," I said.

She squinted at me, unconvinced, and popped the mint into her mouth.

A health care assistant in blue scrubs approached our little group. "Are these the Lopez children?"

"Yes," I said. "Are you the gamekeeper?"

Her chuckled *yes* satisfied the boys. She took their hands, and they trotted with her toward the playroom door in the hall off the lobby.

Maria lingered in front of Nick. "Can I have magic pills for my Mom and baby brother, too?" He gave her two mints. She thanked him and ran after her brothers.

Nick caught me shaking my head. "What?"

"Oh, I don't know—advocating magical thinking, giving candy to children?"

"All children engage in magical thinking. The mints made the kids feel safe and in control."

"Nice. But I'd rather stop the hex rumor from snowballing," I said.

"We could wait for the whole family to come out, then weigh them down with facts. While we're at it, we can tell them about Santa and the Easter Bunny, too. And about your story that only quiet children are allowed in the playroom. Don't judge me while you swap truths with lies for your convenience," Nick said with a cheeky grin.

I put out my hand. "I'll take a mint."

"Hex insurance?"

I put the mint on my tongue. "No, I'm hungry."

"I'll take one of those," Jackson said from behind her desk. "I want the insurance. Mrs. Lopez was the third patient today blaming her problems on the hex. The whole neighborhood is in an uproar about black magic. Take my advice, don't either one of you go near the witch across the street. Mind your own business. That's my medical advice to everybody today."

"Lucia Rojas was upset yesterday," I said, walking to the desk. "She just lost her husband. She doesn't mean to hurt anyone."

"Honey, upset or not, black magic is black magic." Jackson called across the room to Nick, "Hey, boyfriend. Where's my magic pill?"

Nick tossed Jackson the box of mints and then opened the front door. As we stepped outside he said, "I called Lucia's apartment while I was waiting for you. Lucia is taking a nap so we have to kill some time. How hungry are you?"

"Very." I touched the cotton ball taped over the pinprick on my arm. "And I want a cookie."

When we reached the street, three young men with bandannas dangling from their jean pockets leaned against the low cement wall bordering the parking lot. They chewed on toothpicks, watching traffic pass like fans at a tennis match.

I cocked my head in their direction. "Those guys are here every time I come to the clinic or visit Lucia."

"I noticed them, too. They're gang members," Nick said.

"How can you tell?"

"The tattoos, the colored bandannas, the attitude," he said.

"Maybe they know something about the men who shot Paco," I said as we walked along 7th Street toward MacArthur Park.

"If they know, they won't tell you. You're an outsider. They'd take your naïveté as an invitation to snatch your purse." Nick glanced across the street. The "CLOSED" sign was in Botanica Rojas's front window. "I think I'll spend a few afternoons at the botanica to talk to Paco and Lucia's customers."

"Talk about outsiders. You look like—"

Nick shook his head and swept his fingers through his sandy brown hair. "A wealthy financier? A sports agent? I was going for both when I dressed this morning."

"A professor. A cute professor."

We passed the line of people waiting outside Langer's Deli, home of the legendary #19 Pastrami Sandwich. Across the street in MacArthur Park, children played soccer and couples sunned themselves on the grass.

"No wonder people write song lyrics about MacArthur Park—it's so beautiful," I said.

"The park was renamed for General MacArthur after World War II, otherwise Donna Summer and Richard Harris would be singing about a soggy cake in rainy Westlake Park."

"Soggy cake?"

"The song, 'MacArthur Park.' The cake in the rain?"

I laughed. "Right. My Mom loves that song. I never understood the lyrics."

We rounded the corner onto Alvarado Street and headed south, sauntering amid shoppers at stalls lining the sidewalk. Merchandise spilled from table and wall displays of jewelry, stereos and cell phones, games, fabrics, and food. Banded bundles of socks and underwear were stacked outside a dress shop with rows of party dresses, First Communion suits and dresses, and pastel *Quinceañera* gowns on the walls inside.

Ahead of us, a toddler, fluffed out in red and white polka dots and a crinoline petticoat, stretched out her arm to a stuffed pink pony hanging on a display. Barely able to reach the pony on her tiptoes, the tot pulled at the old woman holding her other hand.

"*Quiero, Abuela.*" I want, Grandmother.

I smiled at the woman and said, "Your granddaughter is adorable."

The woman gaped at me in horror. She picked up the tot, spat into the child's hair, and rubbed the gob in. Then she darted into the shop with the little girl in tears.

I turned to Nick, surprised and repulsed. "What was that about?"

"She spat on the girl to protect her from the evil eye."

"The evil eye? I called the child adorable."

"You called her *adorable* but you didn't block your envy

by touching her. The compliment triggered the evil eye."
Nick spoke like I had ignored a well-known fact.

"Why would she take my compliment as envy?"

"Some cultures believe compliments mask envy with a
wish for harm. Babies and young children are the most vulnerable. Touching erases the envy. Some people use spit."

I pretended to spit on my hand then patted his head.
"You're so smart. I promise not to insult any more children
today."

Two shops down we came to a botanica with a handmade
sign in the window: *Protección de la Maldición.* Curse protection.

Nick stopped. "Talk about opportunism."

Oscar Estevez waved through the botanica window and
came outside. With his shoe polish–black pompadour, black
chevron mustache, and blackened eyebrows, I likened him
to an old-school cowboy bandit with a bad dye job. His beer
gut pushed at the black buttons on his long-sleeved white
shirt. Heeled cowboy boots brought him close to my height.

He raked his eyes over my body, then cocked his head at
Nick. "What are you doing here?"

"We came down for a late lunch."

"You can forget Fidencio's," Oscar said, pointing down
the block. "A fire gutted the place last night."

I stepped off the curb to look, and saw yellow police tape
cordoning off the sidewalk on the next block. Black soot
covered the bricks on the front of Fidencio's restaurant. The
windows were boarded.

"What happened?" Nick said.

"Grease fire in the kitchen. The cook blamed it on the
hex. My protection spell business tripled this morning. I

sold out of protection oils and candles before noon." Oscar smirked. "Lucia did me a big favor by scaring the shit out of everybody. She'll probably lose her business because of it. Maybe I'll buy her out."

"She won't sell," Nick said.

"So you say," Oscar said. "But she and Paco should have left the neighborhood a long time ago. The old man was losing friends with his anti-gang crap."

Nick spread his hands. "The man just died, Oscar. Have a little respect."

"Respect?" Oscar shrugged. "Paco wasn't the beloved old *santero* he pretended to be. I'm not the only one thinking good riddance."

A punk with a shaved head and goatee sashayed to the botanica door. The muscles on his arms and chest, covered with tattoos, popped beneath his black T-shirt. He lowered his sunglasses, spit on the sidewalk, and eyed at Oscar to go inside.

"Customer," Oscar said. "Later, Nick."

After they disappeared into the shop, I said, "Tough guys or just crude?"

"Oscar caters to the criminal element Paco and Lucia didn't want in their shop—the gangs and drug cartel members who worship Santa Muerte for protection from the law. There." Nick pointed through Oscar's window to a statue of a skeleton shrouded in a cloak of play money, with the scales of justice in one hand and a globe in the other. "Santa Muerte, the saint of death."

"Is Oscar in a Santa Muerte cult?"

"He feigns neutrality, but he plays up a resemblance to Jesús Malverde, a twentieth-century Mexican bandit often worshipped with Santa Muerte." Nick pointed again, this time to a crude bust of a caballero with the same black-buttoned white shirt, black hair, brows, and chevron mustache Oscar wore. "Malverde was Mexico's Robin Hood, the saint of drug traffickers. Oscar collects everything he can find on Malverde. C'mon." Nick took my hand, tugging me up the block. "Lupita's Taco Truck should be right around the corner."

"Truck food?" I said, skeptical.

Food trucks were big business in Los Angeles. Most were innovative and fun, but a few were downright scary. When we crossed the street, I turned the corner with hesitation, but customers were lined up outside Lupita's Taco Truck like it was free food day. We ordered and ate on a bus bench, balancing plates on our laps while afternoon traffic crawled by. My doubts were erased with the first bite of my carne asada, heaped with grilled steak in a jalapeño and tequila flavored marinade, topped with avocado, tomatoes, panela cheese, and fresh cilantro. Hot sauce heaven.

"If José Saldivar was dealing drugs, maybe he was into Santa Muerte. Oscar might have known him." I popped a radish in my mouth.

"Saldivar was in a gang from Boyle Heights. I doubt he shopped in a rival neighborhood."

"But Saldivar was shot in rival territory. Maybe Oscar heard something on the street from the local gangs," I said.

"The street isn't talking. You heard Dave and Bailey. Gang members would rather go to jail than snitch and face retaliation. Paco and Saldivar were shot on a city street without witnesses? Teresa Suarez didn't recognize the shooters or remember anything she saw? No one stopped or came forward?" Nick sneered. "Without witnesses the case will go cold. Paco and the kid deserve better."

"If Oscar knew something, would he tell you?"

Nick took the last bite of his carne asada, crunched the paper plate into a paper bag, then smiled. "Maybe. He's arrogant. He likes to show off. He might confide in me. For a price."

I stood up. "Then we should go back."

"He won't talk in front of you. I'll come back alone and catch him off-guard." Nick tossed our garbage in a trash can and took my hand. "Ready for that cookie?"

We crossed Alvarado to a *panaderia*, following the nutty scent of baked goods inside to a row of glass cases filled with fresh *conchitas*, *empanadas*, and sugared *galettas*. I bought a dozen Mexican wedding cakes, a favorite of Lucia's, and ate one while Nick paid. We made our way up the block at a quick pace. Trotting in heels through a crowd kept me from dipping in the bag for a second cookie. When we rounded the corner onto 7th, the sidewalk traffic thinned to a trickle.

"I see lights on inside," Nick said as we neared Botanica Rojas. "Lucia opened the shop."

"I'm glad. Going back to work is a positive step for her."

Flower bouquets on Paco's sidewalk memorial withered under the sun. A handwritten sign, there since Sunday, asked for witnesses to call the police. Another sign read simply: *I love you, Paco.*

A new sign, scrawled in Spanish, stopped me.

Arden en infierno con tu diablo marido, bruja. Burn in hell with your devil husband, witch.

Nick yanked the placard from the grouping and ripped it into pieces. "Idiots."

Chapter Nine

Statues of the Virgin Mary, St. Christopher, and assorted saints, plus plaster angels and wooden crucifixes, filled the front window of Botanica Rojas. Nick and I went inside and were enveloped by a haunting *ranchera*. The sadness in the singer's voice, crooning for her lover's return, made me ache for the familiar sounds of Paco's chatter and Lucia's light laughter.

Nick called down the aisle. "Lucia? Cruz?"

We walked along the rows of candles and religious icons displayed on shelves lining the turquoise walls. Assortments of labeled oils and herbs stood in the glass cases that bordered both sides of the shop. "Attract Love," "Go Away Evil," "Drops of Luck," "Come to Me," "Forget Me Not," "Uncrossing," and Lucia's custom potions. Promises. I used to tease Lucia and Paco about trying to drive my profession out of business.

"Back here." Cruz waved over the antennae of the old

TV on the back counter. "Lucia is in the storeroom, packing herbs."

The music stopped. Lucia's voice came from the back. "Who's there? Who is it, Cruz?"

"It's me. Nick. Are you decent?" Nick pulled the red curtains apart and disappeared toward Lucia's giggles.

I wavered, undecided whether to follow him or stop and chat with Cruz. Curiosity and concern for Lucia won. I set my purse and the cookies on the counter, smiling at the caregiver, who looked rather un-nurselike in her navy zip sweatshirt and jeans.

"How is Lucia today?" I said.

Cruz, eyes on the TV, tilted her head from side to side, *so-so*.

"Did she calm down last night, or did Victor have to stay the night?"

"Dr. Morales didn't stay. He gave Lucia a pill, went over some papers with her, then got a phone call and left around seven."

Papers? Odd way to distract a grieving woman. "Did he come back this morning?"

"Not yet. Lucia's better today. She decided to come down here after her nap." Cruz cocked her head. "Are you and Nick related to her?"

"No, but we're very close. Paco and Lucia treated us like de facto grandchildren," I said. "We think of each other as family."

She glanced over her shoulder at the curtain. "I don't think you should stay too long. Lucia needs to go upstairs before she gets too tired."

"I'm impressed she came down here. I think this is the

first time she opened the shop since . . . Well, since Saturday," I said.

"She came down to find Paco." Cruz circled her finger at her temple.

Was her unprofessional gesture supposed to be funny? "Excuse me?"

"I meant that Lucia was confused. I thought being down here would make her happy, not so mopey and depressed. Dr. Morales asked me to keep her busy. Working in the store is better than being cooped up in her apartment all day."

"Did any customers come in?"

"No customers, no visitors, no phone calls," Cruz said. "I don't know how she'll get by without customers or someone to help her in the back room. I didn't take this job to work retail."

"If you're worried about your pay, don't be. I have plenty of money." Lucia, wearing Paco's long burgundy sweater over a striped housedress, came through the curtain with Nick. "I don't want strangers working here, eavesdropping, and helping themselves to my merchandise."

Cruz put up her hands. "That's not what I meant. I was explaining how I don't have experience in a shop if a customer comes."

I hugged my elderly friend, picking up the scent of dark chocolate mixed with layers of patchouli and nutmeg—her own private blend of oils. "I brought you a present, Lucia."

She accepted the bag of cookies, opening it with the innocence of a child at Christmas. A smile as warm as sunshine broke over her face, and her eyes shone with delight. "Mexican wedding cakes? My favorite. Thank you, Teresa. You're a sweet girl."

I swapped uneasy glances with Nick. "I'm Liz. Remember?"

"Liz?" Lucia knitted her brows and searched my face. "Liz. Oh, Liz. I'm sorry. All the customers today confused me. So many faces and names to remember."

"You didn't have customers, Lucia." Cruz glanced at me and shrugged. "She gets mixed up. She called me Teresa, too, when she woke up this morning."

"I know who you are," Lucia snapped. "I made a mistake. I'm old."

Cruz moved toward the curtained door. "I'll go make some tea. You can take your afternoon medication with a cookie. Would you like that?"

"Not too strong," Lucia said after her. "And turn Lola back on."

"Lola?" I said.

Nick leaned on the counter. "Lola Beltrán was the most famous *ranchera* singer of all time. Lola was to *ranchera* what Madonna was to dance."

Lucia grabbed his arm, lowering her voice. "Cruz is horrible in the kitchen. Worse than Liz was."

"But you redeemed me, turned me into a world-class tamale cook," I said.

"You're smart. You listen," Lucia said. "Cruz burned Mrs. Pena's casserole when she tried to heat it for lunch. I'm not going to cook for *her.*"

"Do you want me to bring you dinner?" Nick said. "I will."

"You're a good boy." Lucia shifted her attention to me. "Do you love him?"

She should have asked how much money I had in the bank: an easier question to dodge on the spot. Nick and I danced around every adjective to express our feelings for each other, but neither one of us had brought up the *L* word. Yet. "He's very lovable."

"That's not an answer." She reached for Nick's chin. "Do you love her?"

"I adore her, Lucia," he said.

That wasn't an answer either.

"Paco tells me he loves me whenever I walk into a room. He makes me feel adored every day of my life." She looked between us. "Now, do you love him? Do you love her?"

"We love *you*. That's why we're here," Nick said.

"Fibber," Lucia said.

Cruz came back with a cup of dark tea and Lucia's pill. Lucia took a dainty bite of a cookie then popped the pill in her mouth.

"What medication are you taking?" I said.

When Lucia couldn't answer, Cruz said, "Xanax. Twice a day. Dr. Morales's orders."

"Victor scolded me about my hex last night, but Paco approved." Lucia grinned.

Nick brushed a wisp of hair off her forehead. "Lucia."

"Don't." She pushed his hand away. "I'm not imagining things. I feel Paco all the time. His spirit won't cross until his killer is caught. And Victor was here last night, too. I know he was."

"Yes, he was," I said. "He brought you home. But Lucia, I'm a little worried about your memory. Do you mind if I ask Victor about the medication you're taking?"

"She'll be better after the pill kicks in. Maybe you should go," Cruz said.

"Don't handle me, Cruz. I'm not a baby." Lucia turned

to me. "You can talk to Victor. I trust you. But I don't want either you or Nick to leave yet. I cast the hex to draw out and punish the guilty. I want to put a protection spell over you so my orishas will know you're my friends."

"We came to visit, Lucia. We don't need protection," I said.

"Yes you do. The hex is powerful and directed." Lucia stood and started pulling bottles off the shelves. "Nick, while I prepare, look in the case and select two *resguardos*—amulets to ward off evil."

I raised a hand to protest. Nick held me back, whispering, "Go along with her, Liz. Performing the spell will make her happy."

Lucia's inner sanctum consisted of a small altar and a stool in the back room storage closet. Framed images of saints in faded robes with golden scepters covered the aged red walls. Dried fruit, half-smoked cigars and cigarettes, and hurricane candles lined the baseboards. With room for only two people, Nick volunteered me to go first. Fine with me. There was time for Lucia's hex to work some hoodoo on him for goading me.

Lucia lit a candle in a bowl of water on the altar and gestured for me to sit on the stool. Muttering an incantation under her breath in Spanish, she dipped into a small bowl of oil and touched her finger to my forehead. I knew Spanish well, but her mumblings were too garbled for me to translate.

She held the bracelet Nick chose for my amulet in front of the altar in offering. The bracelet was fashioned with half-inch wooden pieces banded together, each square painted with a saintly image. She slipped the bracelet onto my right wrist, reciting the Lord's Prayer in Spanish, and set my palms together in prayer fashion. She took an aerosol can marked "Go Away Evil" and sprayed a mist around my head and body.

Repeating the ceremony on Nick, she placed the etched brass coin he selected as his amulet into his hand, then prayed and sprayed him. "*Bueno*," she said, setting the can on the floor. "Done.

"The images on your bracelet represent the Seven African Powers," Lucia said to me. "Wear it and trouble will avoid you. Nick, keep the amulet in your pocket. An orisha will protect you. I'll petition Orúnla to watch both of you—he has power over destiny and is very wise."

We filed back into the botanica, where Cruz waited on her stool at the end of the counter, watching TV with her chin on her fist. She looked at her watch, then at the front door, a not very subtle hint for us to leave already.

I collected my purse and hugged Lucia good-bye. "I'll check with Victor on your meds. I'll come back to visit after my session at the clinic on Saturday."

Nick kissed Lucia on the cheek. "And I'll call you in the morning. If you need anything, call me. You know my number. Make sure you set the alarm when you go upstairs."

As soon as we hit the sidewalk outside, I took out my phone and dialed.

"Who are you calling?" Nick said.

"Victor." Voice mail answered. I left a message. As we crossed the street to the parking lot I said to Nick, "I wish someone else, a closer friend, could stay with Lucia."

"You don't like Cruz already? You just met her," Nick said.

79

"Here's how she described Lucia to me." I circled my finger at my temple, mimicking Cruz. "Victor was in a rush to hire her. Lucia deserves compassion, a companion who will care for her, and I don't mean her gods and saints."

"Lucia is comforted by her beliefs," Nick said. "Santeria is centuries old. The orishas she prays to originated in tribal Africa."

"I'm worried about her immediate state of mind. She confused me for Teresa again today, the third or fourth time this week. Her confusion about identities and the delusion that Paco is with her could be reactions to medication or dementia."

He waved me off. "Her quirkiness is part of her charm. And she explained why she senses Paco."

"What you consider quirky I see as an elderly woman at risk for mental disorders and complications."

Nick stopped by the car. "You're angry because Lucia put a spell on you."

"No. I know she meant well. But I think you enjoy watching me participate in meaningless supernatural stunts."

"What's with you today? First you criticize me for placating frightened kids, now you indict me for humoring Lucia. Lighten up. Have Victor check Lucia's medication, take her to a gerontologist or a psychiatrist, reorganize her life if you want to, but give me some credit for caring about both of you," Nick said. "Let Victor handle the medical diagnoses."

He was right, of course. I had acted out my frustrations by lashing out at him and the spell. "I love how you care, Nick. I'm sorry." I took his hand. "Let's go back to the clinic. Maybe Victor decided to show up."

Chapter Ten

Patients packed the Park Clinic lobby, most standing in front of the reception desk and talking over one another. Jackson handed out and collected clipboards, barking at the insistent patients to wait their turn.

"Busy place," Nick said to Jackson after the last person sat down.

"Everyone thinks the hex is contagious and they're at death's door. I had to send Miguel to the market to buy your magic anti-hex mints for the hypochondriacs. I tell them I got the antidote special delivery from an expert. That would be you, honey." She winked at Nick. "That was a good idea."

Nick leaned on the counter. "What flavor?"

"Same as yours. White peppermint," Jackson said, smiling.

"Good choice. Though I prefer orange for severe cases," Nick said.

"This isn't funny," I said. "What if someone is really sick?"

"Honey, I been a clinic receptionist since my first baby was in diapers. I can tell the sick ones from the lonely or crazy ones in a blink. The sick is in their eyes. I'm not just flippin' through magazines back here, you know. I pay attention." She straightened a stack of papers with a crisp bang. "Did you forget something, Liz?"

"We stopped by to see if Dr. Morales decided to come in," I said.

"No, hon, he didn't. Want to leave a message?"

I shook my head, disappointed, and thanked her.

Miguel stopped us at the door. "I saw you come out of Botanica Rojas. Did the police tell Lucia anything about the shooting? Did they catch the guys who shot Paco yet?"

"No. I'm sorry, no news," I said.

"Were you friends with Paco?" Nick said.

"*Si*." Miguel dropped his head. "He was a good man. Paco was nice to everyone. He told me stories about my parents and grandparents from back in the old days. He and Dr. Morales bought me lunch sometimes, too. I never thought the gangs would get Paco. Let me know if I can help Lucia."

"You can. Keep an eye out for her until things settle down. If you see any trouble around Botanica Rojas, call the police, and then let me know, too." Nick handed him a business card.

"I will." Miguel held the door open, waving as we crossed the lot to Nick's car.

We drove toward the Valley, beating the rush hour traffic by . . . Well, we didn't. There was no such thing as beating L.A. traffic on a weekday. Nick turned the radio to sports talk and fixated on a basketball discussion about his hometown Chicago Bulls versus the L.A. Lakers. A guy-guy, Nick liked every sport, in any season, on any field. Throw a ball in the air and Nick would get two beers out of the refrigerator and invite friends over to watch the ball land. I limited my love for sports to football—my Dad and brother's passion—and to baseball, the sport I spent fifteen years virtually married to.

As traffic crept along the 101 Freeway, I settled back to make a call. Mom answered on the second ring.

"I'm glad you called," she said.

"Are you still at the hospital with Carmen?"

"I just left there. Her surgery went well. Her doctor wants her to rest. Now I'm on my way to the mall to pick up a pair of slippers for her. I was going to call you when I got home. Dilly Silva wants to know where you want to live, and how much you're willing to pay for your house."

"We can talk about that later," I said. "Did you reach Victor?"

"I left him a message. Dilly wants to organize listings for you right away. You have to find a place and go through escrow before you can move in, you know."

"I haven't had time to think about moving. Tell Dilly I'll call her over the weekend."

"Well, I wouldn't be so casual about this, Liz. Although . . . You could move in with me and Daddy for a few months while you're house shopping."

My brain flashed a Terror Alert. I loved my Mom, I adored my Dad, but I was too old to move home with my well-meaning parents. "Thanks for the offer but Daddy is allergic to cats."

"Your brother Dave can take the cat." Mom called him

your brother Dave in case in the last thirty-eight years I forgot we were related.

"Erzulie goes where I go. And vice versa," I said.

Grinning, Nick whispered, "Want some privacy? I could step outside."

I covered the mouthpiece. "Cute. Mom is orchestrating. I'll be off in a minute." I said into the phone, "Can we pick up this conversation when I get home, Mom? Nick and I are driving into the Valley now. I'll call you when I get there."

"Don't. I'll stop by your place as soon as I finish at the mall. I'll see you around seven." The phone clicked, and Mom was gone.

"She invited me to move back home," I said to Nick.

"My offer must be sounding better and better."

When my doorbell rang at seven, Erzulie darted up the steps out of sight. I opened the door to my smiling mother.

Although Carmen and Mom were both in their sixties and the best of friends, they were physical contradictions. Carmen, at five feet nine, was four inches taller than Mom. Carmen had her shoulder-length raven locks colored at a salon. Mom wore her white hair in a perfectly coiffed short pageboy. Carmen dressed in bright colors. Mom chose designer pastels. But they shared the laugh of a sailor on leave, and if plied with enough drinks, their stories about their nights on the Sunset Strip during their youth made polite company blush.

Mom settled into the plush chair by my living room window, tucking her Chanel flats beneath her pleated gray slacks. "I'm glad you have to move out of here. This place is too small for you. No one lives in one-bedrooms anymore. And why on earth is it so white?"

"It calms me," I said to the woman who redecorated the family homestead entirely in beige. "I just made a pot of coffee. Would you like a cup?"

"No thank you, dear. We'll hire a decorator for your new house. Dilly can house hunt with you on Sunday. I told her to find listings in Encino and Sherman Oaks, maybe Tarzana?"

So much for waiting for me to decide. I went to the kitchen and poured myself coffee. As I stirred in milk, I said over the counter break, "I prefer Studio City or North Hollywood. The neighborhood is fun, it's close to my office, and I'd like having Robin and Nick nearby."

"Where does Nick live?" Mom said.

"He owns a Craftsman cottage in North Hollywood. Comfy. Great, in fact. I wouldn't mind living in a house like his." I smiled, warming to the thought.

"You're not thinking about moving in with him, are you? Nick Garfield won't settle down. He's a bachelor. You're used to more than what someone like Nick can offer."

I took my coffee to the sofa and sat down. "What do you mean by 'someone like Nick'? You and Nick got along famously when you knew him as Dave's best friend. Why are you opposed to my relationship with him?"

"I'm not. I'm glad you're having your fun. But don't get hurt. Who knows how many women he's been involved with? He never talks about any of them. The two of you are moving too fast."

I didn't know where to begin short of throwing the snow globe from the coffee table into the fireplace in a snit. "Fast? You and Dad got married six months after you met."

"That was a different time and place, Liz."

"And forty years later you still blush when Dad comes in the room."

"What if you and Nick have a fight? Then what? Nick throws you out and moves on to his next girlfriend?"

"I didn't say I was moving in. You did. I don't know what's going to happen. Right now I need a place to live."

"Dilly and I will help you." She took her phone out of her purse and clicked her tongue as she scrolled the screen. "Victor still hasn't returned my messages. Did you see him at the clinic?"

"No. He didn't come in. Nick and I saw Lucia at Botanica Rojas this afternoon. She didn't hear from him today either. He took her home after the wake yesterday, got a phone call, and left."

"Maybe he's at the hospital with Carmen and not answering his phone. You know how he fawns over her."

"But he fawns over Lucia, too," I said. "Paco was his best friend."

"Lucia? The hex woman?" She lifted a brow. "Maybe Victor is locked in her attic."

"She's in her eighties, half his size, and she doesn't have an attic. I'm sorry you haven't met Lucia yet, Mom. You'd like her. She reminds me of Grandma Gordon in Chicago."

Mom fiddled with her necklace, smiling wistfully. "Your Grandma Gordon didn't approve of me. She almost didn't come to our wedding."

"And she was wrong. Hmm, you two had a lot in common."

"We both worried about our children." Mom checked her watch then stood. "I have to go, dear. I have fund-raiser calls to make tonight, and your father is waiting for his dinner.

Don't forget we're delivering underwear and socks to Park Clinic tomorrow after your morning clients. Meet me in front of Good Samaritan Hospital. We can visit Carmen afterward. Dress nice. Make a good impression. Love you, dear."

We swapped air kisses at the door. Erzulie trotted downstairs for her dinner then curled onto a cushion. I made a melted Brie sandwich on cranberry-walnut bread and settled on the couch with a glass of red wine. After two big, gooey bites, I dialed Robin at her office.

Robin Anderson Bloom and I became fast friends in the fifth grade at Encino Elementary School three lifetimes ago. We became cheerleaders together in high school and shared the crazies for boys and clothes. Our friendship remained strong through both of our marriages, my divorce, and the death of her husband, Josh. Her daughter, Orchid, now in college, was my godchild. Robin knew Nick would be my boyfriend before I did.

"Collins Talent, this is Robin."

"Still no receptionist?" I said.

"We just hired one. Took forever to screen out the sociopaths with dreams of stardom and homicidal tendencies," she said.

I laughed. "So why are you answering the phone?"

"Because the overpaid, prima donna, agent-wannabe receptionist we hired insists on leaving at seven. Therefore, I'm left to wrangle calls until Sam leaves," Robin said. "What are you doing?"

"I'm taking my third bite of a grilled Brie cheese sammy. Thought of you."

Robin's soft, plump figure reflected her skills in the kitchen. The girl made stupendous macaroni and cheese, and her brownies were applause worthy.

"Show-off," she said. "I'm on a yucky, microwaveable frozen-food diet. How have you been? How's Nick? More important, how is poor Mrs. Rojas?"

"Lucia has a live-in caretaker now, but her state of mind is wobbly. I'm sad for her. Nick is good. I have news on the personal front."

"Good news? Wait. Don't tell me Nick proposed," Robin said.

"Not quite. I got a notice in the mail yesterday. I have to vacate my town house in six weeks. The owners want it back. Nick invited me to move in with him until I decide what I want to do."

"Awesome. You will, right?"

"No."

"You must be kidding," Robin said. "Nick is amazing. Move in. Have some fun together."

"We are having fun. But I won't make the mistake of moving in too soon."

"Brilliant answer, Liz. Not. Nick is nothing like Jarret."

"I know. But I haven't tested my freedom enough yet. What if I meet someone else?"

"Sit down. You're having an outburst of stupid. This is huge. Perfect timing. The universe made the decision for you," Robin said.

Erzulie hopped on the coffee table. I reached under her belly and dropped her on the floor before she could sniff at my sandwich.

"I like making my own decisions," I said. "I like having my own home. Do you realize the town house is the first place I ever lived in by myself?"

"I'd trade my house and everything I own if Josh were

still alive and waiting for me when I got home. What the hell are you thinking?"

"I'm thinking I want it all. Nick and I can have our fun together in separate houses until we're ready to make a commitment."

"Now I'm really confused. Are you in love with Nick or not?"

"I'm in deep infatuation. He hasn't seen me in the morning without makeup yet," I said.

"If I gave you an excuse this confusing—"

"I'd make you talk until you came to your senses. I know. I can counsel someone else through their issues, but I'm clueless about my own," I said.

"I wouldn't call Nick an issue. Well, you have a standing invite to stay in Orchid's bedroom if you can't find a place in the next six weeks."

"Lovin' you for that, Robin."

"Love you back. Just don't stand too firm on your principles. Let your heart and the universe lead you. I'll help with the garage sale."

"What garage sale?"

"All your leftover married furniture has got to go," Robin said.

"Slow down. I'm not moving yet."

"You will soon. Anything else going on?"

"Not much. Lucia put a 'protection spell' on Nick and me to ward off the hex she cast at the wake, her neighbors believe her hex burned down a restaurant last night, and her doctor might be missing. Normal stuff."

Chapter Eleven

L ate Friday morning I bid my last client of the day good-
bye and locked the door to my Ventura Boulevard office.
The early gloom had burned off, leaving a clear sky over a
day warm and sunny enough for the beach or tennis. Taking
a deep breath of fresh air, I started through the daffodil-
lined brick courtyard to my car for the drive downtown to
meet my mother.

As my car approached the Silver Lake exit on the 101
South, traffic bottlenecked to view a stalled van on the side
of the freeway. I reached for my earphone to make a house-
hunting appointment with Dilly Silva. Nope. I put the earphone down. I wasn't ready. But I had to move. I reached
for the earphone again, and then realized I didn't have Dilly's number in my contacts. I flipped on the radio and sang
along to a Fleetwood Mac triple play.

I merged onto the Harbor Freeway and found the exit

that would take me to Wilshire Boulevard. When I pulled into the circular drive in front of Good Samaritan Hospital, I saw Mom standing at the entrance, her bobbed white hair tucked behind diamond-studded ears, her shoulders squared in a dancer's pose with the silver and black braided chain on her pocketbook crossing her thin frame.

"You look adorable," she said, sliding into my passenger seat.

We both laughed. Of course she'd approve. We wore the same outfit, down to the shoes. The mother/daughter dress-alike might have been cute except our matching black slacks and white shirts made us look like two caterers on our way to work.

"How is Carmen this morning?" I said, steering out of the driveway and following Mom's directions to her car in the parking lot across the street.

"Sore. Loopy on drugs. Worried about Victor. She asks for him constantly."

"No call? Nothing?"

"No, and that man will get a piece of my mind when he shows up," Mom said. "Take that ramp, over there. My car is near the elevator."

I parked. We got into the silver Cadillac Dad gave Mom three years ago for her sixtieth birthday, thinking the luxury car would slow down her driving. Dad was wrong. She sped through three yellow-lit intersections on the one-mile drive east to Park Clinic. Miguel helped us unload the three boxes out of her trunk while the same three gang members loitered on the sidewalk wall, as usual, watching us.

Compared to yesterday's late afternoon commotion, the Park Clinic lobby was tranquil. A man in construction boots, his arm in a sling, flipped through a magazine in a chair against the wall. A middle-aged couple sat in the corner, filling out papers.

Jackson, in a loud pink turtleneck, peered at us over her computer screen. "Hello, ladies."

"Ms. Jackson." Mom set her carton on the desk and straightened her blouse. "Is Dr. Morales here? I want to speak with him."

Jackson shook her head. "Not here, Mrs. Gordon."

"Where is he?"

"I don't know, hon, maybe on a golf course somewhere? Friday is Dr. Morales's day off." Jackson craned her neck, looking past Mom's shoulder. "Miguel, don't stand there with that box. Show Liz and Mrs. Gordon where we keep the supplies."

The three of us paraded with the boxes down the hall to the supply room near the back door. After we stacked the cartons on a shelf, I thanked Miguel and then started toward the lobby with Mom. At the turn of the hall, I spotted Tony Torrico standing at the dispensary.

"Liz, I didn't expect to see you until your group session tomorrow," Tony said, smiling.

"We brought new socks and underwear the Cherries donated for the homeless." I motioned at Mom. "This is my mother, Vivian Gordon."

Mom tilted her chin, smiling. "We met in December at the fund-raiser meeting."

"Yes, I remember well. It's kind of you to deliver the supplies personally." Tony put his hand to the chest of his starched white coat. "We appreciate everything your organization does for the clinic. I wish I could spend some time with you, but the clinic is short staffed today. If you'll excuse me, I have patients waiting." He started toward the exam rooms.

Mom reached for his arm. "A moment, Dr. Torrico. I have to talk to Dr. Morales. He's not returning my calls. Do you know where he is?"

That was my Mom—she loved a compliment but not a dismissal.

"He may be at the hospital with Dr. Perez," Tony said.

"He's not," Mom said. "I was with Carmen all morning. She hasn't heard from him."

"Oh." Tony hesitated. "How is Carmen?"

"Resting comfortably, no thanks to Victor who doesn't return *her* calls either. She's worried and I'm disappointed, Dr. Torrico. Really, how rude. I expected Carmen's business partner to be more responsive at a time like this." Mom crossed her arms. "I hope his behavior doesn't make the Cherries regret our decision to raise money for this clinic."

Tony glanced down the hall. Helen and an intern watched us from the nurse's station. He set his hand on Mom's shoulder. "Let's talk about this in private, Mrs. Gordon."

He escorted us past the dispensary to his office. Mom and I settled into the guest chairs facing his desk and the array of wall photos. Tony sat across from us and folded his hands on his desk.

"I can't explain why Victor wasn't at the hospital when you were there, Mrs. Gordon. Please don't judge the clinic and all the work we do for the neighborhood by his failure to return a phone call. Today is his regular day off. It's possible he had a prearranged commitment." Tiny beads of perspiration glistened at his temples.

I shifted in my seat. "Carmen's emergency surgery threw

us off. I think we expected Victor to step in to keep everyone calm and reassured."

"I promise you"—Tony pointed his finger at Mom—"Victor is a good man, dedicated to the clinic and to his friends. He's had an extremely difficult week, Mrs. Gordon. His best friend was murdered, and Victor took on the responsibility of the funeral arrangements and care for the widow while managing his patients here. He could be home, resting, unaware that you're trying to reach him. He would be devastated if his actions affected the fund-raiser. The Cherry Twists' generosity and support will benefit hundreds of people in the years to come. What can I say or do to assure you all is well?"

"Have him get in touch with me or Carmen," Mom said.

He breathed in, nodding. "I will. If you want, leave your number and I'll let you know when I reach him." Tony rose from his desk. "But I have patients waiting. You understand they come first."

I realized I hadn't checked to see if Lucia had seen or heard from Victor. As Tony and Mom walked through the hall ahead of me, I phoned Lucia's apartment.

Cruz answered. "Lucia is taking a nap. She fell asleep right after her lunch."

"I'm across the street at the clinic. Has Dr. Morales called her or come over?"

"He didn't come. Lucia got a phone call last night. Do you want me to ask her if it was him?" Cruz said.

"No, don't bother her."

"Liz?" Helen Leonard waved me into the empty nurses' station across from the exam rooms. "I heard you talking to Dr. Torrico about Dr. Morales. I haven't heard from him either. The e-mail he sent Wednesday night was strange. I assumed he was busy. He usually checks in with me on days he doesn't come to the clinic, and he calls me every Friday morning before he tees off. But he didn't call—yesterday or this morning. I'm worried, too."

"Where does he golf?"

"The Wilshire Country Club." Helen clenched her hand, rubbing her wrist with her thumb. "He always tees off at eight thirty."

I did a quick search on my phone for the number, dialed, and asked for the starter.

"Pro Shop, this is Chad."

"Hi. I'm trying to locate Victor Morales. Can you tell me if he played this morning? He would have teed off close to eight thirty," I said.

"I know Dr. Morales. Let me check." Chad came back and said, "Nope. He wasn't here this morning."

I hung up disappointed, but the call gave me another idea. "Helen, where does Victor live? I think I'll drive over and check his house."

"Oh good." She wrote out his address from memory and handed me the slip. "Will you promise to call me when you find him? I just want to know that he's okay."

"Promise. Thanks, Helen. You've been a big help."

Mom was waiting for me by Jackson's desk. "There you are. What happened to you?"

"I was with the head nurse. Come on, Mom." I edged her out the front door to the sidewalk. "We're going on a mission."

She cocked her head. "To?"

"Victor must be somewhere. Home is the most logical

place to check." I showed her the note in my hand. "His address. We're going to pay him a visit."

"Brilliant. Why didn't I think of that?"

"I don't know," I said as we got in the car. "You spent forty years married to a detective and you raised another. Good thing I picked up a hint or two from Dad and Dave."

"You picked up hints. I gave them *lessons*."

Mom started the car and punched Victor's address into her dashboard GPS. "Hold on, dear. We're going to Silver Lake."

She drove across town like a dancer elbowing to the front of a chorus line. Twenty minutes and two arguments on speed and caution later, Mom turned the Cadillac onto Victor's street. Cement driveways separated rows of postwar stucco houses with manicured lawns. We parked in front of Victor's cream Tudor home in the middle of the block and climbed the steps to his front door. Drapes covered the windows, blocking the view inside. A jumble of flyers and letters crammed his mailbox.

Mom rang the bell. No answer. She rang again with her ear to the door and shook her head. "I can't hear anything."

"Look." I pointed to the newspaper on his driveway. "Either he didn't come home last night or he hasn't left yet today."

"Maybe he's too sick to answer the bell." Mom banged on the door. "Victor? Are you in there? Yell if you can hear me." She put her head to the panel again and waited. Nothing.

"I wonder if his car is in the garage." I scurried across the lawn to his driveway. The garage door was windowless. A tall, gated fence blocked access to the backyard.

Mom called to me from the sidewalk. "Let's ask the neighbors if they've seen him."

We rang doorbells of the houses on both sides of Victor's. No response. Up and down the block, driveways were empty and the sidewalk vacant. We started back to Mom's car with my good plan feeling like a waste of time.

The garbage cans lined at the curb caught my eye. I started to wheel the neighbor's blue recycle can up Victor's driveway.

"What are you going to do with that?" Mom said, following me.

"I'm going to crawl on top and peek in his backyard. Maybe I can see if his kitchen lights are on." I positioned the can at Victor's back gate. "Steady me."

Mom clenched the handle with both hands while I bolstered myself to a sitting position on top of the plastic bin. With a hand on the fence I swung myself around to kneel, then peeked over the gate. White flowers bordered the house, and a grapefruit tree stood in the center of the yard. A lounger, patio table, and chairs sat on the back porch with a kettle barbeque. Another unopened newspaper lay on the ground. I reached over the gate, slid open the inside lock, and hopped off the can.

Mom moved swiftly across the yard to the back porch, cupping her hands to the sliding glass door to see inside. "No lights on in the house."

I tiptoed over a flowerbed and peered through the garage window. "No car."

Loud, agitated barks coming from the driveway vaulted my heart into my throat. I spun around and stopped short. At the gate, a black and brown dog with paws the size of softballs crouched to attack.

Chapter Twelve

The dog bared its teeth, snarls rumbling deep from its throat. I froze in place under the tree, searching for something to use to protect myself. Grapefruit were scattered at my feet. Pummeling an angry dog with fruit wasn't an option. Mom stood on top of the lounge chair, bracing herself against the house.

A stern female voice called out from the driveway, "Rusty, sit. Now."

The dog sat. Its master, a stout middle-aged redhead in a ragged hoodie, sweats, and hiking boots stopped at the gate. The woman looked at me, then at Mom, and scowled. "Who the hell are you?"

I held up my hands in surrender. "We're Victor's friends."

She took stock of us. "What are you doing with my trash can and why are you sneaking around his yard? Where is he?"

"We don't know where he is. He hasn't been to work in two days and he doesn't answer his phone or the door. We're worried," I said. Rusty eyed my leg. "If you call off your dog, I'll show you my identification."

She snapped her finger. "Rusty, come."

The dog turned its head to her call. Then it turned back to us and growled again.

"Rusty. Now." Her bark was more intimidating than the dog's.

Rusty backed off, giving us one last look, and sat at the woman's side. She clipped a leash onto the collar, patting the dog's head.

Mom stepped off the lounge chair and crossed the yard. "If you don't believe us, call the police. My son is a detective."

The woman didn't blink. Clearly unimpressed, she snapped her fingers toward the porch next door. "Rusty. Home."

Once the dog settled on the porch, I reached into my back pocket and handed her my business card. "I'm Dr. Elizabeth Cooper. This is my mother, Vivian Gordon. As I explained, we're Victor's friends. Concerned friends. Have you seen him in the past two or three days?"

"No." She pocketed my card then set off to roll her trash can down the drive.

I closed the backyard gate. Mom and I followed her to the curb.

"Do you remember the last time you saw Dr. Morales at home?" Mom said.

"I don't remember. I don't keep track of him."

"What about the neighbors on the other side of him?" I said.

"If he's on vacation and Richard and Suzanna are watching his house, they're doing one crap-ass job of it. If it wasn't for Rusty and me picking up newspapers, the whole damn block would be a target for burglars." She raised an eyebrow. *Like you.*

"Was that yesterday's paper in his backyard?" I said.

When the woman didn't answer, Mom said, "We don't want to be pushy."

"I'd say climbing a fence to unlock a gate is already pushy," she said.

"We're worried," Mom said. "We tried the house next door. No one responded. Can you give us Richard and Suzanna's number so we can call them?"

The woman shook her head. "I don't give out numbers to people I don't know. The doc keeps erratic hours. I rarely see him come and go. It takes an earthquake, fire, or flood to gather the neighbors outside at the same time. We keep to ourselves."

The dog whined from the porch.

"Rusty wants his treat. I can't talk anymore." She left us on the sidewalk.

On the drive back to Good Samaritan, I braced one hand on the glove compartment and clutched my armrest with the other while Mom wove through traffic.

"I think we should report Victor missing," I said. "He wouldn't just take off like this."

"I hope he wouldn't," Mom said.

"Come on, Mom. You've known Victor for years. You, Carmen, and the other Cherries would have unearthed his personal secrets or criminal tendencies by now."

Mom smiled at me. "Everyone keeps secrets, dear, but

you know how suspicious Kitty is. Before she let us commit to the fund-raiser for the clinic, Kitty ran a secret background check on Victor to be sure he wouldn't misappropriate the money."

Cherry Twist member Kitty Kirkland acted as the group's legal counsel. Kitty knew about secrets—the beautiful attorney surprised her conservative law partners by coming out and marrying her partner, Quinn, during the 2008 window of time when California allowed same-sex marriages

"And? Did Victor pass Kitty's evaluation?" I said.

"Yes. On paper he's a saint," Mom said.

"How much money have you raised for the clinic so far?"

"Our goal was two hundred thousand dollars, the estimate for the plumbing and shower renovations. We're almost there." Mom pulled into the Good Samaritan lot and parked on the second level. We descended the steps and crossed the street to the hospital.

"Funny," I said as we passed through the hospital reception area to the elevators. "What if Carmen and Victor both miss the gala?"

"That would be unfortunate, not funny," Mom said.

"I meant funny as in odd."

"Carmen will be at the fund-raiser if we have to wheel her in in a hospital bed. You don't know that Victor won't be there," Mom said.

"I hope he is. I hope he's upstairs apologizing to Carmen right now," I said, though I was convinced he wasn't. "Mom, who has access to the money you have collected so far?"

"If you think Victor sweet-talked Carmen into a scheme to raise funds, and then took off with the cash while she's in the hospital, you're wrong. He couldn't." She lifted her chin confidently. "The donations go directly into our fund-raising account. Two signatures, one of which is mine, are required for withdrawal. The money is safe."

Mom stepped out of the elevator and led me to Carmen's hospital room. The windowsill overflowed with cheery "Get Well" balloons and flower bouquets.

Carmen perched in bed with a needle and tube taped to her arm, her raven hair bed-head flat, and her face pale sans makeup. Her forehead creased when she saw us. "Viv, Victor is definitely missing. I just talked to Cruz and Tony. He hasn't been to Lucia's since Wednesday, and he hasn't called the clinic in days."

"I know." Mom rested her purse on a side table and sat next to the bed. "We were just at his house. He didn't answer the door and his car wasn't in the garage. Try to relax, Carmen."

"Relax? How can I?" Carmen touched her stomach, wincing. "Why did I have to end up in the hospital now? I keep thinking about Lucia's hex. I know she didn't mean to hurt her friends but look what's happening to us. Victor's disappeared, I had emergency surgery, Liz was evicted. What kind of madness did Lucia stir up?"

I wasn't about to add Fidencio's burned restaurant. "This isn't about Lucia, Carmen. You got sick. You needed an operation. I have to move because the owners wanted their town house back. Victor could be—"

"In trouble," Carmen said. "What if he was in an accident? Tony is managing the patients at the clinic by himself. Cruz told me no one except you and Nick has visited Lucia since the wake. And here I am, stuck in a hospital bed with railroad tracks of stitches up my middle because I thought I could put off this surgery."

I sat at the side of the bed. "Congrats, Carmen. You're human. We love you for that. Everyone is pitching in while you heal. Nick and I were with Lucia yesterday. I'll visit her tomorrow after my session. I promise we'll keep an eye on her. Tony has the clinic under control. Mom and I saw him this afternoon."

"Did Victor call you after the wake, Liz?" Carmen said.

"No. As far as we know, Lucia and Cruz were the last people who saw or talked to him."

"I have to find him." Carmen pushed back her blanket, flustered, and tried to get out of bed.

Mom stopped her and eased her back onto the pillow. "*You* have to lie down. We'll find him. Your job is to rest." She turned to me. "Liz, call your brother Dave. Tell him Victor is missing and I want him to find him. Then call Nick Garfield and tell him to erase Lucia's hex."

"A hex has nothing to do with—"

She threw a *not now* glare at me. "Go make the calls, please."

I took her instructions as my cue to leave. When I got to my car I called Dave. "Heads up. Victor Morales is MIA. Can you report him as a missing person?"

"You can," Dave said. "Call the Missing Persons bureau. Want the number?"

"Sure. Give me the number, and then repeat it to Mom when she calls you in a few minutes. Or I give you what I know right now and maybe you can help."

He sighed. "Tell me what you know."

After a quick recap, I finished by giving him Victor's address. Dave put me on hold. He came back and said, "Someone already beat you to it. Victor Morales went on the missing persons wire this afternoon."

"Do you know who filed the report?"

"By the address I'd say it was his next-door neighbor," Dave said. "Victor could have taken off on his own, Liz. Adults do it all the time."

"Not the Victor you and I know. I have a bad feeling." Then, knowing Dave had a soft spot for her, I added, "And Carmen is frantic."

"I can't pull Victor out of a hat, but I'll poke around and make sure his case gets attention," Dave said.

During my traffic-hell, forty-minute drive home I updated Nick on the phone. As I pulled the car into my garage, I prepared myself to face the awaiting headache: readying Erzulie's carrier for our weekend at Nick's.

To Erzulie, the carrier was either good news—Nick's house—or it was the road to terror: the vet. She didn't know which when she got in. So the telltale sound of the cage door would send her upstairs under the bed, putting me on the bedroom floor, flat on my stomach to coax her out. Not pretty.

Before I went in the house I eased the carrier out of storage and onto the top of my dryer. I covered my hand and the carrier's wire latch with a towel, opened the door without a sound, and then slipped into the kitchen and shut the door behind me.

Erzulie sat in the center of the kitchen floor, eyeing the door. I set my purse on the counter and smiled down at her. "What do you think? Tuna Treat tonight?"

I took a can of cat food out of the cabinet. Erzulie's

eyes—one amber, the other blue—were on me. Self-conscious of every move, I rinsed out her dish. She usually hopped up on the counter to watch. She stayed on the floor. I got the can opener. Punched the can. Slowly twisted the handle, peeled back the lid, and tossed it in the trash. Took the spoon and—she jumped on the counter. Success.

While Erzulie scarfed down Tuna Treat with abandon, I went upstairs and packed my pin-striped slacks, a black cashmere turtleneck, jeans, a red sweater, an extra T-shirt, the lace bra and panty sets I wore only for Nick, and two pairs of shoes. I zipped my weekend bag shut and looked around my bedroom, feeling bittersweet. Soon I would pack all of my things and vacate my town house forever. Couldn't think about that now.

After a shower, I reapplied my makeup and lifted Erzulie off the bed, cuddling her against my bathrobe. She sensed trouble the second I left the bedroom with her in my arms. She wriggled, arching and reaching to escape, as I carried her down the stairs and into the garage. I put her in the carrier. She cried, her little eyes pleading as I latched the door.

"I promise I'll be right back." I felt like a traitor with a breaking heart for leaving her alone in the carrier. The world's worst kitty mother.

I ran upstairs and pulled on my flowered green dress, grabbed a dark green cardigan, and shoved my bare feet into low-heeled tan sandals. Back in the garage in less than five minutes, I threw my bag into the car, set Erzulie in the carrier on the seat beside me, and started fast-talking as I backed the car out.

"Honey, we're going to Nick's. You like Nick's house, remember? You can play outside. Explore under the house.

Fuzzy toys. Treats." My litany of babble to my howling kitten continued on the short drive to Nick's.

Early spring buds winked from the branches on the oak tree in his front yard. The red, gold, white, and pink zinnias Nick and I planted together in early March circled his brown-shingled, one-bedroom Craftsman cottage. I parked in the drive. Nick came out and collected Erzulie in the carrier and my bag.

He opened the carrier door in his living room and Erzulie crept out, sniffing the black, rust, and beige Aztec rug on his dark hardwood floor. Satisfied with familiar surroundings, she disappeared into the hallway to explore with her tail in the air. Trauma forgotten. I envied her ability to adapt.

Nick turned and drew me close. His warm lips caressed mine with promise. He brushed a strand of hair from my forehead with a light, tender touch. "I have a surprise for you."

The burning logs in the fireplace filled the room with an earthy, woodsy scent, but the smell of garlic coming from the kitchen made my mouth water. Nick was an excellent cook, tutored as a boy by an elderly Italian woman in the kitchen of her Chicago restaurant.

I grinned at him. "You cooked? I like my surprise already."

"I made the lasagna and picked up tiramisu from Vitello's on my way home from class. But that's not the surprise. First I have something for Erzulie. Come see." He led me through the mustard-colored great room into his jade green kitchen. He stopped near the patio door and pointed at a small, hinged panel, eighteen inches square, cut into the wall.

"It's a cat door for her to go in and out at will. I'll latch the door at night when she comes inside." Nick waited with expectant eyes and an eager smile. "Do you like it?"

I pushed the flap open with a light touch. "I love it. When did you do this?"

"The handyman came last week."

Erzulie nudged between us, sniffed at the door, and then walked away.

"Don't worry," I said. "She might not be impressed yet, but I am."

"Your turn." He led me to his bedroom and, with great flourish, opened a huge empty drawer in his large oak dresser. "For you. So you have a place to put your things."

An unexpected lump rose in my throat. Not a happy lump. Tears burned behind my eyes. Not tears of joy.

Nick's smile dropped to a confused frown. "Liz, what's wrong?"

I couldn't answer. I backed my way to the living room and sank on the sofa. With my face in my hands, I let the tears fall. My feelings about leaving my town house, feelings I pushed aside for two days, spilled out. The empty drawer triggered memories of moving from town to town with Jarret, packing and unpacking closets and drawers to move to unfamiliar settings, never knowing how long we would stay before he got traded to another team. Now I had to move again. Yes, empty drawers made me sad.

Chapter Thirteen

"Talk to me." Nick sat down next to me as I cried on his sofa.

"I can't. I feel so foolish." I didn't shed a tear the night Paco was shot, or at his wake, yet I was blubbering like an idiot over a drawer. I fought off an irrational urge to collect Erzulie and go home. My cell phone rang in my purse across the room. I wanted the distraction, and went to Nick's desk to answer.

The number on the screen was blocked. "Liz? This is Matt Bailey, LAPD. I heard Victor Morales was reported missing today. Can we talk?"

"Of course," I said. A light flashed in my mind. "Did my brother call you?"

Bailey paused. "He did. So did Nick. And so did Carmen Perez. The Missing Persons division told me that when Morales's neighbor filed the report, she gave our detective

108

your name. I'm in the Valley. I'd like to talk to you tonight. Are you at home?"

"Yes. I mean no. I'm at Nick's house." I gave him the address, wondering if my slip meant my subconscious had already made a decision about my living arrangements.

"I'll be there in fifteen minutes."

I hung up and looked at Nick. "You called Bailey about Victor?"

"The coincidence of Victor going missing just days after Paco was shot is too odd to ignore."

"Well, Bailey is on his way here." I started to the bathroom to fix my face.

Nick caught my elbow. "Before he gets here, I have something to say."

I braced for a letdown, certain my reaction to the drawer convinced Nick I was not quite sane.

He touched my chin, searching my eyes. "It's just a drawer. My house is open to you. Take all the drawers, every closet. Want to throw my stuff away to make room for yours? Go ahead. Repaint? Tell me the color. All I want is for you to be safe and happy. The drawer was to show you I'm serious. A drawer for this weekend, the whole house if you want to move in."

How could I argue with his utter sweetness? I pressed my forehead to his T-shirt. "I'm sorry I overreacted. The reality of moving hit me in a way I can't explain. I need time to sort out my emotions."

"Take all the time you need. I'm not going anywhere."

By the time I transferred my weekend clothing into the drawer, the doorbell rang. Nick answered. As I fixed my tearstained face in the bathroom I heard Bailey and Nick in the living room joking about my brother's stubborn loyalty to the Rams football team.

"Want to really piss off Dave? Bring up the eighty-five championship game," Nick said.

"The Rams versus 'da Bears,'" Bailey said, laughing. "McMahon was my hero, man."

"You're a Bears fan?" Nick said.

"Born and raised in South Chicago."

"Beverly—St. Ig."

"Swear?" Bailey said. "Me too. Where'd you go to college?"

"Undergrad at Illinois in Champaign, where Dave and I were roommates," Nick said. "I earned my PhD at Oxford. You?"

"U of I—Chicago, then the Police Academy."

"The Bulls and Lakers are on TV tonight if you two decide to pop some beers and settle in," I said, entering the living room.

"That's exactly what I'll be doing at home as soon as I finish here, Liz." Bailey grinned as he pulled out his notebook. "Thanks for meeting with me tonight. The fact that Paco Rojas's best friend went missing has my attention. How well do you know Dr. Morales?"

I tilted my head side to side. "Carmen Perez introduced him to my family years ago when she and Victor became partners. We socialized at parties and fund-raisers. We became closer recently, after Nick and I began having regular dinners with him, Carmen, Paco, and Lucia. Victor was very supportive when I started working at the clinic on Saturdays. He's a wonderful man."

"When was the last time you saw him?"

"Wednesday at Paco's wake." I settled on the edge of the sofa. "First I want to apologize if my mother and I upset Victor's neighbor. If he was inside the house and needed help, we were prepared to do whatever it took to get to him."

"You don't have to apologize," Bailey said. "Your visit prompted the woman to file a missing persons report. What made you think Morales was missing?"

"When Carmen Perez went into the hospital Wednesday night for emergency surgery, she tried to reach Victor. He didn't return her calls or any of mine, didn't go to work at the clinic, and didn't call Lucia Rojas yesterday. When he didn't show up again today, Mom and I decided to go to his house. His car is gone."

"Let me back up a few days. A few things happened at the wake after you left, Bailey." Nick draped his arm behind me and detailed the conversations with Victor at the wake, Lucia's breakdown, the hex, and Victor's exit with Lucia and Cruz. "Victor wouldn't abandon Lucia or the clinic."

"Or Carmen. They're too close," I said.

"The timing makes me wonder if there's a causal connection to the Rojas/Saldivar shooting," Nick said. "Do you have any leads on the case yet?"

Bailey shook his head. "Not much. I know Saldivar lied when he told Teresa Suarez he worked in Westlake. Saldivar was a street hustler from Boyle Heights. I don't know what the hell he was doing in Westlake those three or four nights, but I have a feeling it was connected to the Suarez woman, Rojas, or even Morales. Save me some time—do you know if Morales and Paco Rojas were involved in business together?"

"Not that I know of. Ask Carmen Perez. She's closer to Victor than anyone," I said.

"I already spoke with her at length. I'd like to hear what you know about him. I'm curious about a business connection because Botanica Rojas trades in the occult. Some gangs are heavily involved in that scene," Bailey said.

"Paco refused to deal with the Santa Muerte crowd," Nick said. "Paco and Lucia practice Santeria as their religion. There's nothing illegal or immoral about their beliefs or their trade."

"Maybe Rojas's refusal pissed off the Santa Muerte followers," Bailey said. "Was Dr. Morales into the occult?"

"Not at all," I said.

Bailey pulled at his lip, pensive. "The department views missing elderly as endangered even if they wander off voluntarily. Did Dr. Morales appear sick or disoriented to you at the wake?"

"No," I said.

Nick shook his head. "The man is remarkably capable."

"I'll stop at the clinic then talk to Mrs. Rojas again in the morning," Bailey said. "She was the last person who saw him?"

"She and her caretaker," I said. "Be easy with Lucia. She's still in shock from her husband's death. She has bouts of delusion."

"She's grieving and gets confused," Nick said. "Talk to the caretaker, Cruz DeSoto. Cruz left the wake with Victor and Lucia."

"Carmen Perez told me Morales doesn't have family. Did Morales talk to you about any other close friends I could contact?"

"The people at the clinic. I'd start with his nurse, Helen Leonard," I said.

Bailey made another note. "I don't recall—remind me what Morales wore the day of the wake."

"A maroon sport coat, blue shirt, gray slacks, gray tie with black and white diamonds," Nick said.

"You remember his tie?" I said, impressed.

"My Dad had a similar tie," Nick said. "You wore a red dress, Bailey wore a black sport coat, and Carmen had on a black dress with red roses."

"Show-off," I said.

Nick grinned. "Observant."

"Detective Bailey, what do you think happened to Victor?" I said.

"Most likely his absence is voluntary. But it could be medical, or—" Bailey spread his hands.

"Violence?" Nick said.

"What do you think?" Bailey said.

"A responsible, reliable doctor disappears for no reason? I don't want to, but I could suspect violence was somehow involved," Nick said.

"I'll check his phone records and financials, talk to a few neighbors. If one of them has a key, we'll check his house. I'll get a warrant if I have to but, as I said, most adult missing persons disappear of their own accord," Bailey said. "He might not want to be found."

"I can't believe that. Not now. Not Victor," I said.

Bailey got up to leave. "If Morales contacts you, let me know. The missing persons report was released citywide this afternoon. Maybe we'll get a break and hear from someone who saw him. With any luck, this will all be just a misunderstanding."

When he shook my hand good-bye, I noted the lack of a

wedding ring on his finger. Bailey was smart, handsome, and single. Under better circumstances I would call Robin and have her drop by to meet him, casually. By accident. *How could I introduce them?*

"Good guy," Nick said as we watched Bailey walk to his car.

"After the Chicago lovefest I heard when he came in, I expected you to invite him to dinner."

Nick tickled my chin. "You're far more interesting." He moved his hands to my ribs. "And softer." His fingers teased the flesh at the neckline of my dress until goose bumps ran down my arms. "And tastier." Then he dropped his hands and went into the kitchen. "Hungry?"

I called after him. "Tease."

"Payback. It took me hours of pouring sweat to empty that drawer."

Nick took the lasagna from his stainless-steel oven while I set plates on the counter. I pulled two wineglasses from the cabinet and turned smack into Nick uncorking a bottle of red wine.

"Are you sure this house is big enough for both of us?" I said, laughing.

He pulled me in then kissed me. "The closer the better."

We sat side by side on chrome stools behind the counter. I took a bite of Nick's lasagna, the gooey cheese, spicy meat, hint of basil, and a touch of garlic baked into homemade pasta, and I forgot about Victor, Paco, hexes, and moving for one contented moment.

"I think I'll drive downtown with you tomorrow and hang out with Lucia while you're working. I came up with an idea today," Nick said between bites.

"Where to find Victor?"

"No. To create positive attention for Lucia. Botanica Rojas is a cultural gem. Lucia and Paco's history makes for a compelling human-interest story. I called Sydney Tenbrook at the *Times* and a friend at the Spanish daily about an article. Both were interested. If I can write the story by Monday morning, the feature could run in the online editions a week from Sunday."

I winced. *Would the article draw positive attention or invite trouble?*

"What's with the pained look?" Nick said.

"People are wary of Lucia. What did they call Botanica Rojas? The witch's pantry? What if someone writes a negative response to the article and mentions the hex?"

"With or without the hex, the history of the shop will draw positive and negative attention. That's a given. I'm sure Lucia has been dealing with both sides for decades."

"Good point. By the way, I have a message for you. My mother demands that you erase the hex."

"Demands?" He laughed. "Ah, win Viv's heart and put the neighborhood fears to rest. If only I could. Maybe when Bailey finds Paco's killer, the hex will be forgotten."

I took our empty plates to the sink. "*If* Bailey finds the killer."

Chapter Fourteen

Saturday morning I rolled over and opened an eye, greeted by sunlight streaming through Nick's bedroom shutters. Dessert plates and a wine bottle sat empty at the feet of the fertility goddess on his Mission nightstand. The strand of hair stuck to my forehead was tacky from the tiramisu Nick and I fed each other in his king-sized bed the night before. Nick shifted on his pillow, hair smushed, chin rough with stubble. He sighed in his sleep, a content smile on his face. Erzulie, nestled between our feet at the foot of the bed, perked her ears then stretched with her belly to the mattress and her butt in the air.

I wriggled out of bed and padded to the bathroom for a long, hot shower. I dried off, tucked the towel around me, and opened the bathroom door to the aroma of coffee brewing.

Nick, in bare feet and pajama bottoms, set two cups of coffee on the dresser. "Good morning."

"Is this a hard sell to convince me to move in?"

He kissed the spot on my shoulder that made me tingle, then flicked my towel to the ground. "Yep."

Despite our sexy detour and another shower, Nick and I pulled into Park Clinic's crowded parking lot in time for me to prep for the Wellness Group. We parted with an affectionate peck before Nick crossed the street to visit Lucia. I scanned the lot for Victor's car, hoping he was sidetracked the last two days by some mysterious task and would be at work. No car. No Victor.

Jackson, in a disconcerting explosion of peacock blue ruffles, shook her head as I walked in the clinic. "Hon, you missed it. A police detective was here this morning talking to Dr. Torrico and Helen about Dr. Morales. Nobody knows where he is."

"I heard," I said. "Do you have any ideas?"

"All I know is somebody's got to stop the witch across the street before her hex disappears the rest of us," she said.

"Come on, Jackson. Lucia wouldn't hurt Dr. Morales. They're friends. You don't really believe in hexes, do you?"

"You better believe I do." She fingered the crucifix around her neck. "Restaurants burning down, doctors missing, people coming in here all freaked out with their babies? Girl, I won't even cross the street near her. Hell if I want her hex getting me. I hope somebody takes her away."

"She's in pain, Jackson."

"She's a public nuisance. After the hex got Dr. Perez, I bet Dr. Morales skipped town to avoid being next. I would if I could," she said.

117

"Hexes are fiction. The notion of a hex can't hurt you unless you give it power." As I picked up the Wellness sign-in sheet, Lucia's bracelet peeked from under the cuff of my black sweater, mocking me: *Then why are you wearing me?* I pulled down my sleeve. "Lucia is heartbroken. She needs compassion."

"You don't know who and what you're messing with, hon," Jackson said.

I knew I couldn't change her mind in the time left before my session. "I should get the room ready for group. Any new inquiries?"

"A couple," Jackson said. "I don't know who will show up, though. Don't forget to sign court cards when you're done."

Miguel unlocked the session room at the back of the clinic and flicked a switch, flooding the empty room with fluorescent lights. He opened the double storage closet and pulled out stacks of folding chairs. "Let me know if you want help putting these back when you're done. I put fresh coffee, cups, and supplies in the overhead cabinet this morning."

"Thanks, Miguel." I turned off my cell phone and put it with my purse into a gray metal locker near the door.

"Dr. Cooper?"

"Yes?"

"Jackson is wrong. Mrs. Rojas, she's a good lady."

"I agree, Miguel."

I started a pot of coffee and arranged seven chairs in a horseshoe at the center of the room. The first client to arrive was a surprise. Erica, the Realtor's wife with the bubble hairdo I saw at Paco's wake with her husband, breezed into the session room in an olive green sweater and slacks.

A second surprise followed Erica—Teresa Suarez. The two women separated like opposing magnets. Teresa hiked her purse over the shoulder of her oversized black blazer and headed for the coffee. Erica crossed to the wooden benches under the high windows with her phone in hand.

Next in was Ruby Harvey, a repeat from the week before. She had burnt almond skin and cropped black hair; her thin frame swam under her oversized gray T-shirt. The cuffs of her jeans dragged on the floor as she scuffed to the kitchenette and poured herself coffee. Ruby took the chair to my right, sipping in a continuous rhythm and tapping her flip-flop on the linoleum floor.

At ten fifty-seven, a cocksure young girl in a black leather jacket, flowered sundress, and scuffed leather boots sauntered in. Her stringy blonde/brown/magenta hair looked about a month past needing a shampoo. She got coffee and sat to my left.

The women waited in their seats, staring at the floor. Not at one another, or the walls, or their hands, or me—at the floor. I waited until the clock clicked a notch to eleven A.M. then cleared my throat from my chair at the top of the horseshoe. Time for interpersonal action to begin.

"Good morning. I'm Dr. Elizabeth Cooper, a clinical psychologist and your session leader. You can call me Liz. I won't spend a lot of time talking. This session is for and about you. For those of you who are new, the conversations we have in here are confidential and cannot go beyond this room. In order for us to get to know one another, let's begin by going around the circle with introductions."

I gestured for Teresa, at the end to my left, to begin.

"I'm Teresa Suarez. This is my first time." She turned to leather jacket girl.

The girl twiddled at the skirt of her sundress. We waited. And waited. Her manipulations tested my composure, but I let her show herself, knowing her controlling actions reflected insecurity. Erica coughed. The girl didn't budge.

Teresa tapped the girl's knee. "It's your turn."

"Oh. Me?" She eyed the circle then folded her arms, a protective behavior. "I'm Juanita Sharpe."

Ruby took a gulp of coffee, then said, "Ruby Harvey. I was here last week."

Erica sat erect. "It's nice to meet you, Dr. Cooper. I'm Erica Gates. My husband and I are supporters of the clinic. This is my first visit to the group."

I waited with expectation, wondering which woman would be first to fill the loud silence that followed.

Teresa broke first. "When do we talk?"

"Anytime you like," I said. "You can start by telling the group why you're here, Teresa."

"I guess I'm here because I had a horrible week," she said. "I can't sleep. Last Saturday my landlord and another guy were shot and killed right in front of me. This morning I heard Dr. Perez is in the hospital and Dr. Morales is missing. I don't feel safe."

"No kidding," Ruby said. "I bet the hex got them. None of us are safe from the hex."

Erica rolled her eyes.

Juanita pulled her leather jacket closed. "What hex?"

"The *bruja* from the botanica across the street put a hex on the neighborhood. We're all cursed," Ruby said.

"Her name is Lucia and she's not a witch," Teresa said, picking at the sleeve of her jacket. "I live in her building. She's my friend. I don't believe in the hex, but I'm worried about Dr. Morales. Lucia needs him and trusts him. If she gets sick or has to sell the building, I can't afford to move out. I'm already working two jobs."

"You live with a witch?" Juanita snickered. "We better watch out, girls. Maybe Teresa is a hex carrier."

"Lucia Rojas should shut down her shop forever and come to church. The Lord will protect her. He protects all of us." Erica gripped her hands together.

"What do you need protection from, Erica?" I said.

"People like Lucia Rojas and her friends try to tempt us into damnation," Erica said.

"Hypocrite," Teresa said. "I saw you at Paco's wake with all us sinners."

"I was there with my husband on business." Erica glared at Teresa. "Unlike certain people who invite trouble with their loose morals and dangerous friends."

"Who are you talking about, Erica?" I said.

Erica pointed at Teresa. "Her. The whiner. She made Paco Rojas's death and Dr. Morales's problems all about her. She needs to get outside of herself and help other people. Everybody has problems."

"Oh really?" Teresa said. "You have problems, Mrs. Gates? You drive your new car and parade around in new clothes. Looks like the only problem you have is where to spend your husband's paycheck."

Ruby sneered. "Who cares about her clothes? Until we

get rid of the *bruja*, life will be hell for all of us. My old man and me worked at the restaurant the *bruja* burned down. How are we supposed to pay our rent without jobs? Who buys my husband's booze and drugs? You got problems?" She set her cup on the floor. "My old man told me if I don't get a job by the end of next week, we'll end up on the street. So brag about your church and preach redemption, Erica, but we're doomed by the hex. I need some good luck and a job."

Juanita crossed her booted foot over her knee. "Maybe the doctor took off with somebody's wife."

"Dr. Morales is an old man," Teresa said.

"Ew. Oh." Juanita turned to me. "Can old people have sex?"

"Sure," I said. "Seniors can enjoy an active sex life."

"So maybe the doc took off with somebody's grandma," Juanita said, chuckling.

"Oh, please. Dr. Morales is a respected, moral man." Erica dismissed Juanita with a sniff and pointed at Teresa again. "But *you* have a lot of nerve showing up here complaining. Everybody knows your husband's friends shot your boyfriend and Paco Rojas instead of you. Maybe your friends hated Dr. Morales for not dressing bullet wounds and went after him, too. All the depravity in the neighborhood circles around you, your criminal husband, and the botanica you live over."

Teresa stood, her face raging red. "You stupid, mean bitch. You don't know what you're talking about. I never cheated on my husband. I didn't even *know* José. And how would you know what patients Dr. Morales does or doesn't treat? Mind your own business, you ignorant hag."

"Teresa, sit down," I said. "Erica, stop making sweeping

accusations. Focus on your own feelings, what's going on with you. You're angry. Tell us more about that."

"I don't feel sorry for you." Erica locked her eyes on Teresa. "You married a gang member. Move out of that cursed building and make some friends who follow a righteous path. Save yourself."

"Are you talking about me or about you?" Teresa said. "Maybe you're not so happy with your old man and your friends. I like where I live. Lucia and Paco were good to me. What gives you the right to be the judge and jury on happy?"

"I take my direction from the Lord," Erica said.

Ruby leaned forward. "Then why are you *here*, church lady?"

"My name is Erica," she said, slowly and deliberately. "I came because I need a safe place to talk about my relationship in private. All my husband thinks about is selling real estate. He doesn't pay attention to our marriage. I don't know what I'm doing wrong."

"Plain as day, sister," Ruby said. "You need to lighten up. Have an affair. That'll get his attention."

Erica's face softened. "I don't think he'd care. He hasn't touched me in a year."

"At least your husband comes home at night," Teresa said.

"Sexy lingerie works." Juanita opened her jacket and snapped her red lace bra strap. "And I never met a man who could say no to some nookie."

The tension dissipated into laughter.

"Juanita, will you share why you came to group?" I said.

"A judge sent me. It was either counseling or jail."

"Hah," Ruby said. "If you live in this neighborhood, you're probably safer in jail."

* * *

At the end of fifty minutes, the women helped me stack the chairs into the closet. Erica left with a hasty *thank you*. I wondered if she would return. Ruby and Teresa rinsed the coffeepot and cups at the sink.

Juanita handed me her court card. "You have to sign it to prove I was here. A cop pulled me over and spied a joint in the ashtray. I have to go to three months of AA meetings and counseling."

"Then I'll see you at our next session. Have a good week." Smiling, I handed Juanita the signed card. She and Ruby left together.

I went to the kitchenette to help Teresa put away the rest of the coffee supplies. "I'm happy you decided to come today, Teresa. Getting your feelings out in the open will help you. Have you seen Lucia since the wake?"

Teresa didn't look up. "Once. I still don't know what to say to her. I can't tell if she blames me for Paco's death."

"Talk to her from your heart," I said.

She glanced toward the hall, lowering her voice. "Are we still being confidential?"

"Yes. Our conversations in and out of session became privileged once you joined the group. I'm bound by a code of ethics not to repeat what we talk about," I said.

"You won't or you can't?"

"I can't, unless your life is in danger or you overtly threaten to hurt another person."

"Ever?"

"Ever. Everything we discuss is confidential, and in the state of California that privilege extends even past death."

Her questions put me on alert. "Is there something you want to talk to me about?"

"You can't tell anyone?" Her eyes darted over my shoulder at the door again.

"No one, Teresa. I promise. What's wrong?"

She gripped my arm. "I need your help. Paco wasn't a bystander—he was the target. I'm afraid Dr. Morales knew why."

Chapter Fifteen

Teresa's bold statement about Paco's death jolted me. Unsettled, I brought her to a bench under the session room window and sat down. "Who told you Paco was targeted?"

"Privilege, right?" Teresa searched my eyes, as if waiting for more reassurance.

"My state license requires me to keep discussions with clients confidential. As I told you—unless your life is at stake or I believe you're going to harm someone, whatever you say to me stays between us. Who told you Paco was targeted for murder?"

Her hands shook. "I called in sick yesterday and took the train to Lancaster to visit my husband in jail. I was afraid he thought I was cheating on him with José and told his friends to teach us a lesson. I wasn't cheating on Carlos. I love him. Carlos said he didn't have nothing to do with it."

"But he knew who did?"

She nodded. "He told me a rival gang killed Paco and used me and José to cover it up."

"Then the police already know. Conversations in jail are recorded, Teresa."

Teresa smirked, signing at me with her fingers as she said, "Prisoners use sign language to get messages to the outside. The guards didn't hear anything."

"You have to tell the police what you know."

"I won't." She set her elbows on her knees. "There's a code of silence in the gangs. If anyone even thought I snitched to the cops, they would kill me, and maybe Carlos, too."

"The police will protect you."

"The cops can't protect Carlos. If the rivals can't get to me, they'll get Carlos in jail just to teach me a lesson."

"They know Detective Bailey questioned you the night of the shooting," I said.

"And they know I told him I didn't see the shooter."

"Were you lying?"

"No. But now I know what really happened last Saturday night. I think José was in on it. He showed up at the Chicken Shack the day before the lock was broken. The next night he walked me home and saw Paco come downstairs to let me in. José started a conversation with him. Saturday night me and José passed the black SUV while it was parked up the street. They could have shot us right then but they waited for Paco to come out," Teresa said.

"Are you positive you didn't recognize the shooter?"

"I swear," Teresa said. "You don't know gang life, Liz. Dr. Morales and Paco, they were good friends. When I heard the doc disappeared, my gut told me maybe the same guys went after him. I think he knew something, like maybe who was after Paco."

"If Dr. Morales's life is in danger, we have to tell the police," I said.

She shook her head passionately. "No. Not yet. I only have a feeling, not proof. I'm your client. You swore you couldn't repeat our conversations. And my life will be in danger if I talk to the cops. I'm not threatening Dr. Morales. I'm trying to help him. Through you."

"I'll go to the police with you," I said.

"No way. We have to do this my way. I'm working here at the clinic today. I'm going to find an excuse to search Dr. Morales's office this afternoon. If I find something, you can go to the cops pretending you found the info in the doc's office yourself. I'm taking a big chance, but I want to help Dr. Morales and Lucia."

"I won't lie for you, Teresa. Dr. Morales already told the police everything he knew. And if the police or someone at the clinic hasn't searched his office already, they will soon."

"But they won't know what to look for. Maybe Dr. Morales knew something, but he didn't know he knew," she said.

I blinked at her screwy logic. I had an urge to call Bailey, but I couldn't act on it. Not only would I be breaking the laws of privilege, but I could be putting Teresa's life at risk. My head hurt.

"If Paco was their target, why not stage an armed robbery at the botanica?" I said. "Why did they use you and José?"

"José was a decoy to make Paco look like a bystander. His homies found out the kid was siphoning a lot of money off the top of his drug deals. They turned on him," Teresa said.

"And why did they involve you?" I said.

Her words came out sliced with bitterness: "To warn me and Carlos to stay out of rival business. I know the cops are watching me, but I'm more afraid of who else is. Carlos warned me to be careful. Don't trust anyone, Liz."

"Teresa, why are you involved with these people? You have a good chance to start a new life."

"I'm trying but it's not that simple. Carlos and me got into drugs and the life before we were teens. The gang is my family. They came to our wedding. After Carlos got sent up, I stopped doing drugs and got my job here." Teresa reached in her pocket and brought out a Narcotics Anonymous chip on a key chain. "See? One year."

"Congratulations. It takes courage to fight addiction. It also takes courage to do the right thing. Paco and Lucia were good to you. Dr. Morales gave you a job. I'll say it again, Teresa—talk to the police."

"No. This is the way it's gotta be. This way no one else gets hurt. You're an outsider. No one will ever know I talked to you."

"I won't play this game with you." I went to the locker, retrieved my purse, and then copied Bailey's number onto the back of my business card. "Call Detective Bailey. Tell him what you just told me. He will see that you get protection. Or phone an anonymous tip to Crime Stoppers."

Teresa grabbed my wrist. "Please. I can't. I don't have a choice. Give me this afternoon to go through Dr. Morales's office. If I find anything—" She jerked her head toward the rustle of movement in the hall.

Tony Torrico poked his head in the doorway, smiling. "Am I interrupting? Teresa, we need your help in the file room so Helen can get back to the patients."

"On my way, Dr. Torrico." Teresa turned to me with a final pleading glance then left.

I closed the locker, shut the session room door behind me, and walked down the hall with Tony.

"How did your group session go today?" he said.

"Good. I heard the police came this morning about Victor."

"Yes," he said. "I was going to call the police myself when I didn't hear from him last night or this morning. The detective arrived before I had an opportunity. We told him everything we knew, which wasn't much. We couldn't get into Victor's computer. I asked Helen to go through Victor's calendar entries and the papers on his desk."

"Puzzling," I said.

"Yes. Carmen and I are very concerned." Tony slowed his pace, rubbing the back of his neck. "I hold to my promise that this won't affect the fund-raiser. I refuse to let the clinic suffer in his absence."

"The Cherries will handle the fund-raiser without a hitch, don't worry. Does Victor have any health issues? Could he have had a heart attack or seizure in his car?"

"The detective asked the same questions. After I confirmed Victor was in good health, he left. Frankly, I don't know how seriously the police will treat his disappearance."

"Matt Bailey doesn't strike me as apathetic," I said.

He glanced at me, questioning. "You know the detective searching for Victor?"

"I met Bailey the night Paco was shot. He's investigating both cases because of Victor's relationship with Paco. He didn't tell you?"

"No. Maybe Paco's death, coupled with the pressure of

the clinic, was too much for Victor to cope with, and he took off. It's not a crime for an adult to disappear."

"But it's out of character for Victor." We walked in silence for several steps, and then I said, "Have you talked to Lucia in the past few days?"

"I spoke with her caretaker. She'll check in with me during Victor's absence. Lucia is taking her medication and resting." Tony stopped to sign a form for a nurse, and then we continued down the hall.

"About the pills, Tony. Lucia is having bouts of delusion."

"Lucia had a severe shock. If Victor doesn't return soon, I'll bring her in for an examination," Tony said.

The ladies' room door opened as we passed. Erica Gates came out and fell into pace behind us.

"I'm on my way to Lucia's now," I said to Tony. "Nick is writing a human-interest story about her and the botanica for the *Times* and the Hispanic daily. The story might run next week."

"Nice gesture," Tony said as we reached Jackson's desk. "I wish Lucia the best. She has a tough road ahead."

Erica, still on our heels, clicked her tongue. "Why promote an evil business? Let the Lord be the judge, not some intrusive, outside writer. Botanicas promote sacrilegious propaganda. A story about Lucia and witchcraft invites heathens to come to our neighborhood and draw people into damnation. Lucia Rojas is a consort of the devil."

"Amen," Jackson said under her breath. "That witch—"

"Ms. Jackson." Tony glared at her, pointing to the crowded waiting area. "Don't you have something to do? Are all these patients signed in?"

"Yes, Dr. Torrico."

As Tony and I crossed the lobby to the front door, he glanced over his shoulder at Jackson and Erica whispering at the desk. "I'd walk you out, Liz, but I need to have a word with Jackson. I'll see you at the benefit on Monday?"

"Nick and I will be there with the whole family," I said, smiling. "I hope Victor will be there to celebrate with us."

"I do, too. Please give Lucia my regards this afternoon and tell her or Cruz to call if she needs me. Wait here. I'll have Miguel walk out with you." Tony ignored my polite refusal, called for Miguel, and then said good-bye.

As Miguel and I strolled together toward the street, he said, "Dr. Cooper, do you think something bad happened to Dr. Morales?"

"Please call me Liz. I don't know what to think, Miguel. We'd all like to find him. Do you know of any patients who didn't like Dr. Morales? Someone he wouldn't treat, or someone who complained about him?"

"No ma'am. The policeman asked me the same question this morning. All the patients like Dr. Morales. But I've been thinking about it—I bet Ynez knows where he is. Those two are real close."

I stopped. Miguel's inflection tweaked my imagination. *As in secret-lover close?* "Who is Ynez?"

"Ynez Briano. She's Dr. Morales's patient. They're really good friends. She has a dress shop around the corner on Alvarado. My little sister works there on weekends sometimes. Ynez is a nice lady. She comes to visit Dr. Morales at the clinic a lot."

"I can go to Ynez's shop and talk to her now. Do you think she's there?"

He reached into his back pocket and took out his phone. "I'll call my sister and find out." After a brief conversation, he shook his head. "Ynez won't be in until tomorrow. She's working the farmer's markets today."

As we rounded onto 7th Street, the same three men in muscle shirts lingered at the concrete wall bordering the sidewalk. Their bandannas were tucked into the back pockets of jeans riding so low on their hips I couldn't imagine—and didn't want to know—what held them up. I thought only teenage girls dressed alike on purpose.

The tallest of the three had a buzz cut and a number tattooed on his skull. Another had a snake tattooed around his neck. The third was younger and stocky, with veined biceps bulging from his muscular shoulders. They chewed lazily on toothpicks, watching over the top of their sunglasses as Miguel and I approached.

"Hey-hey, the Boy Scout is on a field trip with a hot mama," Tattoo Neck said. "You think he's hitting that?"

Buzz Cut twirled his toothpick between his lips, looking me up and down. "Nice."

"Oh yeah. I could hit that." Biceps Boy snickered and elbowed Tattoo Neck.

"Ignore them," Miguel said to me. "They're showing off." We edged close to the curb, quickening our pace toward the corner.

Buzz Cut fell in beside us. "Slow down, Boy Scout. Don't be afraid, mama. We don't hurt."

"What's your hurry?" Tattoo Neck blocked our path.

I sidestepped off the curb. Tattoo Neck dodged with me. Buzz Cut made kissing sounds behind us. The two were so close I could smell their sweat.

"Back off." Miguel stepped nose-to-nose with Tattoo Neck.

Biceps Boy closed in on me. "I like older women. Where's your car, mama? Let's go for a ride."

As Biceps Boy reached out to grab at me, Miguel spun around and jammed a knee between the kid's legs. Biceps Boy doubled over in pain. Buzz Cut grabbed the back of Miguel's shirt.

Chapter Sixteen

"**D**amn it, knock it off." Teresa marched down the sidewalk, her loose hair swinging with each angry footstep. "Let go of him."

Buzz Cut let go. Miguel stumbled for balance. Biceps Boy gripped the parking lot wall, his face drained from pain. Tattoo Neck backed away and walked toward Teresa, shaking his head like nothing happened. The three thugs gaped at her like their teacher had just caught them smoking in the schoolyard. A horn blew on the street. Turning, I saw Nick dodge through traffic, unaware of a delivery truck speeding toward him.

I threw my hand to my chest. "Nick!"

The truck swerved. Nick reached the curb, breathless but unharmed, and stalked toward Teresa and the men.

She ranted at Tattoo Neck and his obnoxious pals with the cocky attitude of a woman from the streets, her hand on her hip, head thrown back. "How stupid are you? It's broad daylight. You trying to get arrested?"

Tattoo Neck tolerated her outburst with a stoic face. "Hey, T. It was a guy thing. We were playing around with Miguel. No harm."

Biceps Boy pointed at Miguel. "Until he freakin' attacked me."

"You were obnoxious to Dr. Cooper," Miguel said.

Biceps Boy gave him the finger and walked away.

"Go back to work, Miguel. Jackson needs you," Teresa said. "Tell her I'll be right there."

Miguel spread his hands and shrugged *sorry* at me as he backed down the sidewalk toward the clinic.

Tattoo Neck glared at Nick. "What are you looking at? This is none of your business."

"She's my business," Nick said, thumbing at me.

"They're Lucia's friends," Teresa said to Tattoo Neck. "Apologize to the lady so I can go back to work."

Tattoo Neck and Buzz Cut seethed restraint through clenched teeth and fists. Nick and I watched as spectators to an inside confrontation where Teresa had the upper hand.

"Come on, Teresa." Buzz Cut dropped his hands to his side, frustrated. "We weren't doing nothin'."

She cocked her head, mocking him. "Nothin'? I left work to break up nothin'? Should I tell Carlos about your nothin'? Apologize."

Buzz Cut swallowed, looking at me with a tight face. "Didn't know you knew T. We good?"

"We're good," I said.

Tattoo Neck tilted his chin at me. His way of apologizing, I supposed. I nodded, my way of accepting.

"Let's get out of here." Nick took my hand, leading me toward the crosswalk. "What happened back there? What did those men say to you?"

I gave him the thirty-second version. He glanced over his shoulder at Teresa. "Interesting. She has some kind of control over them. I'm surprised they let her disrespect them in front of us. If Teresa wields that much power on the street, I'd say she knows more about the shooting than she admits to."

I couldn't tell Nick he was right. Teresa's attitude toward the thugs made me question if she lied to me in the clinic about being afraid. She tried to manipulate me earlier, but why? Was she really worried about Victor or was she conniving to keep the investigation away from her?

"I think I'll ask Dave to pull her record. I don't like her friends, and I don't like them around you and Lucia." When I didn't comment, Nick said, "Did you hear anything about Victor inside the clinic?"

"Miguel thinks I should to talk to Ynez Briano, a patient who's close to Victor. She'll be at her dress shop on Alvarado tomorrow. Did Bailey talk to Lucia and Cruz this morning?"

"He was there when I arrived. Cruz repeated her story about Victor and Lucia going through papers, and Victor leaving after a phone call. He must have given Lucia a heavy sedative, because she didn't remember the papers or a phone call. Why would Victor have an overwrought woman go through papers?"

"Good question," I said, stepping up on the curb. "But since Lucia doesn't remember the papers, we have no way to know. How is she?"

"Clearer. More animated," Nick said. "After Bailey left,

we talked about the article. She told me about her courtship with Paco, pulled out her book of potions, and even demonstrated the way she dries herbs. I need more background on the building, and a photo or two, but I have enough to write a good feature. We were paging through Paco's scrapbook when I saw you through the window and ran out."

"And nearly got hit by a truck," I said. "I prefer you alive. I don't communicate well with spirits."

"How do you know? I might be a great haunt." He opened the door to Botanica Rojas and we went into the shop. Cruz waved from behind the TV. Nick stopped at a pile of books and papers on the counter close to the front window.

"Is Lucia in the back room?" I said to Cruz.

"No. She told me to wait here for you. She went upstairs."

Nick summoned me to the counter. "Before we go up, I want to show you something. You'll love this."

I knew from experience that few things excited Nick more than old papers. He put on his glasses and opened a faded black leather album. He flipped to a page of blurred black-and-white photos arranged with names and dates scripted in Spanish on their white borders.

He pointed at a photo in the middle of the page. "This is Paco's father, Aden Rojas."

The face in the picture stirred instant memories of Paco. He inherited his father's Latin features—his eyes, nose, and the cut of his jaw. The middle-aged Aden Rojas, his thumbs hooked around black suspenders on a white, collarless shirt, beamed at the camera from the sidewalk outside the building we were in. "BODEGA ROJAS EST. 1932" was painted in a bold arc on the window behind him.

"*Bodega?*" I said.

"This shop was a grocery store before it was a botanica." Nick turned the pages and showed me a progression of building photos.

I identified the eras by the automobiles parked in front on 7th Street, from tinny old Model Ts to round, luxurious, and heavy 1930s roadsters to the sleek, sharp-finned cars of the 1960s.

He stopped at a picture of a dark-haired woman with a stern, heart-shaped face. She wore an off-the-shoulder blouse and a flowered, ankle-length skirt. Her arm was wrapped around a boy in knickers and a baseball cap. "This is Gracia, the Rojas family matriarch. Paco was her only child."

Across the page was a photo of Gracia and a comely young redhead with a familiar, mischievous smile. The women were at the back counter of the shop, surrounded by bottles. "Is that Lucia?"

"Sure is. She and Gracia were close. When Paco and Lucia got married, they tried to have children but failed. Infertility is thought to be a hex in Santeria. Every birth is viewed as an ancestor reincarnated. Gracia tried to help Lucia—she taught her how to make Aztec herbal medicine potions to get pregnant."

"But the pregnancy never happened." I remembered the night Lucia told Carmen and me, with regret, that she and Paco couldn't produce heirs. They loved children. The jar of hard candy they kept for neighborhood kids still stood next to the cash register.

"Gracia schooled Lucia in everything about Santeria and herbal alchemy," Nick said. "They started Botanica Rojas together in the back of the Bodega while Aden and Paco sold groceries in front."

I saw a sliver of yellow paper peeking from behind a full-page photo of Paco, Lucia, Gracia, and Aden. I pinched the edge and slid the paper out. "What's this?"

Nick unfolded the sheet and skimmed the cursive writing on the yellowed document. "This is the original building deed. Check this out—Aden Rojas purchased the land and this building for eighteen thousand dollars in nineteen thirty-two."

"Wow. That's less than most cars cost today. This property must be worth a million dollars by now."

"Easily a million, probably closer to two based on location. Two generations of memories live under this roof." Nick folded the paper into his pocket. "This deed belongs in a safe or Lucia's safety deposit box, not hidden in a scrapbook."

I pictured the Rojas family selling their collection of statues and exotic concoctions to generations of families, while Los Angeles burgeoned into a modern metropolis outside. As I looked around, my eyes stopped at the end of the aisle where Cruz sat enthralled by the heated Spanish dialogue on her telenovela. I assumed Victor didn't hire her to stare at a TV downstairs while Lucia puttered in the apartment above.

Resentment stirred inside me. "Cruz, why is Lucia upstairs alone?"

She turned down the volume. "She wanted to talk to Paco, undisturbed. Go up. She left both doors unlocked. I'll be there in a minute to make her lunch and give her a pill."

I turned to Nick. "Let's take Lucia out to lunch."

"Great idea. She hasn't been out since the wake." He

packed the photo album with the rest of the papers and carried the box to the back room.

"Don't knock when you get upstairs," Cruz said. "Lucia will get mad. She thinks knocking stirs up bad spirits and chases away good ones."

A breeze fluttered the window curtains in the upstairs corridor outside Lucia's apartment. Nick put his ear to her front door then turned the knob. The living room shades were drawn; slivers of daylight peeked through the sides. A bouquet of pink tulips stood sentry in a vase on the table between the armchairs.

Lucia knelt in front of the Santeria altar in an ecru lace veil and a striped apricot housedress. Miniature votives and a hurricane candle flickered among the coconuts, bananas, pears, and trinkets scattered around the picture of Paco propped in front of his urn.

We waited and watched from the doorway while Lucia sprinkled herbs in a bowl of water at the foot of the photograph. She set a small crucifix into the bowl, chanted, and made the sign of the cross with a small bouquet of flowers over the altar.

Lucia kissed Paco's photograph. "*Te amo, Paciano.*" Then she pushed herself up and raised the shades. "What are you waiting for? Come in."

"We didn't want to disturb you." I wrapped her in a gentle hug, her body so thin I feared I'd break her.

She pinched my cheek with affection, then took my arm and pushed back my sleeve, uncovering my bracelet. "Hah."

She wagged her finger at Nick. "I told you the bracelet would protect her. You didn't believe me. You had to run into the street."

"He was very gallant, Lucia. Between Nick, Miguel, and Teresa, I didn't need the bracelet at all."

"It doesn't matter if you don't believe, Liz. The orishas know you're special to me. Both of you are. And you have to be careful. I stirred up trouble by setting the hex in motion. There's no turning back. Before the full moon wanes, Paco's murderers will be punished."

"People are afraid of you, Lucia," I said. "Your friends in the neighborhood need reassurance that you wouldn't hurt them."

"No." Lucia sat in her armchair, scowling. "Someone at the wake was responsible for killing Paco. I felt the evil there, taunting me. I had to fight back. Bad luck and misery can hound Paco's killer until he shows himself. Keep the bracelet on, Liz. Make me happy. Stay out of trouble."

"I promise, just for you. Nick showed me photos of you in the family scrapbook downstairs. I loved seeing you as a girl, the saucy redhead Paco fell in love with."

Her strawberry red hair came from a bottle now, but her eyes sparkled with the same mischievous glint in her pictures. "Paco was too handsome. I had to make him marry me before the other *chicas* got their claws into him. Something you should remember, Liz."

Nick coughed. "Liz found the deed to your building hidden behind a photo." He pulled the paper from his pocket. "You should keep this in a safe place."

"You found the deed?" She clapped her hands. "Paco and

Victor searched all over for it. Put it in the top drawer of the desk. I'll tell Victor when he calls tonight."

"He's calling you?" Nick said with surprise.

"He calls me every night. He promised to visit me soon," she said.

First relieved, then miffed at Victor for not calling Carmen or the clinic, I said, "Did he tell you where he is?"

"Not now," she said as Cruz opened the front door.

"Time for lunch and your medication. Are you hungry?" Without waiting for an answer, Cruz headed into the kitchen.

"Let us take you out," Nick said. "Liz and I will bring you back fat and happy."

"Not today. Victor told me to stay home and rest," Lucia said.

"Does Detective Bailey know Victor called you?" I said.

"I can't tell anyone," she said. "It's a secret."

When Cruz came out, Lucia took her pill and rested her head back in the armchair. "Nick, do you still have the statue of Santa Barbara I gave you?"

"I keep it on my desk. Changó, the orisha of lightning, thunder, and electricity. I think of you when the lights flicker and during spring thunderstorms. *Que viva Changó.*"

"Yes, Changó is that, and more. I wanted you to have the statue because you understand justice the same way Changó does. And because you and Liz are strong together, like Changó and Oyá, his mistress and companion in battle." She grinned up at me. "Their lovemaking is passionate and volatile. Inseparable, like the two of you."

I accepted Lucia's comment—compliment?—with a smile. Leaving her with Nick to talk Santeria, I decided to have a chat with Cruz in the kitchen. I found her rifling through the drawer next to the sink. She took out an opener and then pierced open the can of beans in front of her on the counter.

"We tried to coax Lucia out to lunch, but she refused," I said. "Has she been eating?"

Cruz threw up her hands and sighed. "I know she doesn't like my cooking yet but she won't leave the building. I'm trying to make her happy. Teresa brought us food from the Chicken Shack the other night. The local restaurants won't deliver to this building because of the hex and the fire at Fidencio's. We have casseroles and tamales in the freezer that I microwave. Don't worry, Lucia eats when she's hungry."

As Cruz rattled off explanations, I picked up the prescription bottle from the counter and read the label. *Xanax .125*. Victor Morales was Lucia's prescribing physician, and the scrip was dated the day after Paco's death.

"Is this the only medication Lucia takes?" I said, noting the light dosage.

She took the bottle out of my hand and dropped it in a drawer. "The only one. I have to fix her lunch before she takes her nap. Don't want her to starve," she added with a prickly smirk.

Her attitude grated on me. I was aching to pry into Cruz's background. I couldn't sense her compassion or empathy for Lucia. I trusted that Victor and Father Nuncio checked out her references, so I set aside my feelings and accepted their judgment—for the moment.

"You've been with Lucia constantly for the past few days. Has her state of mind improved since the wake?"

Cruz emptied the beans into a pan on the stove and

turned on the gas. "Lucia is strong. She gets tired in the afternoon, but she sleeps good and she eats good."

"And have the delusions stopped?"

"She talks to her orishas. The orishas talk back. What you call delusion is Lucia communicating with the other side. She's fine. And if she weren't, I would notify her doctor," Cruz said, stirring cooked rice into the beans. "She has plenty of those."

"Has anyone aside from Teresa and us phoned or come over?" If Victor had called, Cruz would have heard the phone ring.

"No one."

"Except Dr.—"

Cruz set the spoon on the side of the stove and faced me. "Please don't upset her anymore with talk about Dr. Morales. The detective this morning was bad enough."

Curious that she assumed I meant Victor. "I actually meant the call from Dr. Torrico. He told me he spoke to you."

"Oh." She paused for a beat. "Yes, Dr. Torrico called me to ask about her. I thought you were talking about phone calls for *Lucia*. When I said she was strong, I meant that she's doing well for what she just went through over her husband. But she sits near the phone all day convinced Dr. Morales or Paco will call. Are we done? I'm kind of busy." Cruz turned to the stove.

I went back into the living room. Nick sat at the edge of Paco's armchair. Lucia relaxed in her chair, grinning at him like a child who couldn't hold a secret.

"Victor's going to call me again today. He's with Paco. You can't tell anybody, Nick. He made me promise not to tell." She leaned back and closed her eyes.

Chapter Seventeen

As Lucia dozed off in her armchair, Nick tugged me to the window beside the altar. Dropping his voice, he said, "What pill did Cruz give her? Lucia was fine this morning."

"Some sedatives have delusional side effects, but I just saw the bottle. The anxiety medication Victor prescribed isn't that strong. Part of me wants to believe her, Nick. What if Victor really called?"

"To tell her he's with Paco?" He glanced over at Lucia. "I don't like this. If her mind is slipping away, what do we do? She doesn't have relatives."

"We find Victor. We're here for her now. Carmen will examine her Monday."

"I don't know if we should leave her alone."

Cruz came out of the kitchen. "She's not alone. I'm here. I take good care of her." She set a glass of milk and a plate on the end table at Lucia's side.

"And I'm grateful you're here." Nick's suave smile didn't cancel Cruz's scowl.

"She missed her lunch. You better go," Cruz said.

"Tell her we'll be back later." Nick gave Cruz his business card. "Here's my phone number. Call me if she needs anything. Anything."

"*Si.*" As we left, Cruz said, "And don't worry. I'll make sure she eats."

Nick and I walked the two blocks to Langer's Deli. We ordered pastrami and Swiss cheese sandwiches on rye with coleslaw and Russian dressing, a Diet Coke for me, and Dr. Brown's Cream Soda for Nick. Between bites of hot pastrami and crunchy french fries, we made a decision to go to the hospital and talk to Carmen.

The cloudless, smog-free sky opened the view of the city from the skyscrapers downtown all the way to the frame of the snowcapped San Gabriel Mountains to the north. We drove stop-and-go to Good Samaritan, bogged down by construction and late afternoon traffic on Wilshire.

As we walked into her room, Carmen sat up in bed with a cheery smile. "I'm so glad you came. Sit down. Sit down. Thank you for the flowers, Nick." She gestured at the vase of white daisylike buds on the windowsill.

"I thought you'd appreciate them. The ancient Egyptians dedicated the flowering chamomile plant to the sun gods because of its healing properties," he said.

"They're lovely. Just looking at them makes me feel better. Detective Bailey and I talked at length about Victor after you left the hospital yesterday. I haven't heard from him today. I assume there's not any news?" Her hopeful look fell into disappointment when we shook our heads.

"Bailey questioned the clinic staff this morning," I said.

"Were you there with them?" Carmen reached for a tissue and blew her nose.

"No, but Nick and I talked to Bailey last night. We'll help as much as we can. Promise," I said.

"Good. I'm going home tomorrow."

"We were just with Lucia," Nick said. "She told us Victor called her last night."

"He did?" Carmen sat up straight in bed. "What did he say? Where is he? Why didn't you tell me right away?"

"I don't know if we should believe her," I said. "Cruz told me the phone didn't ring last night. Lucia might have her days confused, or he called while Cruz was watching TV. Or Lucia is having delusions again. But if Victor actually called, he told Lucia he was with Paco."

"Victor wouldn't say something so cold. I'm glad we had the foresight to hire the caretaker for her," Carmen said. "How is Cruz working out?"

I glanced at Nick. "To be fair, we haven't been around Cruz long enough to judge. She and Lucia need time to get to know each other."

Carmen cocked her head. "That's a judgment in itself, sweetie. What do you think, Nick?"

"Cruz stays clear of me," Nick said. "I'm not sold yet. Did you read her résumé before Victor hired her?"

"I trust Victor," Carmen said. "He needed someone for Lucia right away, and we agreed to give Cruz a trial until Victor and Lucia made a permanent decision."

"Unless Lucia is thrilled with her, I wouldn't make Cruz

a permanent hire. Lucia's state of mind is the bigger concern," I said. "If she falls apart—"

"I'll spend time with Lucia and Cruz before I go into the clinic Monday. Tony is available for emergencies until then." She turned to me. "Tell me something good. How did the Wellness Group go this morning? Did the women play nice, or did they give you a hard time?"

"It went well." I glanced sideways at Nick.

Carmen flapped her hand. "We can talk in front of Nick. He doesn't know any of the people."

"No," Nick said. "You should talk shop in private. I'll go out in the hall and check my e-mail and phone messages."

Carmen watched him back out the door, and then said, "He's a good one."

"I know," I said. What I didn't know was why I wasn't packing to move in with him.

"Are you going to live with him?" Carmen said.

Were my thoughts that transparent? If so, maybe Carmen could decipher them for me. "I'm thinking about it." I sat in the chair by her bed and dropped my purse on the floor.

"Don't do that," Carmen said.

"What? Don't move in with Nick, or don't sit down?" I scooted to the side of the seat cushion.

"Your purse on the floor invites bad luck. All the money inside will drain out."

"I'm not superstitious."

"Pick up the purse and humor me anyway. There's too much bad luck going around. Go on, pick it up."

Carmen could be as stubborn as my mother. Her bedridden state gave her a sympathetic advantage, so I reached down and brought the purse to my lap.

"Thank you," Carmen said. "Now tell me about the group."

"Lively," I said. "Four women came but only one was a carryover from last week. They spent more time complaining about Lucia's hex than I would have liked."

"I can understand their obsession about the hex. Santeria has a strong influence on the neighborhood. Did they blame every flat tire in the area on Lucia?"

"In the broadest sense, yes," I said. "People will talk about anything to avoid their feelings."

Carmen laughed. "Did Erica Gates come? She asked my opinion about the group last Monday. I assured her support groups were valuable to strengthen interpersonal skills."

"Can I hire you to do my PR? You're an excellent spokeswoman. Yes, she came."

"And when the hex came up, did she proselytize about the church as their only salvation?"

"Erica has strong convictions. But I also sensed a lot of loneliness," I said.

"That's why I encouraged her to attend your session," Carmen said. "I think she *is* lonely. Her husband deals in commercial real estate. He'd buy a sandbox if he thought he could develop it. The harder Bernie works, the deeper Erica throws herself into community and church activities. What about the other women?"

I glanced at the door. Satisfied no one lingered close in the hallway, I leaned in. "Can we treat this conversation as a professional consult? I need your advice, but we have to speak under a doctor-to-doctor umbrella to legally protect the privacy issues."

"Of course. You seem concerned," Carmen said.

"I am concerned. The client is Teresa Suarez."

"Really." Carmen creased her forehead. "I wondered how she was coping with the shooting. What did she say in group that concerned you so?"

"It wasn't what she said in group. After the other women left, Teresa approached me in private. She made me reassure her that our conversation was confidential, and then told me she visited her husband in jail. He told her Paco wasn't the bystander last Saturday night—he was the target."

"Oh my God."

"There's more. Teresa thinks Victor's disappearance is tied to Paco's death."

"Does she know where Victor is?"

"No," I said.

"Make her go to the police," Carmen said.

"I tried. She won't. She claimed privilege and made me vow not to say anything, which means neither can you."

"What if the killers are after Lucia and Victor? Go to the police."

"Ethically, I can only contact the police if Teresa is threatened or she is the threat. If I did contact them, I have nothing to offer except Teresa's suspicions and a jailhouse rumor. She didn't tell me who killed Paco. She only suspects Victor's absence is linked to the shooting. She's searching Victor's office this afternoon. If she finds something, she wants *me* to take the information to the police and leave her out of it."

"Tony had Helen go through Victor's office. Teresa is playing games with you," Carmen said.

"I agree. And I don't know if I trust what she told me. When I left the clinic with Miguel today three gang members harassed us on the sidewalk. Teresa came out and bullied them off. It was strange, Carmen. The three full-grown punks were afraid of her. She transformed from a frightened and worried client into a belligerent, I don't know, gang queen? The change in her demeanor was remarkable. But what if she finds a clue Helen missed in Victor's office? I won't go to the police and lie for her. Unless . . ."

"Unless what?"

"You could give Nick and me permission to do another search of Victor's office tonight. We go through his files. We check his e-mail. Then we take what we find to the police and leave Teresa out of it completely."

"Brilliant. You have my permission," Carmen said.

"How do we get into his computer without a password?"

"Victor uses his late wife's name as his password for everything. Remember Beatrice? Maybe her spirit will guide us to him."

"And you're comfortable with us going through his files?" I said.

"Sweetie, I trust you and Nick. If I could get out of bed I would search Victor's office and computer myself. And if I had the key, I'd search his house down to his underwear drawer to find him. I'll tell him the search was my idea after I kiss him for being alive. Victor would do the same for me. We don't keep secrets from each other."

There was a knock. Nick peeked through the door. "Is it safe?"

Carmen waved him in, grinning. "Are you testing us with film quotes again, Nick? *Marathon Man*."

"Caught me," he said. "And who gave the line?"

"Olivier to that adorable Dustin Hoffman."

"You're good, Carmen." Nick handed her a box. "You probably can't eat these chocolates but—"

"You're so right. My doctor would kill me. Give them to me." She unwrapped the cellophane, opened the box, and closed her eyes to inhale the aroma. "Heaven. I'll sneak a bite, and you and the nurses can enjoy the rest of the box for me. Hell, I'm already in the hospital. Save me a piece. Or two."

She passed me the milk chocolate–covered caramels. I took two pieces and bit into one. The sweet chocolate and chewy caramel melted in my mouth.

"We're going to the clinic to search Victor's office," I said to Nick.

"Okay." He popped a caramel in his mouth. "What are we looking for?"

"What do you look for when you do research?" Carmen said.

"Patterns. Breaks from patterns. Something abnormal, out of place," Nick said. "If I can get in his computer, I'll go through his e-mails and Internet browser. If the history is there, we'll have a list of his searches."

"Do that," she said. "His password is Beatrice. Open his mail, too. And Liz, go through the personal folder he keeps in the back of his bottom desk drawer. Call me when you get to the clinic. I'll call and alert Tony in case he stays late. The key to the front door is in my purse in the closet."

"Did you talk to any of Victor's friends?" Nick said.

"I gave Detective Bailey a list, and I contacted his golf partners myself this morning," Carmen said. "None of them have talked to him since Tuesday. I have everyone calling around."

I retrieved Carmen's purse from the closet. She unhooked a thick silver key off a ring and wrote down the code for the security alarm.

"Did anything happen in the past month or so to upset Victor before Paco was shot?" Nick said. "Any threats or intimidation?"

"Toward Victor? No." Her eyes searched the ceiling. "We've been lucky. The only trouble I remember happened years ago, after Paco filed a complaint about kids loitering on the sidewalk in front of the botanica and outside the clinic. Victor told Paco not to, but Paco was outraged about the growing gang problem and insisted we file the report along with him. A few days later someone smashed the front window of the botanica and keyed Victor's car."

"Did Paco or Victor call the police?" Nick said.

"No. Victor didn't want to encourage more trouble. Paco chose a different approach. He went to neighborhood council meetings, demanded increased patrol, and got involved in the Neighborhood Watch. Paco wanted the gangs out of the district, and the gangs knew it."

"Don't forget about the recent broken lock on Paco and Lucia's downstairs door," I said.

"Yes, I know. That was odd. The gangs kept their distance from the building after—" She stopped herself.

"After Teresa moved in?" Nick said.

"Why would you say that?" Carmen said.

"I just wonder if the building was off-limits because of her. Liz and I saw her in action with some gang members today. She's tough," he said. "What if Paco caught her doing something illegal, and was killed out of fear or retaliation?"

Carmen and I swapped glances.

"Paco and Teresa were close," Carmen said.

"So? Even if he liked Teresa, Paco hated the gangs. I wonder if the punks we saw her with today broke the lock on the Rojases' building," Nick said. "I think one of you should talk to Teresa again."

We couldn't tell Nick that Teresa was my client. I had to end the conversation before he pushed further. I turned to Carmen. "Was Victor worried or upset about anything else?"

She picked up on the topic switch with ease. "Like money or his health? No. I would know. Victor wouldn't abandon the clinic or Lucia. You saw him with her. He protects her like family. He has her power of attorney. He wouldn't desert her. Or me."

"He has her medical POA. At the wake he told us the legal POA wasn't signed yet," Nick said.

"Which concerns me," I said. "Without Victor to handle her affairs, she's vulnerable."

"I'll spend more time with Lucia next week," Carmen said. "If I agree with Tony's initial impression of her condition, maybe we should discuss moving her into a facility. She would be safe in a controlled environment with professionals monitoring her."

I waved her off. "It's too soon after Paco's death to force Lucia out of her home. Relocating to an unfamiliar, strange setting would be horribly stressful, Carmen. Lucia is much better off at home with a nurturing caretaker."

A cheery voice interrupted from the doorway. "Well, look who's here."

Glamorous in a ruffle-collared camel pantsuit with her hair coiffed in waves, Mom swept into the room holding up a shopping bag from Bottega Louie, the downtown gourmet market. She flickered her eyes around the room. "The energy in here is troubled. What in the world were you three talking about before I got here?"

"Victor," I said.

"Liz, didn't you tell Dave to find him? The fund-raiser is Monday. Nick, did you reverse the hex like I asked? How far does the effect of the hex spread? Do you feel the strange energy in here?" Without waiting for a response, she rifled to the bottom of her Chanel bag and brought out a tiny gray bundle of dried sage tied with a red thread. Another dip into her purse produced a lighter. "I have to smudge this room right now or Carmen won't sleep a wink tonight."

Mom lit the sage and waved a small stream of smoke around her body, over Carmen's bed, and into the four corners of the room. Nick stood back, grinning as she performed her ceremony. Her smudging was old news to me. I ate another chocolate to pass the time. The sage smoke drifted out into the hospital corridor, drawing a stout nurse in blue scrubs into the room.

"Is there something burning in here?" She barreled to the monitor at Carmen's side. She bent down, checked the wiring, and glanced back at us.

"I'm clearing out the negative energy with sage," Mom said, straight-faced.

The nurse swerved around with her hands on her hips "Put it out, now. You'll set off the smoke alarm. This is a hospital, not a temple. Candles and incense burning are not allowed. They create a fire hazard, and the odor disturbs the other patients."

"I intend to disturb the negative spirits lurking in here."

Mom went into the small bathroom and flushed the remnants of burnt sage down the toilet.

The nurse clicked her tongue and left. Mom settled into the chair by the bed, with a self-satisfied grin. "Some of the negative energy just left. It already feels better in here."

"Where's Daddy?" I said.

"Home, watching sports." Mom moved the chocolates from Carmen's tray to a table. "If you answered your phone, dear, you could have joined Carmen and me for dinner."

"You called? I didn't hear . . . Oh." I dug in my purse and found my phone, muted. I forgot to turn the ringer back on after the group session. The screen told me I had four messages. "Sorry about that, Mom. How many times did you call?"

"Three or four. Dilly can take you house hunting tomorrow. She wanted to know what time," Mom said. "Since you didn't call me back, I made an appointment for us to meet her at eleven."

The thought of house hunting with my mother started a headache at the back of my neck. I envisioned her pushing an oversized box in the suburbs on me, using crazy concepts like resale value. Nope.

"Nick and I made plans tomorrow." I nodded in his direction, counting on his backup.

"Go look at houses. I can write my article while you're out."

I caught the hurt in Nick's eyes before he turned away. Was his accommodating attitude about my future residence a guise? Did I disappoint him when I didn't leap at the invitation to move in with him?

"Then it's settled," Mom said. "I'll call Dilly tonight to confirm. By the way, she told me something odd this morning. At our last fund-raiser meeting for the clinic, Victor asked if she knew a good real estate attorney. Is Victor planning to sell the clinic? Should we alert Kitty?"

I loved how Mom could go straight to an assumption.

Carmen shook her off. "Viv, you know we lease the space for Park Clinic. So does Kitty. Victor and I agreed to sign an extended lease after the Cherries committed to raise money for showers and plumbing."

"Maybe Victor was going to sell his house," Mom said.

"He needs a real estate agent for that, not a lawyer." I got up and moved toward the door. "We should leave, Nick. Maybe we'll find the answer in Victor's office."

Chapter Eighteen

On the way back to Park Clinic with Nick, I picked up the three messages Mom left about the meeting with Dilly. Robin called to say she found a dress for the fundraiser.

No message from Teresa. I hoped that meant she changed her mind about involving me and went to the police on her own. Or it meant she searched but didn't find what she was after in Victor's office.

I tucked my phone back in my purse. "Nick, what if the papers Victor went over with Lucia after the wake were for her legal power of attorney? What if she signed them?"

"And then he took the papers and disappeared? What would that accomplish?"

"I don't know. I'm grasping," I said. "I hate to say this, but maybe we should have Lucia check her bank account. What if Victor had hidden money problems?"

"Bailey can check his finances. That's a pretty cold turnaround. Do you think Victor is that heartless?"

"I don't. I'm trying to avoid thinking he's dead," I said.

We parked in front of Park Clinic near dusk. Nick used Carmen's key to unlock the dead bolt, then disabled the alarm. We turned on the lights behind Jackson's desk and strolled through the corridors to Victor's office in back. I tried the knob. Locked. I reached for my phone to call Carmen.

Nick stopped me. "Wait here. I'll be right back."

He disappeared down the hall toward reception. I heard a drawer clatter open, then a jangle and a bang. He came back with a set of keys, trying several until he found one that opened Victor's door.

"How did you know?" I said in wonderment.

"I saw Jackson pull them out for an intern the other day. I assumed she wouldn't take a mess of metal like this home with her."

I turned on the overhead lights in Victor's small, windowless office. His medical school diplomas hung on the wall behind his wooden desk. The credenza was topped with pictures of Victor with Beatrice, a lovely, open-faced blonde in her midsixties. They both appeared relaxed and happy, sitting at the edge of Rome's Trevi Fountain, and standing side by side in Hawaiian shirts by a waterfall. A group shot showed Victor and Beatrice with Carmen, Paco, and Lucia posed behind a birthday cake. The photo on his desk displayed a much thinner Beatrice waving from a wheelchair.

Nick turned on the old desktop computer and entered the password at the screen prompt. The computer hummed and a sky blue background appeared. "I'm in."

While he searched the computer, I sifted through the stack of mail at the corner of the desk: *Global Health Magazine*, letters addressed to Victor from pharmaceutical companies, medical journals, and a small "Thank-You" postcard with "You're the best. xoxo, Ynez" written on the back. I paged through his At-A-Glance calendar. Paco's wake last Wednesday was the lone entry for the week. The following week he had penciled in "fund-raiser" on Monday evening, "Ynez" at noon on Tuesday, and a haircut appointment on Thursday. I fanned through the remainder of the pages and found nothing. No cryptic notes; no other notes at all.

"Look at this." Nick pointed at the e-mail he had open on the computer screen. "This came in Wednesday night."

I read over his shoulder:

Will do. Should I reschedule your patients for Friday afternoon or move to next week?—Helen

"We knew Victor e-mailed Helen that night," I said. "That must be her reply."

Nick scrolled down. "But read the original e-mail he wrote her at seven thirty."

Helen, I won't be in Thursday for personal reasons. Reschedule my appointments.

"A little brusque for him," I said. Victor restrained himself in person but the keyboard unleashed his inner verbosity. The congratulatory e-mail he had sent when I joined the clinic went on for pages. "What do you want me to see?"

"Helen replied with a question a minute later, and he didn't respond. Unless he called her?"

"She told me they didn't talk on the phone," I said. "What about the rest of his e-mails?"

"All business. None of his incoming e-mails have been

161

opened since Wednesday." Nick sat back in the chair. "Why did he e-mail Helen instead of calling her?"

"She didn't answer her phone?"

"She answered the e-mail instantly."

"I'm more curious about why he only told Helen," I said. "I would assume he'd phone or write Carmen or Tony if an emergency came up. We need to see his phone records."

Nick grunted agreement then went back to his screen search. I opened the bottom desk drawer.

Labeled manila folders were arranged in alphabetical order to the back. I skimmed through the headers and stopped at the light blue file marked "Payroll" to check for recent firings, perhaps someone holding a grudge. Helen Leonard and the rest of the medical staff earned standard wages for their positions. Jackson and Miguel were paid just above minimum wage. Teresa's entry stopped me.

"Teresa made two hundred dollars a week, in cash. That's a lot of money for a part-time Saturday job," I said.

"Maybe she works more hours than you thought."

"And is paid in cash?"

"Do you think it's relevant?"

"Just odd."

I flipped through the remainder of the files and then pulled out the folder I found tucked behind a black three-ring binder in the back of the drawer. I opened the file inside. The two letters on top were both addressed to Paco Rojas, dated three weeks ago.

Bernard Gates signed the first on Gates Realty stationery. He thanked Paco for their recent discussion about the progressive changes coming to Westlake. Gates outlined his background and success stories, and then requested a follow-up meeting with Paco to discuss the value and sale of his building. Gates assured he would personally help relocate the Rojas family to a new home. Stapled to the letter was a copy of a recent newspaper article, touting the wisdom of selling commercial property in the current market for the best price before a decline.

The second letter was from Raymon Cansino of C&C Commercial Properties and Investments. In it, Cansino insinuated that Paco's building was targeted for inspection and a fast sale would protect Paco from a burden of fines and fees. He claimed his interested buyers would absorb all penalty costs on top of a generous offer to buy.

Beneath the letters I found an Internet article about city plans for the Subway to the Sea, the controversial extension of the Metro Purple Line from downtown Los Angeles to the Westside for traffic-challenged Angelenos.

"Liz." Nick drew my attention up to the computer screen. "Victor's latest Internet searches were about real estate: the county assessor, the Los Angeles housing department, commercial property law, eminent domain, and property values in Westlake."

"Maybe because of these." I set the letters in front of him.

He read them, and then opened the drop-down "History" menu on the browser. "Victor searched those companies and the individual men several times. And he researched the value of Paco's building and searched property liens and possible complaints."

"Cause and effect?" I said. "Victor researches the building, Paco gets killed, and a few days later Victor disappears. Both Realtors were at the wake. Bernie Gates was the Realtor who said he had Paco poised to sell."

"It's worth talking to one or both of them."

"But this information doesn't tell us where Victor is. Did you find anything else before we call Carmen?"

"He bookmarked senior dating sites," Nick said, laughing.

"No. Don't tell me Victor was two-timing Carmen on the side. Makes me curious to meet Ynez tomorrow."

Nick saw how serious I was and stopped laughing. "In his defense, they could be old bookmarks. Can't blame a guy for looking."

"Any cybersex e-mails hinting he took off with a cougar?"

"Considering Victor is in his seventies, his cougar would be at least eighty. No web winks from octogenarians. His online reputation is intact."

We dialed Carmen's hospital room from the speakerphone. After we ran down the details, she couldn't account for the real estate searches and drew the same conclusion we had—Victor was helping Paco research the value of his building.

"Except Paco Rojas wouldn't sell for any amount," Carmen said.

"Everyone has their price," I said.

"Not Paco. He lived in the same building his whole life, through wars, riots, and earthquakes. I'd be more than shocked if he and Lucia planned to retire somewhere else. They would have said something. Did you find anything else in Victor's computer? Notes? Letters?"

"Ynez Briano sent a thank-you note. He wrote her in for lunch next week on his calendar. Miguel mentioned they're close. How close?" I said.

"Victor seems very fond of her. She's been a patient at

the clinic for a few years. They planned a lunch date together? I have no idea why. I didn't realize they saw each other outside the clinic," Carmen said.

"I'll find out when I see her tomorrow. But I think the lunch date is telling. Putting future events like lunches and haircuts on his calendar strengthens a theory that his disappearance was unplanned," I said.

"And confirms that something awful happened to him," Carmen said.

"We'll find him, Carmen," Nick said.

We ended the call with a promise to be in touch the next day.

Two pops echoed through the empty halls, like distant fireworks. Tires screeched from the alley behind the clinic, the engine fading south, away from 7th Street.

Nick jerked back in the chair. "That sounded like gunshots. Is there a back door?"

"Around the corner past the dispensary, and down the other hall. But you're not going out there, are you?"

"No. I want to be certain no one can get in. I'll be right back."

My mind darted to Lucia across the street. The gunfire could have triggered flashbacks to Paco and upset her. I pulled out my phone and dialed.

Lucia picked up on the first ring. "Victor?"

"It's Liz. Are you and Cruz all right? Nick and I are right across the street."

"Come over. I can't talk. I'm waiting for Victor to call." A click and the line went silent.

She didn't mention the gunfire. That was good. Waiting by the phone for Victor to call? Troubling.

Nick came back and said, "The back door is metal with a steel bar. No one can get in, but I heard shouting in the alley. Someone was shot."

Sirens blared outside. I returned the files to the back of the drawer and put Victor's desk back in order. We locked up and exited Park Clinic into a sea of flashing red and blue lights. LAPD patrol cars blocked off the alleyway. When we reached the sidewalk, an ambulance pulled out of the alley with lights and siren on and turned east onto 7th. Small groups of people, including Buzz Cut and Tattoo Neck, were gathered on both sides of the street under the glare of the streetlamps.

From the midst of one of the small groups, an unshaven youth in a plaid shirt and jeans pointed a longneck bottle of beer across the street at Botanica Rojas. "The *bruja*'s hex again. This is her fault. Let's get her."

Others took up the cry, turning their attention from the alley to Botanica Rojas, and chanting, "Get the witch, get the witch."

"Burn the building!" The ragged group marched across the street, away from the squad cars. New people joined the mass heading toward Botanica Rojas.

"Damn it. Wait here." Nick followed the crowd into the street.

Lucia and Cruz were at the second floor window looking down. I fumbled for my phone and hit redial as I darted across the street, panicked that the mob would see them.

When Cruz answered, I said, "Get Lucia away from the window. I'm almost at the door. Don't buzz anyone in unless you hear my voice on the intercom."

Angry and threatening shouts surrounded me. My heart

pounding, I desperately searched through the swarm of faces for Nick. Police, in helmets and riot gear, poured en masse into the street. The growing mob hurled empty bottles at the officers and rocks at the botanica. I bumped my way through to the sidewalk, with my purse clutched to my chest.

As I reached the curb, the front window of Botanica Rojas shattered into pieces. A teenager in an overgrown fade haircut lit a rolled newspaper with a lighter. Nick pushed through the group and tackled the torchbearer at the waist, wrestling him to the ground through a din of shouts, sirens, and the rapid click of Tasers. A kid in camouflage pants picked up the burning paper and backed into the street. Buzz Cut grabbed the kid, throwing him to the ground. Tattoo Neck stomped out the flames.

I ducked into Lucia's downstairs stoop, panting, and hit the intercom button. "It's Liz. Buzz me in."

When I entered the vestibule, Lucia and Cruz appeared at the top of the steps.

"What should we do?" Cruz said.

"Is the back door secure?" I said.

Lucia nodded. "Bolted and chained. But our botanica—"

"Nick is in front of the shop with the police. I want both of you to stay inside the apartment and keep away from the windows."

Cruz put an arm around Lucia and eased her back to the apartment. As soon as I heard the door close behind them, I went back outside for Nick.

Police outnumbered the crowd that remained. Five people, including the youth who incited the riot and the two torchbearers, were hauled off in a police van. Police barricades blocked off the squad cars and the officers investigating the alley shooting. I spotted Nick in front of the broken window at Botanica Rojas, talking with a patrolman in riot gear.

"My friend owns the building, damn right I defended it. I have to find my girlfriend. She's five feet five, dark hair—"

"I'm here, Nick." I locked onto his arm. His clothes were filthy but, aside from a swollen cheek, he appeared to be unscathed. "Lucia's upstairs, safe. What do we do about that?" I pointed at the window.

"Will you find a glass repair company to board it tonight? I'll wait out here and guard the shop."

My face was damp with perspiration and my hair matted to the back of my neck as I climbed the steps to Lucia's apartment. Music poured into the corridor. Cruz was at the open door. Inside, Lucia was at the dining room table singing along to Lola Beltran.

"It was the only thing I could think of to distract her," Cruz said.

"Good idea." I slipped into the chair next to Lucia. "I'm sorry. The botanica's front window is smashed. Nick will make sure no one gets inside the shop. I have to find someone to board the window tonight."

"My hex is working. It won't be long." Lucia went to the desk and opened her address book. "Paco has a glass repair service he uses. Here's the number. You tell them Paco needs them."

The 24-Hour Glass Repair agreed to come within the hour. I sat by the desk for a minute to catch my breath.

"Liz? Are you all right?" Lucia said.

"Don't worry," I said, more to assure myself than to

answer her. "The botanica is safe. The police will be outside investigating all night."

Cruz clutched her waist. "I heard shots. Are you sure we're safe?"

"Yes. Keep the doors locked, especially the one downstairs. Is Teresa home?"

"She came in a few hours ago then left again," Cruz said.

"I'm going to wait outside for the repairmen with Nick. We'll come up after the window is boarded." I sidetracked to the kitchen, put a piece of ice in a paper towel, and took it downstairs.

Nick sat on the curb, hands folded, his elbows resting on his knees. I gently put the ice on the red welt on his cheek. "Does it hurt?"

"No."

"Did you find out who was shot in the alley?"

He shook his head. "People aren't exactly stopping to chat with the guy protecting the 'Witch's Pantry.' The whole neighborhood is against her. Lucia's followers believed in the good she practiced as a *santera*, and now they believe she hexed them."

"Could Osaze help us?" I said.

Our friend Osaze Moon was a respected Vodoun in Hollywood. Last autumn Nick and I witnessed him perform a ritualistic voodoo hex-breaker over a curse cast in the 1800s. Osaze's ceremony was convincing, even to a nonbeliever like me.

"Asking a Vodoun to break a *brujeria tie* is like asking a rabbi to perform a Catholic exorcism. Two completely different cultures." He thought for a while then said, "Some

Santeria followers practice Catholicism. Father Nuncio might be able to stir up compassion among them."

A horn tooted from down the street. The 24-Hour Glass Repair truck stopped behind the police barricade. We asked a policeman to let the truck bypass the roadblock. Two repairmen nailed large pieces of plywood over the Botanica Rojas window. Nick paid with a credit card, and the men left with a promise to replace the glass early Monday.

When Nick and I reentered Lucia's apartment, the overhead lights were off. Candles flickered on the altar, and the floor lamp in the corner emitted a restful glow. Lucia sat alone at the desk, talking on the phone.

She broke into a huge smile. "It's Victor. I told you he would call."

Chapter Nineteen

Nick and I swapped looks, surprised and relieved. I beat him in a close race through the living room to the desk. Lucia gave me the phone. I put the receiver to my ear, and then set it into the cradle.

Lucia glowered. "Why did you do that? That was Victor. Why did you hang up on him?"

"No one was on the line. I only heard a dial tone." I was perplexed—Victor, or whoever called, had hung up. Or Lucia imagined the call. "Are you sure it was him?"

Her face clouded. "It was Victor. He calls me every night. If you don't believe me, ask Cruz." She called the caretaker out of her bedroom for confirmation.

"The phone rang five minutes ago. Lucia answered," Cruz said. "I thought it was one of you or Teresa."

"It was Victor," Lucia said. "He's with Paco."

The buzzer to the downstairs door interrupted further debate. Nick answered the intercom.

"Los Angeles Police Department," a male voice said. "We need to speak to the building manager."

Lucia marched out to the dimly lit corridor with Cruz, Nick, and me following. Two uniformed LAPD patrolmen came up the stairs.

The first officer, middle-aged with a military haircut and squared jaw, approached us and said, "I'm Officer Mac-Cauley. Are one of you the building's manager?"

"I'm the owner," Lucia said, folding her arms. "What do you want?"

"Ma'am, does a Teresa Suarez live in one of these apartments?"

"She's not home. Come back later." Lucia turned her back on him and went inside, slamming the door behind her.

Cruz opened the apartment door and went in after her.

The second officer, Wynant according to the name on his uniform, eyed the welt on Nick's cheek then glanced at the apartment. "Everything okay in there?"

"Mrs. Rojas is rattled," Nick said. "Her husband was killed last week. A mob just trashed her storefront."

"What happened to your face?" Wynant said.

"I got clocked protecting the shop downstairs," Nick said.

"Does Teresa Suarez live here?" MacCauley asked, pointing to Lucia's apartment.

"Down the hall," Nick said.

MacCauley and Wynant went to Teresa's door and pounded. When she didn't answer, they came back and Mac-Cauley said, "Can you describe Ms. Suarez?"

"She's Hispanic, curly brown hair and brown eyes," I

said. "She's medium height, about a hundred forty pounds. I know her. Is there a problem?"

"A woman of that description was shot in the alley across the street. Her purse and identification were taken, but a witness at the scene identified the victim as Ms. Suarez and gave us this address," Wynant said.

A chill crept through me. "How is she?"

"I don't know. She was unconscious when they took her away in the ambulance. Can you let us in her apartment? We have to check for minors," MacCauley said.

"I'll get the key," Nick said.

As I waited in the corridor with the patrolmen, Mac-Cauley said, "You know Mrs. Suarez?"

"I work with her at Park Clinic, across the street," I said, stunned. "I just saw her this morning."

"Do you know her family?"

"I don't. I know her husband is in jail, if that helps. His name is Carlos."

"Have you been here all night?"

"Mrs. Rojas and her caretaker were. Nick and I were across the street at Park Clinic when we heard the shots," I said.

Nick came back and gave MacCauley the key. The officers walked down the corridor, knocked at Teresa's door again, and then used the key to enter.

"Someone should be at the hospital for her. Maybe we should go," I said to Nick.

"We barely know her, Liz. If the police confirm Teresa is the victim, they'll find and contact her family. I doubt if the hospital would let us see her tonight anyway."

MacCauley brought back the key. "The apartment is

empty. Our detectives may come back later tonight or tomorrow to search after we confirm identity and her condition. We'll need a contact number for Mrs. Rojas."

"I'd like to talk to the other woman who was just out here. The younger one," Wynant said.

I called Cruz into the hall. Wynant asked if she or Lucia heard any arguments or saw anyone with Teresa that day. Cruz told them Teresa came home earlier, alone, then left again without incident. The policemen thanked us for our cooperation and left.

Nick and I found Lucia inside her apartment, kneeling at her altar.

"She's been there since I told her the news," Cruz said.

I closed my eyes and sighed in frustration. "Why did you upset her? The police didn't confirm Teresa was the victim yet."

"She asked me why the cops wanted to talk to me, and I told her. What was I supposed to do? Lie?"

I turned to Nick. "Maybe one of us should stay here tonight."

"No," Cruz said. "She wants to be left alone. I'll watch her. She'll be safe. The police are outside."

I went to the altar. "Lucia?"

"I want to perform a healing ritual for Teresa before I go to bed," Lucia said. "Go home."

Nick took me by the elbow. "Come on, Liz. Let's get some rest. We'll come back in the morning." He turned to Cruz. "If you hear suspicious noises, call the police. Understand?"

We left the apartment and crossed to the parking lot. One lane of 7th Street remained blocked off for the squad cars lining the alley. Nick started the car, turned left out of the lot, and drove past the police blockade.

I reviewed the timeline since Nick and I left Teresa earlier in the day. I knew she went back to the clinic to work. She intended to search Victor's office, unseen. If she found something and decided to call Bailey, could their conversation reach the street fast enough for retaliation against her? I should have called Bailey myself. Instead, I did what I was supposed to do and kept my mouth shut. My principles left a bitter taste.

Nick drove toward the 101 Freeway North. "You're very quiet. Any thoughts about what happened tonight?"

"A lot. Paco is murdered. Then Victor, his best friend, disappears. Then Paco's tenant, who has gang ties, is allegedly attacked. I can't sort out the connections, if they exist. And then there's the phone call Lucia just got. Whoever was on the line hung up. What if Cruz made the call from her bedroom and pretended she was Victor? I know it sounds crazy but . . ."

"Why Cruz?"

I shrugged. "To control Lucia."

"For what reason?"

"To steal from her."

"How does that connect to Victor's disappearance?" Nick said.

"Maybe it doesn't. But without Victor there to monitor, Cruz could try to coerce Lucia into withdrawing money from her bank account. I want to check Cruz's background."

The drive home was quick for a Saturday night. We parked in Nick's driveway and opened the front door to face a little kitten with a bad attitude. Every cabinet in the kitchen was opened wide, and the full dish of dry food we left was pitifully empty. I opened a can of cat food, apologizing profusely to Erzulie, while Nick poured two glasses of much-needed wine for us and heated the leftover lasagna.

Sunday morning I rolled to the side of the bed for a quick trip to the bathroom. Nick was still asleep, and I intended to brush my teeth and put on lipstick, counting on my good looks to cheer him up before I reminded him about my house-hunting appointment with Dilly.

Erzulie leapt off the foot of the bed to the top of the dresser. Nick stirred, pulling me back into bed before my feet reached the Konya Turkish rug. My knee bonked the edge of the nightstand. The mica shade on the lamp wobbled over the alarm clock. I caught the stone fertility goddess before she toppled over.

"Ow, ow, ow." I rubbed my knee.

Sleepy-faced Nick kissed the front of my knee, tracing his lips up my thigh. I melted into the mattress. Who needs lipstick? He lightly kissed my hand, my shoulder, my neck, and ended with a fast smooch on my lips before he reached over me for the phone.

He dialed then said, "Cruz? It's Nick. How did it go last night?" He listened, nodding. "Good. We'll see you at eleven."

I donned my robe and padded into the kitchen to start the coffee and feed Erzulie. She followed me with her tail straight up, yesterday's abandonment forgotten. My kitten taught me a strong lesson in forgiveness.

"What do you fancy this morning?" I said to her. "Tuna

or shrimp? I feel sunny just looking at you, so how about the yellow can?"

She hopped onto the white-tiled counter next to the refrigerator. I punctured the lid of cat food while she sat with her nose four inches from my hand. Her eyes were fixed on the opener, once again intent on learning how to liberate her food and eliminate the middleman. Another lesson: the desire and need for independence. *Or was I projecting my own needs through her? Hello? Dr. Freud?*

Nick's cell phone rang in the bedroom. I sipped my coffee at the counter. Erzulie attacked her breakfast. A perfect picture of urban tranquility: the kitten, my man, and me in our house in the Valley. Correction. Nick's house in the Valley.

The morning sun beamed in, bouncing off the stainless-steel appliances and white tiles in the kitchen, and brightening the mustard-colored walls in the living room. Oddities and antiquities from Nick's travels stood between the books stacked on his mantel. Masks, figurines, and metal crosses decorated shelves and tabletops throughout the room. His Aztec rug, a souvenir from a trip to South America, covered the dark wood floor. The statue of Santa Barbara from Lucia stood on the desk at the front window.

Nick's home reflected his unique taste, studies, and travels. If I moved in, even temporarily, would the pieces of my life—my books, my snow globe from Dad, my scented candles, comforter, photos of my friends—fit in? Or would the pieces of my life, everything I treasured, be boxed in storage to go—where?

Nick came out of the bedroom barefoot, shirtless, and in jeans.

"We should call the hospital and check on Teresa," I said.

He poured a cup of coffee and sat down next to me. "I had Dave call. I figured he could cut through the hospital red tape faster. He just called back and confirmed it was her."

"How is she? Can we visit her?"

He put his arm around me. "Teresa is dead, Liz. She died at the hospital this morning."

I covered my mouth, gripped by sorrow. During the short time I knew her, Teresa's life was fraught with tragedy, fear, and conflict. I tried to picture her smiling, and couldn't. I remembered her words during the wellness session—*I don't feel safe*—and later, her passionate plea for my help. Did my flat refusal contribute to her death?

"Bailey was interviewing witnesses at the crime scene all night," Nick said, gently. "He's on his way to the state prison in Lancaster to talk to her husband right now."

Chapter Twenty

"Lucia," I said to Nick. "We have to tell her before she hears about Teresa on the news."

I started toward the bedroom to get dressed and heard my phone ringing in my purse. I didn't recognize the number on the screen. "Hello?"

"It's Mom. I'm at the hospital, waiting to drive Carmen home. I just want to be sure you're meeting Dilly. She's going to church then she'll meet you in Du par's parking lot at eleven."

"I can't go. Something important came up. Nick and I are on our way downtown," I said. "Let me talk to Carmen."

"No," Mom said. "Liz, you can't cancel on Dilly. She set up three houses for you to see. You can't just make people change their day like that. Can't Nick Garfield take care of this himself? You have to find a place to live before you're out on the streets."

"I won't be out on the street. I told you, something happened. One of Carmen's employees was shot in the alley behind the clinic last night. Dilly will have to understand." I paced the living room while Mom ranted about responsibility, manners, and taking care of myself first.

"Put Carmen on the phone," I said.

Carmen answered in a flash. "What happened?"

"Teresa was shot behind the clinic last night. She died this morning. I'm so sorry."

"Teresa? Oh my God, what next? Why?"

"Nick and I are on our way to be with Lucia now."

"Call Tony if you need him. And tell Lucia I'll come by to see her first thing tomorrow morning," Carmen said.

I could hear Mom in the background. "The hex. Carmen, you are not going back to work until you hire someone to guard that clinic and everyone inside. And I don't mean bodyguards. Give me the phone . . . Elizabeth?"

"I'm here," I said.

"I don't want you going to that neighborhood with Nick Garfield or anyone else until Carmen and I find someone to undo the hex. Nick obviously didn't listen to me or he doesn't know what he's doing. Victor is still missing and now someone else is dead? Stay away from that woman. Do you hear me?"

"I want to be there for Lucia when she hears the news. I don't know if she can handle another shock, Mom. And enough with the hex. It's a distraction. Drop it. Nick has better things to do."

"Go look at houses," Nick said from the kitchen. "Find a place to live. Lucia doesn't need both of us. I'll go. You can meet me there later."

I covered the phone. "I don't think so, Nick. Lucia—"

"I'll take care of her. Go." His tone was final.

"All right," I said to Mom. "I'll meet Dilly for an hour."

"Good," Mom said. "Carmen is ready to leave the hospital. Call me after you see Dilly. And be careful. I worry about you."

"There's no need to worry. I'll be with Nick."

"That doesn't comfort me."

I dialed Robin. When she answered, I gave her a brief explanation and asked for her company. "If you're along, Dilly can't hijack me."

"House hunting? I'm in," she said. "Let's take my convertible."

"Pick me up in forty minutes at my house. I want to take Erzulie home first. Poor thing. We both need to find a place to live, fast." I hung up, wincing at my poor choice of words in front of Nick. I turned to him. "I'm sorry, I didn't mean—"

"Don't worry. I get it."

"I didn't mean I don't want to be here with you. I meant I have to settle my living arrangements before Mom gets more involved than she already is."

He drank his coffee while Erzulie, paws folded beneath her on the counter, watched in adoration. I went to shower and dress. When I came out of the bathroom, Nick stood in the hall, ready to leave. He packed his laptop in silence and started for the door.

"Nick?" I said as he picked up his keys.

"Call me when you're done house hunting. I hope you find what you're looking for." His hand gripped the doorknob.

My heart slunk to my stomach. I went to him and put my arms around his neck. "I don't want to mess this up. Us."

"I know. You're right. Where you live won't change how I feel about you." He pressed his lips to my forehead.

"Are you certain? Because yesterday morning you would have given me a proper kiss good-bye."

He dropped the briefcase. He pulled me into his arms and kissed me hard. "I'm crazy about you. Proper enough?"

I steadied myself on the doorjamb, too breathless to answer. After he left, I moved my clothes from the drawer into my overnight bag and then coaxed Erzulie into her carrier without a fight. *So much for a relaxing weekend with just the three of us.*

The streets were Sunday-morning vacant. I made the small trek from North Hollywood to Studio City in record time. When I opened the kitchen door to my town house, I felt like a visitor.

I knew the feeling of detachment. I had it in my marriage each time Jarret was traded and we left another house or apartment for another team and another rental, with never enough time between to set up a real home.

Erzulie trotted out of her carrier, tail up. She didn't care where she lived as long as she had something smelly to eat and someone warm to curl up with. *Something I should seriously consider, except for the smelly food part.*

At ten forty-five, Robin pulled up behind the wheel of her new cream-colored convertible. She bought the car last October, a "freedom purchase" after spending two nights in jail on suspicion of murder due, in part, to my brother. Robin was exonerated and released, but she kept her distance from Dave. She wouldn't talk to him at Mom's Christmas party. At Mom's Valentine's Day party, they were civil but not chatty.

I bounded down my front steps and slid into the front

seat. Robin's golden blonde curls were pulled back from her round face in a ponytail. She wore her extra pounds like an asset in a hot pink sweater, white jeans, and bejeweled sandals. I made stress look sporty in jeans, a red sweater, and white converse sneakers. We both put on sunglasses, and with the wind blowing through our hair, we could have been two teens on the way to the mall. If you layered on twenty-plus years and crow's-feet.

"Okay, what's wrong?" Robin said.

"Can't fool you."

On the way to Du-par's I gave Robin the news about Teresa, omitting her client status. Then I updated her on Victor and Lucia. Robin concluded Victor and Teresa were victims of the hex. Before I could argue her out of that fantasy, she turned into the crowded parking lot on Ventura Boulevard.

The brunch crowd stood in line outside Du-par's. Trader Joe's patrons bumped grocery carts behind open car trunks. Couples pushed strollers across the boulevard to the weekly Studio City Farmer's Market.

Dilly Silva waited for us at the side of her BMW 528i. She had positioned her car between two spaces, oblivious to the glare of drivers searching for parking. A petite bleached blonde, Dilly made midsixties look like fifty. Her bee-stung lips and smooth, celluloid doll-face were the work of her husband, Dewey, a Beverly Hills plastic surgeon. Dilly, one of the original Cherry Twists, spent her late teens with Mom and Carmen go-go dancing on TV and in clubs on the Sunset Strip. Now an Encino power real estate agent, she'd traded white go-go boots and fringed miniskirts for Louboutin pumps, St. John suits, and diamonds.

She backed out her BMW for Robin to park. I slid into Dilly's front passenger seat; Robin settled in the back. Dilly dropped a stack of house photos on my lap.

"Viv told me about the eviction. You only have six weeks to find a place and move? We'll have to negotiate a quick escrow."

I raised a finger in correction. "I wasn't evicted. The owners aren't renewing my lease. They're moving back into the town house themselves."

"They must be getting a divorce. She's keeping the house and making him move into the town house," Dilly said. "That's what you should have done when you left Jarret. I'll never understand why you didn't keep that house for yourself."

"It was too big, drafty, and filled with bad memories," I said. "I like my town house."

"Don't worry. We'll find something fabulous for you. How is Jarret? Dewey and I saw him pitch the home opener."

"I haven't talked to him lately." I shifted uneasily as we sped west on Ventura Boulevard.

"Liz has been busy with Nick," Robin said from the backseat. "Aren't they adorable together? Personally, I think she should move in with him."

"You mean Dave's friend? The *teacher*?" Dilly said.

"Nick is a college professor, and an author," I said.

"Yes, I know. I saw him at Viv's last party. But no, no, no." Dilly shook her head. "A gal your age should own property by now. Really, dear. You have the money."

"What about love?" Robin said.

"Love is good," Dilly said. "But investing in real estate

is more permanent. You'll have so much fun decorating, too."

Robin leaned between the seats. "Dilly, have you *seen* Nick? He's the only decoration Liz needs."

We cruised through Studio City into Sherman Oaks, and under the 405 Freeway. I listened without comment until Dilly's sales pitch on the value of investing in a down market caught my attention.

"Is it common for two Realtors to approach an owner to sell a commercial property?" I said.

"Very common with commercial Realtors. They generate the bulk of their business by soliciting sales. The competition is favorable for the building owner," Dilly said.

"What if the owner wasn't interested in selling?"

Dilly shrugged. "Then there's nothing to talk about. Unless the agent knows something the owner doesn't."

"Like what?" Robin said.

"Future zoning changes or construction in the neighborhood that might increase the property value in the future," Dilly said. "Why the interest?"

"Victor researched the value of the building his friends own across the street from Park Clinic. The owners aren't willing to sell, but at least two Realtors are eager get the property on the market. I'm curious about the interest," I said.

"Hmm," Dilly said. "I wonder if Victor asked me for a real estate attorney to help his friend investigate changes in the area."

"Like the Subway to the Sea?" I said.

"In Westlake? Could be. I'm not an expert on commercial

property, but a property that close to the Metro station would profit nicely from the extension to the Westside because of MacArthur Park."

"How much of a profit?" Robin said.

"Even a small percentage increase could be significant. Commercial property near public transit is very desirable. The Westside extension just ups the ante." Dilly pointed as we passed Benihana restaurant. "They filmed scenes from *The 40-Year-Old Virgin* in there. Isn't that fun?"

I felt a kick on the back of my seat. *A subtle hint from Robin for me to move in with Nick?*

"She was referring to you, Robin," I said over my shoulder. "Virginity renews every three years and you don't have much time left."

"Very funny. It's not like men are knocking on my front door," Robin said.

Dilly made a left turn, and for the next hour I played Goldilocks. The first house she showed us was too big—a sprawling four-bedroom ranch, south of the boulevard on a block with bikes, mommy-vans, and daddy-sedans in every driveway.

The second house was too modern for my taste; a square, two-story, white milk carton structure with squared windows and cacti in place of a front lawn. The third house, built on the edge of a steep canyon with a jaw-dropping price tag, was too small. One bedroom downstairs, and the living room and kitchen on the second story. Charming, if I didn't mind ducking my head descending stairs to the cramped bedroom, or the vertigo I'd get from taking in the breathtaking view from a patio supported by massive steel straws.

I nixed the last house on the list when I saw the address.

The street was walking distance from my parents' ranch home. "What about a bungalow or cottage closer to where I live now? Something old and cozy, with character."

"I agree," Robin said. "Like Sherman Oaks, Studio City, or North Hollywood. Can we go back and look for houses there?"

Dilly furrowed her brow. "When I went over ideas with Viv, she told me you loved Encino. It's a beautiful area. You grew up here."

"I did. And it was great. But now I'd like to be closer to my friends and my office. I should have called you and explained before we met this morning. This was my fault, Dilly. I'm sorry I put you through all this effort."

"We made a good start today. Now I know what you want, and what you don't want." Dilly tapped her manicured fingers on the steering wheel as we cruised east on Ventura Boulevard toward Du-par's. "I'll pull together some new listings this afternoon, and we can see more houses on Tuesday during the broker open."

"Wait, you guys," Robin said. "I parked in front of a house for sale in Studio City yesterday, when I went to Aroma for lunch. Funky. Not much to see from the street. But it's in the right neighborhood."

I turned to Dilly. "Can we make one more stop?"

Chapter Twenty-one

Dilly bypassed Du-par's and, following Robin's directions, turned left off Ventura Boulevard onto Tujunga Avenue, then left again several blocks over the bridge. She parked on a charming shaded side street lined with two-story bungalows and one-story cottages. Robin and I got out of the BMW and stood in front of a yard choked with overgrown trees and bushes.

I nudged Robin. "This made you think of me?"

"You're good with challenges," she said, giggling.

The property was the pimple on prom night, a blemish in the center of an attractive, well-tended block. The lawn consisted of dirt, burnt grass, and weeds. Untrimmed trees sheltered a gray-shingled house with weathered brown trim.

I started up the broken-brick path. Dead leaves littered the roof of the two-story structure. The two upstairs windows, the wide porch below, and the front door in the middle cracked an awkward, homely smiley face at me.

"I didn't notice how big it was from the street," Robin said.

I turned to Dilly. "Can we see the inside?"

"Are you sure?" She brushed a withered leaf off of her skirt. At my nod, she took out her iPhone. "I have to check the MLS for the listing broker."

While Dilly worked the phone, Robin and I wandered to the side of the house. We didn't get far. A fence blocked the entry to the yard on both sides.

"It has a fireplace." I pointed to the bricks rising two stories between the windows on the left exterior. "Love that."

"And lots of windows." Robin smiled. "And location."

Dilly called us to get back in the car. "The house just went on the market. I left the listing broker a message. Meanwhile, I'll get more houses for us to look at. We can do better than this." She dropped us off in Du-par's lot, parting with a promise to call. "And I'll see you at the fund-raiser tomorrow, girls."

After Robin and I climbed into her convertible, she said, "What did Nick say about you shopping for a house?"

"He encouraged me to do whatever I want, but I have a feeling he really wants me to move in with him."

"And I don't understand why you aren't jumping at the chance," she said.

"I'm happy with the way things are. Nick makes me feel adored. And I adore him. He's wonderful and fun and smart. But we've only been a couple for a few months. I haven't seen his warts yet. I don't want to discover them a month after I move in when there's no turning back."

"Warts? That's about the most unromantic thing I've ever heard you say, Liz."

"Metaphorical warts. My heart would love to move in, but my brain is throwing out caution flags. I married Jarret on a whim, and I stayed with him too long after the infatuation wore off. I won't make another moonstruck decision. Make sense?"

"Way too logical. Where is Nick?" Robin said.

"He's with Lucia. I'm driving downtown to meet them now."

"Want some company? It's such a gorgeous day. I'd love to open my car on the freeway with the top down. What do you think?"

"I'd love it," I said. "You can meet Lucia."

Robin sped along the 101 as fast as traffic would allow, which wasn't all that fast. With the sun warming our faces, we listened to oldies on the radio all the way downtown. She took the Alvarado Street exit and drove south toward Westlake.

When we got to MacArthur Park, I said, "Can we make a stop before we go to Lucia's? There's a woman with a dress shop on Alvarado I want to talk to about Victor."

"A dress shop? You spoil me."

We cruised at low speed in the right lane until I saw the Briano Fashion dress shop tucked between a beauty salon and a dollar store on the east side of the street. Robin parked, and we walked up the block. Women strolled in and out of Ynez's open-front store, stopping to pick through the tube socks, underwear, and bras piled on the tables outside.

Inside, Ynez's shop had the festive feel of a disorganized princess's closet exploding with pink, white, lace, and netted gowns. Preteens, teenage girls, and adult women rifled through plastic-protected First Communion and *Quinceañera* dresses on wire hangers hung from the ceiling. Rows of white two-inch heeled pumps lined the back wall.

Robin looked at the pastel frocks surrounding us. "I'm embarrassed to say I still don't understand exactly what *Quinceañera* is."

"A fifteenth birthday party, like a 'Sweet Sixteen,' but much more ritualistic. It's customary to wear pink or white dresses for purity. In the 'Ritual of the Shoe,' the father exchanges his daughter's flats for heels to mark her transition to womanhood. Some of the celebrations last all weekend."

"Remember the 'Sweet Sixteen' your parents threw for you?" Robin said.

"Good grief. I can still picture the frilly pink dress my Mom wore."

Robin laughed. "If I remember right, she sang that night."

"And you and I ducked down to my rec room to make out with the two—"

"Can I help you?"

"Yes." I turned to the woman behind us. "I'm looking for Ynez Briano."

"That's me." Ynez gave us a sweet, crooked-tooth smile. Black hair tumbled down her shoulders and curled around the cleavage of her tank top. Tight, hip-hugging jeans bared her trim midriff.

"I'm Liz Cooper. Are you a friend of Dr. Morales?"

Ynez's eyes lit up. "Yes, I am. Did he send you here?"

191

Robin nudged me. "I'll wait for you outside so you can talk."

"Thanks, Robin." I turned back to Ynez. "Miguel, the guard at Park Clinic, sent me. We haven't heard from Dr. Morales for a few days. Miguel thought you might know where he is."

"I don't." Her face clouded. "I haven't seen Dr. Morales since my clinic appointment last Tuesday. He's my hero. He diagnosed my diabetes and saved my life. What can I do to help?"

"Did he act unusual or out of character when you were with him?"

"He was upset about Paco, and so worried about Lucia. I told him he looked tired. Dr. Morales told me to worry about myself, not him. We made a lunch date for next Tuesday to celebrate my first year on insulin." She furrowed her brow. "How long has he been missing?"

"The last time we saw him was at Paco's wake on Wednesday. The police are searching for him. So are all of his friends," I said.

"I did notice something I thought was strange. I passed the clinic Wednesday night after midnight and saw his car in the clinic parking lot. I remember wondering why he would be working so late, especially after the wake. But the next morning his car was gone. I'll ask around the neighborhood. Do you think he's sick or in trouble?"

"I don't know, Ynez. His friends are getting the word out to as many people as we can. Would you call me if he contacts you, or if you hear anything? Any piece of information would help." I gave her my number.

"I promise, I will." A customer interrupted, asking Ynez

for directions to the dressing room. Before she left to help the woman, she gave me her number. "Will you call me when you find him? Dr. Morales is family."

"I will." I left the shop, unsettled. If she saw Victor's car in the lot late Wednesday, it meant he was either at the clinic a lot longer than I thought, or he left with someone else. *Who?*

Robin wasn't out on the sidewalk. I strolled from shop to shop, searching for her down aisles and through windows. I finally caught a glimpse of her blonde ponytail deep inside the shop I should have steered her away from. She couldn't see me waving at her over the *Protección de la Maldición* sign in the window. I went in to get her.

The inside of Oscar Estevez's botanica was set up like a drugstore, but instead of cough medicine, greeting cards, and toothpaste, I moved through aisles lined with packets of ritual herbs and spell-casters. Spanish periodicals on the news rack touted headlines of secret home remedies, Santa Muerte rituals, and incantations.

I passed an open closet draped with red curtains, lit from above. The altar at the center held a large, red-cloaked, black and beige skeletal figurine holding a scythe and a globe. The sign above the entry read:

Santuario de La Santa Muerte

Para Orar Hacer Sus Peticion y
Mostrar Su Agradecimiento

An altar to Santa Muerte to pray for requests and to show appreciation.

Robin stood at the back of the store, peering inside a glass counter. I called her name, hoping to get her attention to make a fast exit. She waved at me to come back. I shook my head *no*. She bobbed her head *yes*. I gave up and joined her at the counter.

She pointed to a silver pendant engraved with an image of the Grim Reaper. "Isn't that deliciously creepy? I can see it on a black dress for Halloween."

I heard a man speaking in Spanish behind the curtain facing the counter. "I'm moving to a bigger shop on 7th Street very soon."

"Do you think it's expens—" Robin said. I shushed her and pointed at the curtain.

"*Si*," the man continued. "That's the one. All her customers are coming to me now. She won't last much longer. I'll send you an invitation to my grand opening." He laughed. "*Adios*."

I grabbed Robin's sleeve. "Let's get out of here."

As she picked up her purse, the curtain parted and Oscar came out. He narrowed his eyes at me, then Robin, then at me again. "Looking for something?"

"Just browsing." Flashing an insincere smile, I hastened Robin out to the sidewalk.

In true L.A. fashion, instead of walking we drove the three blocks to Botanica Rojas and parked in the lot next door. *La dispensa de la bruja 187* was scrawled in red on the east wall of Lucia's building. Nick stood beneath the graffiti with a bucket of paint, a pan, and a paint roller.

I gazed up at the writing. "When did that happen?"

"Sometime last night or this morning." He wiped his hands on a rag. "Hi Robin."

"Hi Nick." Robin eyed the inscription. "Witch's pantry? What's 187, a gang?"

"187 is the police code for murder." Nick poured paint in the pan then dipped in the roller. "This is the latest largesse from the friendly neighbors after last night's arson attempt."

"Lucia can't protect her building from her own hex?" Robin said.

"You mean conjure a magic fence?" I waved an imaginary wand in the air.

"Think this is a joke?" Nick's attitude reeked irritation. He turned his back to us and rolled paint on the edge of the graffiti.

"You know I don't," I said. "How did Lucia take the news about Teresa?"

Nick stopped painting and turned around. "She knew. When I walked in her apartment Lucia said, 'Teresa is dead,' then offered me a cup of tea. We talked about Paco and the article over lunch. When Cruz came back from the market, she told me about this graffiti. And here I am. What took you so long?"

"We stopped on Alvarado to talk to Ynez," I said.

"And?"

"She saw Victor's car parked at the clinic after midnight on Wednesday." I pointed to the second-floor windows. "Are Lucia and Cruz upstairs?"

"Lucia is in the botanica. Cruz took a few hours off to visit her family. I decided I'm going to spend the night. I'll ask Bailey if he can up the patrol. I don't like the thought of Lucia and Cruz being alone in this building." He started painting again.

As we moved toward the front of the building Robin glanced over her shoulder. "He's in a foul mood."

"I can't blame him. It was brazen to graffiti the wall with the police right across the street investigating. Lucia is isolated until the hex business wears off."

"Can't she end the hex?"

"She wouldn't. At least not until Paco's killer is caught."

Robin followed me into Botanica Rojas. The boarded window blocked out the daylight, creating a twilight atmosphere inside. Counter lamps lit the back shelves; lemongrass incense scented the air. Lucia, in a blue and green print dress and Paco's sweater, swept pieces of glass and broken statues off the floor while music played from the back room.

Lucia smiled when she saw me. "I'm glad you came. Nick is outside. Did you see him?"

"We did," I said. "Lucia, this is my friend Robin Bloom. Robin, this is Lucia Rojas."

"It's lovely to finally meet you, Lucia." Robin offered her hand. "I'm so sorry for your loss. I'm a widow, too."

Lucia covered Robin's hand with hers. "How sad for you. I'm sorry my shop is a mess. All this petty vandalism and graffiti is the way of the neighborhood now."

"Your shop is wonderful."

"Thank you. I trust my orishas to protect us from thieves. And, of course, we never keep money in the register. Can I show you around?"

"Yes, I'd love that." Robin trailed Lucia through the shop,

pointing at statues and asking about the healing properties of the packeted herbs.

I had commandeered the broom to finish the sweeping. When I tossed the last shards of glass into the trash, I said, "Lucia, do you mind if I use the bathroom upstairs?"

"Go ahead. My keys are next to the register," Lucia said.

I collected the keys, estimating I had about fifteen minutes to search Teresa's apartment.

Chapter Twenty-two

I unlocked Lucia's upstairs door, leaving it open to hear the intercom. Then I hurried through the corridor to Teresa's apartment, unlocked the door, and went inside.

Her tiny studio smelled of old cooking grease masked by cheap perfume. A welcome rush of fresh air from the open corridor windows followed me in. Her walls were dusty white, and alabaster mini-blinds were drawn closed over the windows. To my right, a card table and chairs created a makeshift dining area between the bathroom door and the tiny kitchenette. On the far wall an open convertible sofa was covered with a brown-print comforter and disheveled pink sheets. Scarves and jewelry dangled from the mirror above her dresser with bottles, brushes, and beaded jewelry scattered on top. An array of purses and shoes were lined up beneath the window.

According to Cruz, Teresa came home after work, and

then left again for the evening. From the looks of the mess in the apartment, Teresa wasn't a put-it-away type of woman. If she took a tangible clue out of Victor's office, it was in her apartment or at the morgue.

I scanned the card table. *People En Espanol*, *Us Weekly*, and old issues of the *National Enquirer* were stacked next to supermarket flyers, store catalogs, and bills from a department store and a phone company. No notes scribbled in haste. No phone book. Next stop, the kitchenette. A sticky mess of dried coffee cup rings, plastic utensils, and cookie crumbs covered the counter. Coffee mugs crowded on the dish rack next to the sink. Empty Chicken Shack containers were heaped on top of a full trash can. A loaf of bread and a bag of Oreo cookies topped the refrigerator. I rummaged through the lone drawer filled with sugar, ketchup, and hot sauce packets then moved back to the main room.

First stop, the dresser top, to see if she left a note or a paper between the jewelry, makeup, and bottles of perfume. So much for plain sight. I had no idea why I was looking for a note, but I gently rifled through the clothing in the drawers. In the back of the bottom drawer I found a purple velveteen bag with a gold drawstring pull. I reached inside and repressed a gag. *I couldn't go that far.* No way Teresa would hide a clue in her vibrator bag. I winced and looked anyway. No papers, though I left behind a fragment of my dignity when I closed the bag.

I was ignoring the obvious—when people get home from work, they change their clothes. What was Teresa wearing yesterday? I closed my eyes, visualizing her storming through the parking lot toward Buzz Cut in a . . . black blazer.

I unfolded the closet doors to a clutter of shoe boxes, clothes, and a basket full of laundry. Dresses, blouses, jeans, and skirts on wire hangers jammed the wooden pole. The black jacket stuck out from the middle of the cluster. I dug into its pocket and found my business card with Bailey's phone number on the back. Beneath Bailey's number, Teresa had scribbled something barely legible. *6h vivev caw51no*.

Couldn't be a phone number. Too odd for a local address. I went to the window, opened the blind, and read again in the sunlight. As I squinted to let her scribbling blur, the numbers morphed into letters: *bh vivev casino*, or maybe *bh river casino*.

Beverly Hills River Casino? There wasn't a river or a casino in Beverly Hills. I got out my smartphone and searched the Internet for "river casino," "Beverly Hills casino," and "b.h. casino." The results came up blank for metropolitan Los Angeles. I stared at her writing again and saw the *n*. Cansino. Raymon Cansino. Again. The letter writer who called himself Paco's friend and whose secretary called Lucia on Monday. But what was *bh river*? I wouldn't find out standing in her apartment. I tucked the note back into her jacket pocket, closed the closet door, locked up both apartments, and went downstairs.

I didn't see Nick outside. Lucia and Robin were in deep conversation at the rear of the botanica. Robin hooted with laughter, and Lucia's merry response delighted me. It was the first time I'd seen her truly joyful in a week.

"What happened to Nick?" I said.

"He went out to do an errand," Robin said. "He said he'd be right back. Lucia is showing me how she uses herbs and candles to create spells. Do you know almost every herb has an orisha—like a god or goddess—connected to it? It's amazing how much she knows about casting spells, Liz. Fascinating. She offered to create a love spell for me."

"A pretty girl like Robin should take a lover to make her laugh." Lucia patted the side of Robin's face. "Too much sadness behind those eyes."

"What do you think, Liz?" Robin said.

"I'm all for you taking a lover, but I thought you swore off spells."

"From amateurs. Lucia is an expert." Robin turned to her new friend. "Would you do a weak little spell maybe? Something innocent for starters?"

"Real passion is not weak or little," Lucia said.

"Be easy on her, Lucia. Her last innocent spell landed her in jail," I said.

"And brought Nick back into your life," Robin said. "It wasn't a complete disaster."

"Aha. Destiny. I know just what Robin needs." Lucia pulled a white phallic-shaped candle off the shelf behind her. "Burn this to attract a new lover." She presented the erect wax sculpture to Robin.

"Oh, I, no, uh, not." Robin recoiled backward.

Embarrassed and utterly self-conscious, I shut my eyes to avoid the sight of Lucia's veined hand around the wax male organ. Didn't work. "Maybe something a little more subtle?"

"But this is the best tool for finding a lover." Lucia pumped the candle with emphasis.

I smothered a laugh.

Robin turned scarlet. "A little too much, too fast. I was thinking a dinner date, not all-night sex."

"So you want romance, not passion. For that I use a 'Come To Me' candle. I'll fix one up for you." Lucia put the white candle back on the shelf and moved down the aisle to a row of hurricane candles in tall glass jars. She selected one filled with pink wax and gathered a collection of packets and tiny amber vials from a shelf beneath the counter.

Lucia began to anoint the eight-inch, seven-day candle with oil and herbs, explaining the process as she worked.

"Pink is for new love, sweet love, innocent and cherished love. Light the wick and allow it to burn through the veil between the material world and the other realm. The flame opens a path to the gods waiting to grant your petition. Always watch the candle as you work. A steady flame and clean glass means your spell will be successful and your wish granted. A flickering flame or smoky glass will tell you if the time is not right for your petition. And if the flame hisses at you, a spirit is trying to get a message to you."

Robin rubbed her arms, nervously. "What if Josh doesn't want me to date yet?"

"Josh always, always wanted you to be happy," I said. "We all do. You don't need a candle flame to tell you that."

She put a hand to her heart and took a deep breath. "I'm ready. Tell me what to do, Lucia."

"Before your evening bath, drink a cup of chamomile tea with honey to honor Oshun, the patron of love and sensuality. Bathe and let your body dry naturally, no towels," Lucia said. "Stand naked at your altar and light the candle with open intention. Burn a stick of sandalwood incense to grant your wish. Meditate on the candle and allow your heart to fill with love while you breathe in and out. Extinguish the flame with a plate on top of the glass cylinder. Never blow out a candle. Start the ritual tonight while the oils hold the strongest potency. Soon your lover will come, and you will get your heart's desire."

Lucia dripped rose-hip oil on her palm and rubbed her hands together. "Rose hip heals the aching heart and empowers helpful spirits. I anoint the candle from top to bottom for positive attraction." She guided her oiled palms down the sides of the glass. Her skill and self-assurance made her spell crafting appear believable, a bit of magic to create hope. "Whose name will I etch into the wax to attract?"

"There is no one," Robin said.

"Then we let fate decide." Lucia tied a pink ribbon around the candle, wrapped the whole package in foil, and gave it to Robin. "This will bring you lasting love."

Robin slipped the candle into her shoulder bag like a treasured totem. "Thank you. How much do I owe you?"

"Paco and I are romantics. The candle is my gift to you. The orishas guide your spell. Make whatever offering you want to them." Lucia sat on her stool.

"I want to give you something." Robin pulled bills from her wallet and tucked them into Lucia's pocket. "I'll let you know what happens."

"You don't have to. I already see the fire between you and your new lover in your eyes," Lucia said. "I wish Paco were here. He loved when I joined hearts together."

"Nick is writing an article about Botanica Rojas and Lucia's talents for the Sunday edition of the papers," I said to Robin.

Lucia smiled. "I told Victor about the article last night before you came. Paco will be so proud." She read my doubt and flapped her hand at me. "I know my husband is dead, but his spirit is here. He will be proud of the article."

"He'll always be with you," Robin said. "Believe me, I know."

The front door opened. Nick came in, jaw set, and stopped at the entrance. He crooked his finger at me. "Can I talk to you outside?" He left the door slamming behind him.

Lucia and Robin raised their eyebrows. I shrugged, clueless, and followed him out to the sidewalk.

Nick paced from the door to the curb and back to me, and then cocked his head in the direction of Alvarado Street. "I just was at Oscar's botanica. Remember him?"

I nodded slightly.

"He asked why I didn't bring back the babes I sent to spy on him earlier. The blonde and the brunette. Sound familiar?"

Chapter Twenty-three

Nick glared at me on the sidewalk in front of Botanica Rojas's boarded window while afternoon traffic sped past. "Are you out of your mind?"

"Honestly Nick, it was no big deal," I said. "I only went inside Oscar's botanica to get Robin. She wandered in there while I was talking to Ynez Briano."

"Do you have any idea how dangerous Oscar Estevez is? I told you I'd talk to him. What were you thinking?"

"Right now I'm thinking you're overreacting. I didn't say more than two words to him. Calm down. It was innocent. I found Robin and left. I'm sorry I didn't tell you. But I did hear him—"

"*I'm sorry* is a cheap excuse for an ignor . . ." He pressed his lips together. "For a bad move. You could have . . . You're in the crosshairs of a man who shouldn't even know who you are."

"He already knows who I am. He saw me with *you* the other day. Sorry is all I have to offer. But in the two minutes I was there, I heard him bragging about moving his shop to Lucia's building. Do you think Oscar had one of the Realtors contact Paco?"

"Oscar doesn't have that kind of money. And even if Paco was willing to sell, he wouldn't sell to Oscar," Nick said. "They hated each other."

"Did you ask Oscar if he knew anything about Paco's shooting? Did he give you any information?" I said.

"Aside from his lewd comments about you and Robin? Not yet." He spun on his heels, and I followed him inside.

I rolled my eyes as a warning to Robin and Lucia at the back counter. Nick stopped short in mid-aisle, turned, and began to say something to me when the front door opened behind us.

Cruz entered, glanced at the scowl on Nick's face, and frowned. "Is Lucia all right?"

Nick and I snapped in unison, "Yes."

"Lucia spent all afternoon in the shop?" Cruz said.

"I came down with her after lunch. She wanted to clean up," he said.

"She shouldn't be working. She didn't sleep well last night." Cruz hastened to the back counter and turned off the lamp. "Time for your afternoon medication, Lucia. Let's go upstairs."

"I want to stay down here and visit. Stop telling me what to do. I'll go up when I feel like it." Lucia turned the lamp back on. "Don't be rude to my friends."

Robin gravitated down the aisle toward me. I stood with

her, stuck between the bickering women in the back and my fuming boyfriend by the front door.

"Everything cool with Nick?" Robin whispered.

"Oscar told Nick that he saw us. I'll explain later," I said.

"I think I should leave." Robin dug through her purse and produced her keys. She called down the aisle, "Lucia, it was lovely to meet you. Thank you so much for the spell. I'll let you know what happens."

"Come visit me again. Happiness is your destiny. Your new love is near," Lucia said.

"A mild flirtation would be enough, but thank you." Robin stopped in front of Nick, looking up with an expectant smile. "I'll see you again tomorrow night. You and Liz are picking me up at six for the fund-raiser?"

"That's the plan. But don't leave here yet. Give me a minute to tell Lucia I'll be back later, and then Liz and I will follow you into the Valley."

After he walked away Robin pulled me aside. "Okay, he is acting very bizarre. It's broad daylight. I don't need an escort home."

"I know. Just play along for a few blocks then you can ditch us," I said.

Nick and I followed Robin's car up Alvarado Street to the freeway. We argued in silence. He kept his left fist to his mouth and steered with other hand. I folded my arms and stared out the window. As soon as we hit the on-ramp, Robin crossed into the fast lane and lost us.

"I saw a house," I said.

No comment.

"A bungalow in Studio City," I said. "A real mess on the outside, and we couldn't get inside, but the location is perfect. Close to you, and close to my office. Dilly is setting up an appointment so I can take a tour."

"Good for you." His eyes never left the road ahead.

Ugh.

"Will you look at it with me?"

"Why do you need me to be there? It's your house."

We sped past the concrete embankments bordering both sides of the freeway through the Cahuenga Pass. Concrete— good place to pound my head. *Be patient. Let him work through his anger.*

"I want you to see the house because your opinion is important to me. I wouldn't make a big move like this without talking it through with you."

"Whatever you want."

That did it. "Okay. I get it. We're fighting. I don't know what we're fighting about, so catch me up. Are you still angry about Robin and me going into Oscar's shop, or is this about me not moving in with you?"

"Live wherever you want," he said.

Well, hello Nick's warts. Nice to finally meet you.

I opted for playful. "And you'll be my boyfriend, and let me keep my drawer at your house?"

"Maybe." His lips almost twitched into a smile. He turned away so I couldn't see him.

"Do you want to stop for coffee and talk about it?" I said.

"I can't. I'm picking up some clothes and going back to Lucia's. Bailey hasn't called me back about the patrol, and

I can't let those two women spend the night alone in that building."

"Where will you sleep?"

"I don't care. A chair. I'm worried for Lucia. And on top of it, I'm worried about you. People like Oscar don't trust outsiders poking into their business."

I held up a hand. "Stop. You don't *have* to protect Lucia or me. I won't take any risks, I promise. And as you said, Bailey can get increased patrol around the botanica for a while. You, Carmen, and I should have a serious discussion with Lucia about her immediate living arrangements. Though I hope with all my heart she can stay where she is, her safety comes first. Did you talk to Father Nuncio?"

"He was on retreat this weekend," Nick said. "I made an appointment to meet with him tomorrow at eleven thirty."

"Excellent. My last session is over at ten. I can meet you in the clinic parking lot at eleven."

"Try not to wander into gang haunts before I get there."

"Try to avoid flying fists tonight," I said.

Nick parked in front of my town house and walked me to my front door. We touched foreheads, smiling, in a gentle truce. Before he left, he turned and said, "I'll look at the house with you."

I made a peanut butter sandwich and took it upstairs to my office, determined to unravel Teresa's cryptic scribble. Erzulie jumped on my desk and watched me turn on my computer and enter a search for C&C Properties. The company site header showed the C&C logo above the skyline of downtown Los Angeles with a row of tabs beneath titled Services, Properties, Professionals, and Contact. I clicked on Professionals and scrolled through the alphabetical staff listing. I found a photo of Raymon Cansino posed against a white background in a dark suit and red tie, staring intently at the camera with a self-assured, have-I-got-a-property-for-you grin. With another click I landed on his profile page.

The opening paragraph touted Cansino as one of the "most respected commercial real estate specialists in Downtown and East Los Angeles, with the foresight and knowledge to assist his clients in all aspects of commercial property transfer and management." Blah, blah, blah. Told me nothing.

The bio went on to describe Cansino as one of the top producers at C&C every year since 1996, including 2009, the year the market crashed.

Cansino's biography failed to show me much about the man. No prior job history, no personal background, college affiliations, or professional organizations. His client list was long, but because he was with the company since at least 1996, I assumed it would be. Cansino was a vice president. I checked the other Realtors at the firm and six of the eight were VPs or Associate VPs.

I made a thorough read of his section for clues to *bh* or *river* and came up blank. My last stop was the Contact section. C&C had offices in the San Fernando and San Gabriel Valleys, and offices downtown, in the South Bay, in Beverly Hills, and in Boyle Heights. Bingo. I noted the Beverly Hills and Boyle Heights phone numbers and went back to Cansino's page. The number for the office in Boyle Heights—the mostly Latino neighborhood east of downtown—matched the contact number for Cansino. Then I sat back, wondering what made a Boyle Heights Realtor so interested in Paco's two-story building in Westlake. I assumed Realtors were territorial. Maybe Cansino had a buyer.

Despite several searches, I found no references to *river* on the C&C site. I closed the tab and searched for Boyle Heights on Wikipedia. The Los Angeles River borders the western side of Boyle Heights but the river flows from the San Fernando Valley all the way down to Long Beach—not a defining clue.

But as I scanned through, I noticed two MTA Gold Line subway stations opened in Boyle Heights in the past decade, giving Cansino firsthand knowledge of the effect of Metro expansion on property values. I did a final Internet search for "Raymon Cansino" and the results directed me back to the C&C site.

I had one more resource, closer to home, and more thorough than the Internet. My brother knew current Los Angeles scuttlebutt as well as Mom knew designer clothes and Nick knew religion. Dave inherited talent from both of our parents. He had Mom's love of gossip and Dad's detective expertise. I dialed his number and he picked up. From the TV in the background I could hear a crowd cheering, sneakers squeaking on wood, and a whistle shrieking.

"What, Liz? I'm watching the Lakers."

I was honored he took my call during a game. "Ever heard of C&C Properties?"

"Sure. Commercial real estate. They control acres of land and buildings all over the city. Shoot, shoot, damn it, shoot the damn ball." A whistle blew. Dave groaned.

"And Raymon Cansino?" I said.

211

"Uh-huh. Eastside real estate so-called hotshot. Likes the spotlight. If you turn on your TV right now you can see him. He's sitting three rows behind the Lakers' bench."

"He is?" I rolled back my desk chair and trotted downstairs holding the phone while Dave mumbled something about defensive shot blocking. I picked up my TV remote off the coffee table and turned on the game. Commercial break.

Winded and sorry I didn't bring my sandwich with me, I said, "Is Cansino a good guy?"

"Why?" he said.

"I'm curious. Cansino tried to get the Rojases to sell their building before Paco died." The game came back on. I waited for Dave's answer in silence with my eyes on the screen. After the ball went out of play, the camera panned the bench.

"There's Cansino, behind number forty-five, two rows back. The guy in the gray business suit," Dave said.

I caught a glimpse of Cansino's slicked-back black hair from between the heads of three mammoth basketball players. The players parted, framing Cansino in the crowd. He leaned forward in his seat, elbows on his knees, and looked up at the scoreboard above center court at the Staples Center.

"Good guy or bad guy?" I said.

"He has money and connections. That's all I can tell you."

"All you can tell me, or all you will tell me?"

Too late. The ball went back in play and I lost Dave's attention to the game. At the next break I tossed out my next question, hoping for a spontaneous answer.

"What is Cansino's connection to the river in Boyle Heights?"

The background noise on his side of the call went dead.

Chapter Twenty-four

When Dave muted the Laker game mid-shot from outside the key, I knew I hit a nerve.

"Where did you hear about the river?" Dave said.

"Off the record?" I said.

He groaned. "What record? Unless you're doing something illegal, just tell me."

I knew relating my conversation with Teresa would be unethical, so I said, "Nick and I went through Victor's office last night and found a letter from Cansino to Paco Rojas. Today I found a note in Teresa Suarez's apartment with Cansino's name, the word *river*, and the letters *b* and *h*. I know there's a connection. I assumed 'b. h.' is for Boyle Heights, where Cansino's office is located. I'm curious what the river is."

"Why the hell were you in Teresa Suarez's apartment?"

"I can't tell you why. It's privileged."

"Privileged? What privilege?"

"Teresa was my client. Our conversations are protected. If I gave you the reason I went into her apartment, I'd be breaking her trust."

"She's dead."

"It doesn't matter, Dave. Please just answer my question without asking me to explain."

"Do you know who shot her?"

"No. I don't."

I held the phone away from my ear while Dave blurted out a string of swear words. "And do me a goddamn favor. Set your lofty ethics aside, give everything you found in her apartment to Matt Bailey, and then stay the freaking hell out of the investigation before someone else dies or disappears. Hear me?"

I couldn't help but hear him, and his shouting didn't change my mind. "Just tell me more about the river."

"What do you want to know? The River is the biggest Mexican gang in Boyle Heights."

"Is Cansino a member?" I waited for his answer. "Dave? Is Cansino a member of the River Gang?"

"His nephew is. Cansino may have some old ties from the past, but he portrays himself as a legitimate businessman." Dave put up the volume on his TV again, his artless attempt to close the subject

"So you *do* know about him. Is he under investigation?"

"Leave the crime solving to the police. Watch yourself, Liz. Stay away from Cansino." Dave yelled a profanity at the refs, then said good-bye to me. He could be so affectionate when he wanted to be.

I knew from conversations with my Dad and Dave, and

214

from reading the news, that gangs were intensely territorial. There were a myriad of gangs in Los Angeles separated by geography, nationality, and race. The communities of Westlake and Boyle Heights were miles apart, and the chance of the same gang controlling both neighborhoods was nil. How did Teresa make a connection between Cansino, the River Gang, Paco, and Victor?

I went back upstairs to my computer to search for information on the Rojases' building. The L.A. County Assessor's website estimated the value of the Rojases' land plus two-story structure at well over two million dollars. I located the addresses to the empty adjoining lots and searched for owner names. The assessor's site didn't list them. Time to get creative again.

Twenty minutes of Internet surfing later, with Erzulie stretched out in a contented snooze next to the keyboard, I registered on a subscription real estate research site. Within seconds I located the parcels surrounding the Rojas property and discovered the properties on 7th Street were owned by the Eagle Holding Company and purchased within the past five years.

After my hunt for the names of the company principals stalled, I called Dilly.

"I talked to the listing agent for the bungalow in Studio City," she said as soon as she answered. "Three bedrooms, two and a half baths, hardwood floors, fireplace in living room and master, good-sized backyard. The seller is motivated—we can negotiate."

The fireplace in the master bedroom heightened my interest. "How much are they asking?"

When she gave me the quote, I felt a hopeful tug in my

stomach. The number was almost workable depending on the condition of the structure and how much interior work would be needed. And I knew Dilly was a great haggler.

"When can I see the inside?" I said.

"They're still cleaning things out of the house. The agent won't get the keys until Wednesday. Are you free?"

"Yes. Make the appointment," I said. "Is Carmen home from the hospital?"

"I just talked to her. She sounds much better. I just think it will be a shame if she has to represent the clinic tomorrow night without Victor. Call her. Cheer her up," Dilly said.

"I will. But I actually called you for a different favor. Can you find out who brokered the sale of some properties downtown?"

"Sure. Give me the addresses."

I read off the street numbers to the lots surrounding Lucia's building then said, "The Eagle Holding Company is listed as the property owner. How do I find the names of the principals?"

"I can tell you that now. Eagle Holding Company is Henry Wright's firm. He's a major commercial developer—malls, apartment complexes, and parking lots. A big commercial broker downtown named Kenner Laughton is Wright's buyer agent. I can call a friend at a title company and get back to you tomorrow with the brokers who repped the sellers. Do these questions have something to do with Victor?"

"I think so. I just don't know how yet. Are you familiar with Bernie Gates or Raymon Cansino? They're both commercial real estate agents."

"No. I know of Laughton because he's so big, but I'm

more familiar with residential agents than commercial agents," she said.

"Whatever you can get me might help." I thanked Dilly, hung up, and then dialed again. Carmen's voice sounded weary when she answered.

"Did I wake you?"

"No, sweetie. I'm reading my mail."

"How do you feel?"

"Tired, but I have a lot of catching up to do. I'm planning to see Lucia in the morning before I get to the clinic, then we have the fund-raiser tomorrow night."

"You're taking on too much too fast. Can't Tony handle the clinic one more day?"

"No. He's been an angel the past four days. I can't ask him to carry the patient load anymore. I'm interviewing another doctor tomorrow to help. Did you meet Ynez?"

"I did." I recapped our conversation then said, "I need your advice again, Carmen. This stays within the doctor confidentiality agreement we made about Teresa yesterday. Agreed?"

"Of course. What is it?"

"I found a note in Teresa's apartment this afternoon. Remember the letters from Realtors to Paco that were in Victor's desk?"

"Yes. From Bernie Gates and C&C Properties."

"Raymon Cansino was the agent from C&C. Teresa wrote his name on the back of the business card I gave her after our session. I think she went through Victor's office after all, saw the letter, and made a connection."

"I know that name. Stay there," she said. I heard her

rustling through papers. "Here it is. Raymon Cansino bought a table for the fund-raiser. So did Bernard Gates."

"Victor knew both men?"

"Not necessarily. Quite a few of the local businessmen bought tables or made donations. You can talk to both Cansino *and* Gates tomorrow night."

"Teresa wrote 'b.h. river' ahead of Cansino's name. Are you familiar with the River Gang in Boyle Heights?"

"No. Victor and I have enough problems dealing with the gangs in Westlake," she said with an edge. "Could *river* be another person or a partial address?"

"Could be, but I assume Teresa meant the River Gang because they're in Boyle Heights and so is Cansino's office. Maybe she knew the connection because of her gang ties. If I tell the police what I found, they'll ask why I searched her apartment. I wouldn't be able to explain without revealing what Teresa told me. And even if the information I found would lead them to Victor, or helps to solve Paco's and José Saldivar's murders, under the rules of privilege I'm ethically obligated to keep the information to myself. I've never been in a situation like this, Carmen. I don't know what I should do."

"The police will find the note when they search her apartment," Carmen said.

"On my business card."

"Truthfully? You can't go to the police. They have to come to you. You can tell them she was your client if you're forced to because your business card was in her pocket. But since you have no knowledge of a pending crime involving Teresa, your responsibility is bound to her even though she's dead. Does that help you with your decision?"

"Yes." I sighed in frustration. Diligent Detective Bailey would find the notes on my card in Teresa's apartment, and either decipher what she meant on his own, or call me.

"You helped justify my silence, but it doesn't make me feel good about holding back information. By the way, I saw the payroll file in Victor's drawer. Why was Teresa making so much at the clinic? In cash?" I said.

"I don't remember what we were paying her. You probably misread the file. Accounting forms are complicated. I'm tired now, sweetie. I'm going to bed. Big day tomorrow."

I hung up, troubled again. The payroll document didn't need an explanation. Teresa's cash payments and ballooned salary did.

Monday morning my once adorable bedroom felt like a hotel room on the day of checkout. A cloudy mood determined my outfit—black gabardine slacks, sweater, and boots pulled from the closet filled with clothes I had to weed out to move. Every drawer seemed filled with unnecessary junk to pack or throw away. I needed a strong kick of attitude, so I dressed, fed Erzulie, and headed for the Caffeine Café at Laurel Canyon for a double cappuccino.

The caffeine jolt got me through my morning client sessions and the trek across town to meet Nick in the Park Clinic lot. As I pulled in to park, I saw him on the sidewalk, talking to Tattoo Neck. They nodded at each other and parted.

When Nick and I got into his car, I cocked my head toward Tattoo Neck and his friends. "What was that about?"

"I offered them cash to call me if there was any trouble at Lucia's," Nick said.

"You don't even know them."

"They helped me protect Botanica Rojas from the mob on Saturday night. And they understand money. They're doing it for Teresa," Nick said. "I decided to hire them because of the note in Teresa's apartment."

"How did you . . . ? Dave told you."

"You'd better believe he told me. The River Gang is one of the most menacing factions in the city. José Saldivar was a member."

I winced. I had been so occupied with the link to Cansino that I completely forgot Saldivar's Boyle Heights gang connection.

"Dave tore into me about keeping you out of trouble," Nick said. "Why didn't you tell me you went in there?"

"I couldn't, Nick."

"Were you afraid to tell me because I was angry about Oscar?"

"No, not at all. It was a privacy issue," I said. I made a conscious choice—I had trusted Dave enough to cross an ethical line, I had to trust Nick too. "When Teresa came to my group session on Saturday she became a client, and clients' names are privileged. Our discussions remain confidential, even after her death. I couldn't tell you I searched her apartment without explaining why I went in there. I still can't elaborate. But I didn't know what the River was until I talked to Dave."

I told Nick how I made the Boyle Heights connection by researching Cansino, then about my conversation with Dilly about the Rojas building. "The same developer bought the lots surrounding Paco and Lucia."

"Dave is stepping in to help Bailey investigate Paco's and

Teresa's deaths. Meanwhile," Nick said, pointing outside at Tattoo Neck, Buzz Cut, and Biceps Boy, "our buddies on the cement wall will watch Botanica Rojas and Lucia until the neighborhood settles down."

"Any more trouble at Lucia's last night?"

"It was quiet. Lucia gave me a key, and I treated them to takeout. We ate then Lucia and Cruz went to bed. I spent most of the night polishing the article. I sent it to the newspaper editors this morning."

"Did Lucia receive any phone calls?"

Nick snorted in mocked contempt. "Sure—when I was out picking up dinner. Victor allegedly called while Cruz was in the shower. The timing of the phone calls is remarkable. But the police will have Victor's phone records now. Dave or Bailey can tell us about any activity."

"What if we get Dave to put a trace on Lucia's phone? Can he do that?"

"With her permission he can. Lucia and I had a few minutes alone. Last night's conversation with Victor upset her. Supposedly he's with Paco, and Paco doesn't want her to live alone in the building anymore. He wants her to sell and move to a community with people who could take care of her."

"That doesn't sound like Victor."

"I don't know if the conversations are real, Liz."

"Imaginary phone calls from Victor and Paco could be a subconscious method of rationalizing her choices. If Paco told her to move, she'd be honoring his wishes instead of abandoning her life with him," I said. "Except for one thing."

"Cruz confirmed that the phone rang Saturday night, right before we got there."

"Exactly. What if it was the developer? Or Gates, or Cansino?"

"Or Victor. And don't forget about Oscar Estevez. He wants her out of business." Nick started the car, backed out of the parking space, and swung toward the street.

"Tonight will be interesting. Gates and Cansino will be at the fund-raiser." I checked my watch. "We have a little time. Let's stop at the bakery and pick up some sweets for Father Nuncio."

"Bribe a priest for help?" Nick said.

"That's not a sin, is it?"

Chapter Twenty-five

Nick parked in front of the *panaderia* and the minute I stepped out of the car I caught the mouthwatering scent of baked goods mingled with the aroma of fresh brewed coffee wafting through the open door. Customers jammed the inside of the shop, waiting in line for hot bread from the aluminum racks on the back wall and the goodies in glass cases in front of us. Four clerks in pristine white uniforms efficiently packed orders and poured coffee.

Nick ripped a number from a red dispenser on the counter while I perused the lineup of fresh *conchas, bolillos, pan dulce,* and cookies. When they called our turn, we ordered a dozen *conchas,* the sweet Mexican bread with a shell-shaped sugar topping.

"And three Mexican coffees, please," I said to the clerk. "Liz?"

I spun around, surprised to hear my name. Erica Gates,

elegant in a chic, zip-front white leather jacket and white slacks, elbowed toward me through the crowd.

"Erica, hello. How unusual to run into you here," I said.

"Is it? I don't know why. Everyone comes here. This is the best bakery in Westlake. The women in my church group won't touch pastries from anywhere else. Are you working at the clinic today?"

"No. We're on our way to an appointment."

"Did you hear the news about Teresa Suarez? She was murdered in the alley behind the clinic Saturday night." Erica pressed her lips together, shaking her head. "That girl. Living with that woman in that building, fraternizing with criminals. I told her to move. She just wouldn't listen. Like Saint Matthew said in the Bible: 'Live by the sword, die by the sword.'"

Nick paid the clerk and turned to us. "The accurate quote, 'All they that take the sword shall perish with the sword,' is accredited to Jesus in the Gospel of Saint Matthew, chapter twenty-six, verse fifty-two. The common interpretation alludes to poetic justice. There's nothing poetic about being shot in a dark alley. However, another interpretation suggests he or she who judges will be judged."

Erica's eyebrows shot up. Nick eyed her askance.

I summoned all my grace and said, "Erica, this is Nick Garfield. Nick is a Religious Philosophy professor. He's didactic before his second cup of coffee. Nick, this is Erica Gates."

Erica gave him a pompous "hello," then said to me, "I'm sorry for the Suarez family but something like this was bound to happen. Teresa lived in that hellhole building with a devil worshipper."

A chunky, plain-faced woman interjected from behind us, "Are you talking about the girl who was murdered by the hex Saturday night?"

"*Si. Maleficio*," another man said.

"Forget the hex. Is anyone here willing to help the police find the real, live person who shot her?" Nick said.

"Why should they help?" Oscar Estevez pushed his way through the crowd. "Senora Rojas hexed them and their families. We have our own problems. Am I right?"

A scattering of patrons nodded agreement.

"Lucia Rojas should move away before someone forces her out," Oscar said.

"You're threatening an old woman?" Nick looked down at him.

"I'm protecting my friends from a vengeful *bruja*."

"And cashing in on their fear."

Oscar cocked his chin. "I help my friends when they come to me. We got the *bruja*'s message when she burned Fidencio's restaurant. Her tenant was murdered in an alley. Good people are afraid to go out at night. Yeah, I hope Lucia Rojas comes to her senses and moves." He received approving nods from the crowd.

"Or you could take a stand against the gangs like Paco Rojas did," I said.

"And died because of it," someone said from the back of the crowd. "Gangs are a police problem."

"Lucia's devilish threat provoked unrest. She has to leave the neighborhood," Erica said.

"And Gates Realty would be there to buy her building," Nick said, arching his brow.

Erica darted her eyes at me, then at Nick. "I wouldn't

know. That's my husband's business." She made a show of checking her watch then snapped across the counter, "Juan, where is my order? I've been here forever."

"Coming now, Senora Gates. *Lo siento.*"

Anxious to end the confrontation, I prodded Nick toward the door. "We have an appointment to keep." When he was out of earshot, I turned back to Erica. "I'm sorry. Everyone's on edge."

She ignored me.

When I got into Nick's car, I said, "What were you doing? Trying to start a riot?"

"Oscar shoots off his mouth too much. Or do you mean the self-important prig? I don't like when people misquote the Bible. So she hates Teresa and Lucia—why drag religion into it?"

"Why did you bring up Bernard Gates?"

"Bernard Gates? Erica Gates? Not too hard to make that connection. Let's go to church."

Our Lady of the Wayside Parish, between 8th and 9th Streets, was a short ride from the bakery. I walked with Nick through the parish parking lot, raising my eyes to see the top of the steeple towering into the sky over the light sand adobe church exterior. Father Nuncio, in a short-sleeved blue shirt tucked into black pants, greeted us warmly from the church steps. We strolled together to the rectory next door.

The deep red walls and carved wooden furniture inside the sitting room evoked the feel of a Spanish hacienda. I set the cardboard tray from the bakery on a rustic side table beneath a portrait of the Virgin Mary.

"Ah, Mexican coffee and *conchas*. A treat. Thank you." Father Nuncio smiled serenely and sat in a straight-backed chair near the window. Nick and I settled on the leather sofa facing him.

"Thank you for seeing us," Nick said. "We came to talk with you about Mrs. Rojas."

"How is Lucia?" the priest said with concern.

"We've been with her every day since Paco was shot," I said. "She's coping with his death, but there are times she imagines he phoned or is downstairs in the botanica. Her isolation is the larger, more troubling issue. The neighborhood is in an uproar over the hex she set in motion at the wake. Her friends in the area abandoned her, Father."

"Everyone?" Father Nuncio said.

"The rumor about the hex spread," Nick said. "Lucia is the focus of local unrest. People blame her for the grease fire at Fidencio's, Teresa Suarez's murder, and every illness or accident in the area. Neither Liz nor I have the power to control the word of mouth. We're concerned for her."

"I heard the news about Teresa Suarez. Sad," Father Nuncio said. "I didn't know Teresa, but Paco and Lucia spoke to me about her. They liked her very much."

"I'm curious," I said. "How did you come to know Paco and Lucia? Did they attend your church?"

"Ours is an unusual friendship. I met them at one of our festivals the first year I arrived at the parish. Paco and Lucia were both baptized Catholic as infants. They weren't regulars at Mass, but they attended quite a few of our neighborhood celebrations. I saw them often, and occasionally I visited them at the shop to chat."

"I imagine you had a few interesting discussions on religion," Nick said.

"Lively," the priest said with a chuckle. "Especially with Paco. The origin of Santeria is linked to the Catholic Church, so we had much in common and we had many differences. As early as the sixteenth century, Spanish Catholic priests baptized Africans before they were put on slave ships to Cuba. The slaves simply merged the Yoruba religions into Catholicism. The syncretic religion that evolved was Santeria. It spread from Cuba to South America and Mexico, then here to the States. Yes, Paco, Lucia, and I had strong doctrinal differences but I also considered them friends. How can I help her?"

"Help us convince the locals that the hex won't hurt them," I said.

The priest opened his hands. "They can't be hurt by something that doesn't exist. There is no such thing as a hex."

"I agree," I said. "But as Nick just said, the rumor took life. Lucia won't defuse it."

Nick leaned forward. "I realize you're not in the hex-breaking business, Father, but we came hoping you could stir compassion for Lucia in the parish. I know it's a lot to ask, but—"

"Say no more. I'll visit Lucia myself, and I'll reach out to our lay ministry. Is she living alone in the apartment?"

"No. Cruz lives there with her," I said. "I understand you referred her. I wonder if you would fill in a little more of her background for us?"

Father Nuncio furrowed his brow. "I'm sorry. Who is Cruz?"

"Cruz DeSoto, the live-in caretaker Dr. Morales hired on your referral?" I said, apprehensive. "I was told you recommended her. I saw you talking to her at the wake."

"Lucia's nurse? Yes, we spoke at the wake," Father Nuncio said. "She introduced herself to me. It was the first time we met. Perhaps you misunderstood. Maybe one of our parishioners referred her?"

Or Cruz lied. I closed my eyes. "I'm sorry, Father. I must have made a mistake or heard wrong. I'll check her referrals."

"Thank you for helping us with Lucia," Nick said, standing. "Your support will make a difference."

"Compassion is one of the linchpins of my work. I'll pay Lucia a visit tomorrow. I have faith in the goodwill of my parishioners. She won't be alone." Father Nuncio escorted us out of the rectory.

As we stood outside on the steps, my phone rang in my purse. I took it out, saw the name on the screen, and then excused myself to take the call.

When Nick met me at the car I said, "Dilly just gave me the names of the agents who repped the sellers of both lots bordering Lucia's building. Want to take a guess?"

"Gates or Cansino?" Nick said.

"Both. Gates sold the lot to the west. Cansino sold the lot to the east. The question is, how does this information relate to Victor's disappearance—or does it?"

"Let's see if we can find out." Nick started the car. "Gates Realty is close by, on Wilshire. Buckle up."

I hesitated, trapped. I couldn't tell him Erica Gates was

my client, too. Dropping in on her husband was ethically fuzzy. Despite my urge to investigate, I didn't want to risk crossing another privacy boundary.

"Both of us don't need to talk to Gates. Drop me off at the clinic. Carmen and Tony should be aware that Cruz lied about Father Nuncio's recommendation."

"Gates might be more open to talk to a couple," Nick said. "We won't be there long."

"Nick, I really don't want to."

"After my run-in with his wife, I'll be more comfortable with you there." He turned out of the church lot and drove north.

The Empire Building stood on the south side of Wilshire Boulevard, several blocks west of Good Samaritan Hospital. Nick parked in the building's underground lot, and we climbed a flight of stairs to Gates Realty on the ground floor.

A fortyish brunette with a short, tight perm sat behind the front desk in the modern, industrial office. She smiled pleasantly as we entered. "Do you have an appointment?"

"We don't," Nick said. "We stopped on a whim. My wife reads auras. She felt a strong pull when we passed your sign."

Chapter Twenty-six

The Gates Realty receptionist began to say something, stopped, then cocked her head.

"I was kidding," Nick said, grinning. "We came to inquire about a building in Westlake. My name is Nick Garfield. Is Mr. Gates in?"

She cracked a dimpled smile. "You got me. And here I was, about to ask your wife to read my aura. I love that stuff. Bernie's here. I'll check and see if he's busy. You can wait over there." She directed us to a cove of chairs nestled in front of the street-side window blanketed with property flyers.

"Aura reader, Nick? That's your intro?" I whispered as we sat down. "Did you sleep in Lucia's sanctuary last night?"

"I considered snake charmer but couldn't make it work."

"Mr. and Mrs. Garfield?" Bernie Gates lumbered into the lobby, tucking in his striped shirt as he approached. He pointed to the property brochures on the window, smiling. "A loft in the downtown arts district came on the market today. A decorator's dream." He winked at me. "And I have two spacious upper-floor condos with views from downtown that will make your friends weep with envy." He held out his hand. "I'm Bernie Gates."

Nick stood. "Nick Garfield. And this is—"

"Liz," I said, rising to greet him. "I'll just wait out here while you two talk." I turned to sit down again.

"No, no," Bernie said, stopping me. "You come too, Mrs. Garfield. It's more comfortable in my office."

Mrs. Garfield had a pleasant ring. *Did Mr. Garfield believe in rings?*

"No, really. I should check my phone messages," I said.

"I insist." Bernie cupped my elbow and led us to a large, windowless office in the rear of the suite.

Stacks of papers, sports memorabilia, and sales awards jammed the top of his desk and filing cabinets. He invited us to sit down, and then eased himself into a leather chair behind the desk. "What kind of property are you interested in?"

"I understand you talked to Paco Rojas about selling his building on 7th Street," Nick said.

Bernie's eyebrows darted up. "Are you interested in buying it?"

"No," Nick said. "We're friends of Mrs. Rojas. Several Realtors approached her recently. We're curious about the rush this soon after her husband's death. We heard you have an honest reputation. We came to you for the truth."

"I understand." Bernie folded his hands on his belly, grinning after the compliment. "Well, I *was* very interested until the call I got this morning. I was told Mrs. Rojas went with another Realtor. Bizarre turnaround, if you ask me. Mr. Rojas was adamant about not selling."

"Who called you?" I said.

"Victor Morales. Know him?"

Nick and I exchanged glances. He nodded at Bernie. "We do. And he called you this morning?"

"Not more than an hour ago. I had phoned Mrs. Rojas on Friday to offer my condolences again and my services if she ever decides to sell her building. Morales called this morning, saying she appreciated the gesture, but my services wouldn't be needed."

"Did you speak to Mrs. Rojas on Friday?" Nick's foot tapped on the floor in overdrive.

"No. I left a message with the woman who answered the phone."

Cruz relayed Lucia's messages to Victor while playing dumb with us?

I leaned forward, confused. "Victor Morales returned your call this morning? That's—"

Nick discreetly touched my knee, and said to Bernie, "We didn't know. Will you tell us why you're interested in the building?"

"Everyone who deals commercial wants that listing. I suppose I can tell you why, since I'm not getting it. The developer who owns the adjacent properties offered a bonus to the selling broker who brought him the Rojas building. Paco Rojas wouldn't budge. He wouldn't even take a second phone call. I guess the widow thought differently."

"What kind of bonus?" I said.

"Cash over and above commission. Three weeks ago, I

heard the developer might give exclusive leasing rights on any new development to the selling broker," Bernie said. "Morales wouldn't tell me who the widow went with to represent her. But wait a minute. Did she tell you? How many people are speaking for Mrs. Rojas, anyway?"

"Mrs. Rojas speaks for herself. We want to make certain she has accurate information and is aware of her options," Nick said. "Do you know Raymon Cansino?"

"Sure I do." Bernie blew out a sigh. "Cansino sold the building on east side of the Rojases. Elbowed me out after he heard I sold the building on the west to the developer. Don't tell me Mrs. Rojas is going to use Cansino."

"We don't know," Nick said.

"What is his reputation?" I said.

Bernie looked from side to side. "Between us, because Mrs. Rojas seems like a nice lady? Cansino is a soulless bastard. I wouldn't let my worst enemy do business with him."

"Thank you for the advice *and* the information, Bernie," Nick said, standing.

"Tell Mrs. R. that I'll be glad to make another offer if she changes her mind again." Bernie rolled his eyes at Nick. "Women."

I walked into the hall ahead of them, unshielded against the scowling woman waiting in the lobby. I offered Erica Gates my most gracious smile, wanting more than anything to be invisible.

Bernie bypassed me to reach his wife, and then turned to make introductions. "Erica, this is—"

"I know who they are," she said with disgust.

Nick grinned. "Hello, again. I hope I didn't offend you

this morning, Mrs. Gates. My sincere apologies. Your husband's a great guy."

Erica ignored him and said to me, "Can we talk in private?"

"Of course." I held up a be-right-back finger at Nick and followed Erica.

We went into an empty conference room two doors off the lobby. She shut the door and faced me, her breath reeking of coffee and cigarettes. "What are you doing here?"

"We came on business. Nick needed information from your husband." The truth should have composed me, but her anger had me on guard.

"You told Bernie about our meeting."

"No." I shook my head. "I didn't. I wouldn't, Erica."

"Your actions are as cavalier as your boyfriend's attitude. I was told what was said in the Wellness Group was confidential. You had no right to tell your friend about my family then bring him to see my husband. I'm reporting you."

"Erica, I didn't tell Nick about you or your family. Mr. Gates doesn't know you and I are acquainted."

"He does now. And I'm forced to explain how I know you, unless your callous boyfriend already told him."

"I assure you, Nick doesn't know you're my client. And the sooner we go back to the lobby, the less you'll have to explain."

"You have a lot of nerve talking to my husband without my knowledge. You stepped over a line. Carmen Perez won't think much of your unprofessional actions. Neither will the state medical board when I file my complaint."

I struggled for outward calm. Inside I was panicking.

"Erica, our meeting with Bernie had absolutely nothing to do with you."

"You had no right." She stormed out of the room.

A report to the Board of Psychology would trigger an inquiry. Visiting Bernie, regardless of my inept effort to avoid it, was a foolish blunder that could harm my reputation. I had to apologize, change Erica's mind, but when I returned to the lobby she was gone.

Nick and I exchanged appreciative good-byes with Bernie and left. As we descended the steps to the garage, he said, "Gates is a good guy but the wife is a shrew. What was she so pissed about?"

Easy answer—me. But telling Nick the truth would be another privacy breach. "She was still upset about this morning."

"She'll get over it. How does she know you? Did you meet her at the wake?"

"I've seen her around. What do you think about Victor calling Bernie? Do you believe it was really Victor?"

"Whoever it was, I doubt if Lucia was aware of the call. Why would she spend the past three days helping me write an article about the botanica if she planned to sell?" Nick opened the passenger door for me, and then got in the other side. He started the car then dialed his car phone. "Let's see if Dave or Bailey got Victor's phone records yet."

Dave answered, his voice scratching over Nick's speakerphone as he read off the phone company report. "The last call made from Victor's cell phone was on Wednesday morning to Carmen's home phone number. The last call made *to* his cell phone was from Park Clinic on Wednesday evening at six forty-five. And the last ping registered was from the Westlake area Wednesday night."

"What's a *ping*?" I said.

"Loosely put, a *ping* is a hit from an active cell phone to the closest tracking tower. Tells us the general area the telephone activity originated from. Victor's cell phone has been out of service since Wednesday, and his home phone has been dormant for over a week. If he's making calls, they're not from either line," Dave said.

"We know Victor, or someone pretending to be Victor, called Bernie Gates this morning," Nick said.

"Dave, I'm beginning to think Lucia may be the target of a scam. Maybe through Cansino," I said.

"You mean Cansino working with Victor Morales? That's a wild assumption," Dave said.

"Well, something strange is going on," I said. "Can you trace Lucia's incoming calls? We have to locate Victor or whoever is impersonating him."

"If someone is impersonating him," Nick said.

"I can't get a warrant to trace her phone based on a feeling. Lucia has to give the phone company approval," Dave said.

"I'll get her approval," Nick said. "I'm on my way to talk to Lucia now. The caretaker could be in on the scam, too. She lied about her references. Dave, would you see if you could find an address on her? Her name is Cruz DeSoto."

"Hold on." Dave came back on the line, laughing. "There are about two hundred Cruz DeSotos in Los Angeles. At least thirty in Westlake."

"What about Boyle Heights?" I said.

"Twenty or twenty-five. Sorry," Dave said. "I need more than a name to track her down."

"I'm going to the clinic," I said. "I'll see if Carmen has a copy of Cruz's employment application."

"Did you tell Bailey about the note you found in the Suarez apartment yet?" Dave said.

"No."

"Pick up the damn phone and call him like I told you to last night. Do it. And try to restrain yourself from playing detective. You already have a job," Dave said with a sharp bite of sarcasm.

Some joke. If Erica Gates cost me my license, I could be hunting for a new job along with a new home.

Nick hung up and drove up the ramp to the street. He turned left onto Wilshire Boulevard. As I scanned through my recent calls for Bailey's number, my phone rang.

"Liz? It's Matt Bailey."

"Bailey? I was about to call you."

Bailey's reply came short and clipped. "I want to talk to you about Teresa Suarez. Where will you be this afternoon?"

"I'm in Westlake right now with Nick, on my way to Park Clinic."

"Meet me outside Park Clinic in an hour. Why were you calling me? Did Morales show up?"

"No. But I might have new information about him and maybe Paco Rojas. I'll tell you when I see you," I said. Nick tossed me a disapproving look as I hung up. "What? I'm not confessing unlawful entry to a cop over the phone."

"Learn that from TV?"

"No. At the family dinner table."

238

Chapter Twenty-seven

The Park Clinic mini-mall hummed with lunchtime action. Cars moved through the lot, Tattoo Neck and his friends loafed at their usual post, and laborers ambled toward the restaurant. Nick found an open space close to the street and we agreed to meet at Park Clinic after he stopped to visit Lucia.

Miguel met me at the clinic door. I thanked him for the tip on Ynez. "She told me she saw Victor's car in the lot after midnight on Wednesday. How late did you work that night?"

"Wednesday?" He looked up at the ceiling. "Let's see. I always lock the front door when we close at five, then I check the exam rooms, the dispensary, and clean up the kitchen in the back. I guess I went home right before six."

"Was anybody still here when you left?"

"Sure. The usual crowd. Helen and the interns always work

late. So do the doctors, though Dr. Perez and Dr. Morales didn't come back after the wake. At least not before I left."

"Are there security cameras?"

"Nope. But there's an alarm."

The alarm couldn't show me the cars outside, anyone left inside, or a record of Victor entering or leaving. I thanked Miguel and crossed to the reception desk. Jackson, decked out in bright lime green, chattered on the phone. When I caught her eye, she thumbed over her shoulder. "They're in Dr. Perez's office."

I didn't wait to ask her who "they" were. When I entered the office I found Carmen, Tony Torrico, and my mother, with man I didn't know. He was in his late forties or early fifties, in a khaki sport coat over a denim shirt. The group circled Carmen's desk, studying a scroll of blue and white drawings.

Carmen gestured me in and introduced the stranger as Bob Warnecke, the contractor for the clinic's plumbing upgrade. Our polite greetings were interrupted by Bob's cell phone.

He looked at the screen. "Will you excuse me for a moment? I have to take this outside. I'll be right back."

Tony glanced up from the papers. "The plans look good to me, Carmen. I think we should approve them and move ahead."

"Should Victor see them first?" Mom said.

"I'd like him to, but Tony may be right. Bob needs time to organize a construction timetable. I can't guarantee when Victor will be back," Carmen said, her tone edged with worry. "This morning I heard that Victor might have been calling Lucia all along."

"So he's not missing after all? He's just not coming to

work? I don't like that." Tony glanced into the hall, then turned back and lowered his voice. "I hate to say it, Carmen, but maybe you should check the clinic financials before we proceed."

"The financials are solid. The money for construction is funded in a separate account." Carmen tilted her head to the door and shot Tony a warning glance.

"Carmen, you've been dreaming about this upgrade for years. The donors will expect to see work begin," Mom said as Bob came back into the office.

"You're smart to move ahead with the renovations now, before the neighborhood expands." Bob rolled the papers into a tube and secured them with a rubber band.

"How do you mean expands?" I said.

"I'm hearing strong rumors about parking structures and new businesses planned because of the MTA Westside Extension. Good for the whole area around the clinic, I think."

"Are you talking about the Subway to the Sea?" Mom said.

"Yep. The city is investing billions," Bob said. "An extension to the ocean will affect every neighborhood close to the MTA stations. Property values tripled after the station down the block was built."

"Including the building across the street?" I said.

"The old two-story? In between the empty lots?" Bob cocked his head in the direction of Botanica Rojas. "Yeah. I understand a parking structure or condos with a mall at the base will go up as soon as developers clear the block. I'd like to be in on *that* deal."

"What if the owner won't sell?" I said.

"They'll sell. There's too much money involved." Bob

checked his watch then slid the tube of papers under his arm. "Sorry, I have to leave. I'm late for my next meeting."

Mom offered to escort him to the lobby. I backed into the hall to let them pass. They left together, with Mom chattering about tile colors.

Tony paused in Carmen's doorway. "Do you want me to sit in for your interview with Dr. Ashworth this afternoon?"

"Yes. I think you'll like her. She just finished her residency. I think she'll fit in well. She'll relieve you of some of the patient load. I can't thank you enough, Tony."

"Please." Tony held up his palm. "You have a great staff. Everyone pitched in. The patients come first. The clinic will thrive. The plans for the showers and plumbing are good." He brushed past me in the hall and went into his office next door.

Carmen buried her head in her hands at her desk. "Victor, where are you? Teresa promised we'd be protected. I don't know what to do."

Protected? The facts clicked into place: Teresa's "friends" posted outside the clinic every day. The way they responded to her orders. *How could I be so naïve?*

"Carmen." I put my hand on her shoulder.

She shrugged me off and sat up. "I'm all right, sweetie."

"You paid Teresa for gang protection," I said. "Why didn't you say something?"

She pulled a tissue from the box on the corner of her desk, pretending not to hear me. "Where did your mother go?"

I slid into the chair facing her. "I should have known when I saw Teresa's earnings. Despite the gang problems in the neighborhood, Park Clinic was never touched. No graffiti, no broken windows, no stolen equipment."

Her eyes shot up. "We had to. For our safety."

"Had to what?" Mom appeared at the office door with Nick.

"Carmen and Victor paid protection money to the gangs. Teresa was the middleman," I said.

"You told her?" Mom said to Carmen.

"You knew?" I said.

"Anyone who watches television knows about extortion. Of course she and Victor paid for protection. Every business around here does. And the correct term is bagman, dear, not middleman," Mom said.

I should watch more TV.

"I can't deal with this anymore without Victor," Carmen said. "Maybe we should call off the fund-raiser."

"Good Lord, Carmen, no," Mom said, shaking her head. "Pull yourself together. We can't cancel. We collected *money*. The guests, caterers, and orchestra are coming in a few hours. Everything was perfect until that woman hexed everyone. Nick, do something."

Nick closed the office door behind him. "Lucia means no harm to the clinic, Viv."

"Well, she's not exactly performing a 'Success Spell' or a 'Find Victor Spell' for us either."

"Want to stop the bad luck, Mom? Stop believing in it." I turned to Carmen. "When did the extortion start?"

"Carlos Suarez, Teresa's husband, came to Victor years ago after the first incident," she said. "We knew the trouble he could cause us, and agreed that bending to Carlos's demand was safer than fighting him. We paid him out of petty cash. After he was sent to jail, Teresa went to Victor and told him if we hired her, the protection would continue."

"Why a job? Why not just collect the cash?" Nick said.

"Despite her involvement, I think Teresa wanted to

escape gang life. The clerical job here gave her some experience for her résumé. I don't know how we'll handle protection for the clinic now. And with Teresa dead, I don't know how long Lucia will have protection either."

"Lucia?" Nick said.

"They lowered Teresa's rent in exchange for protection," Carmen said. "Teresa bartered a deal with Lucia."

"While Paco campaigned against the gangs?" I said.

"Paco could say what he wanted as long as the gang collected their money," Carmen said. "The elder gang members are wary of Lucia. Her reputation as a *bruja* keeps them in check. But what's news to you today, Liz, is common knowledge on the street. The gang members outside really do watch out for us. I honestly don't think the local gang is involved with Victor's disappearance."

Her phone rang before I could tell her about Victor's morning call to Bernie Gates. Carmen answered, frowning as she listened. She put the caller on hold and said to us, "Will you excuse me? I need to finish this call in private."

"Cocktails at seven," Mom said as Nick and I accompanied her to her car. "Dinner at seven thirty, speeches at eight, and dancing until eleven. I want you there at six thirty."

"We'll be there. Save me a dance," Nick said.

I swore I saw Mom blushing when she got into her car and left.

"Did you find out anything from Lucia?" I said to Nick.

"She knew all about Bernie's call on Friday. Cruz gave her the message, and Lucia relayed it to Victor, or whoever called her Friday night."

"The mystery man," I said. "Seriously, Nick, how does Victor disappear from home, work, and his friends, but stay conscientious enough to call Lucia? It doesn't add up."

"She refuses to believe Victor is missing. I can't fault her thinking. After all, he calls her."

"And tells her he's with Paco. Conscientious and cruel at the same time," I said, opening the clinic door. We found two empty chairs in the corner and sat down to wait for Bailey to show outside.

"When I asked Lucia why Victor didn't come to see her as promised, I saw doubt in her eyes. That gave me an opening. I persuaded her to approve a trace on her incoming calls." Nick sat back and grinned. "If Lucia gets a call tonight, we'll have the number tomorrow."

"Excellent. Nice work. Does Cruz know?"

"No. Lucia and I talked in the back room of the botanica. Cruz was—"

"Don't tell me." I smirked. "Out in front, watching TV?"

"Right. I also asked Lucia if Victor gave her Cruz's résumé. She asked him to keep it for her. Did you see it in Victor's desk Saturday night?"

"No. But I wasn't really searching for it. And I didn't have an opportunity to ask Carmen." I stood up. "I'll go talk to her now."

I found Carmen outside the open Dutch door to the dispensary, clipboard in hand. "Do you have a minute? Father Nuncio gave Nick and me an interesting bit of information this morning."

"What's that?" Carmen didn't look up. She scribbled her

signature on a form and handed the clipboard to the dispensary nurse. Waving for me to follow, she started toward her office.

"He doesn't know Cruz DeSoto," I said. "He never met her until she introduced herself at the wake. We should review her application. Cruz lied to Victor. I don't trust her."

"I'm certain Victor told me Father Nuncio recommended her." Carmen stopped outside Tony's office door. "You didn't see Cruz's application when you went through Victor's office the other night? It wasn't in the file with the Realtor letters to Paco?"

"I wasn't looking for it," I said.

Her response was curt. "You saw everything else."

"Do you mind if I go through his files again?"

"I do mind." She crossed her arms. "In fact, you and I need to talk. Privately."

We turned into her office. She shut the door. "Sit down, Dr. Cooper."

I took a seat and shifted, nervous. "What is it, Carmen?"

"Erica Gates called me. An extremely angry Erica Gates. Were you at her husband's office this morning?"

"Yes." My stomach lurched. "Nick and I went together. But our visit to Gates Realty had nothing to do with Erica. We thought if Bernie could tell us why Paco and Lucia's building was so interesting to buyers we'd have a clue to Paco's murder or Victor's disappearance. Erica got to the office as Nick and I were leaving. She was already annoyed." I described the morning run-in with Nick. The more I tried to explain, the sicker I felt. "Nick didn't know who Erica was at the bakery. I attempted to mediate but when we left, she was upset. When she saw me at Bernie's, she was livid."

Carmen shook her head. "Did you even consider Erica might be at Gates Realty before you went there? That Bernie might ask how you knew his wife? Last night on the phone, you were concerned about your professional obligation to Teresa, yet today you ignored Erica's right to privacy as a member of the Wellness Group. You put Erica and yourself in an awkward and potentially embarrassing position. She wants your license revoked."

"Carmen, Bernie doesn't know Erica is my client. He didn't ask how we knew each other."

"He didn't ask her in front of you." She rubbed her forehead. "I can't brush this off. She's prepared to file a complaint with the California Board of Psychology."

"She doesn't have grounds."

"She still has the right to file. The state board would weigh your word against hers. Your ethics would be under scrutiny."

Regardless of the outcome, an unprofessional conduct complaint would be in my file, permanently. I took a deep breath to ease the panicked qualm in my chest. "I could talk to Erica again. Apologize."

"You'll only exacerbate the problem. This couldn't have happened at a worse time, Liz. Until I have time to sort this out, consider the Wellness Group on hiatus. Take a break. I want you to keep away from the clinic for a while."

Chapter Twenty-eight

I left Carmen's office downhearted and upset. Juanita and Ruby would be turned away when they came to the Wellness session on Saturday. I hated letting them down. I hated letting Carmen down. Although confident I didn't breach my ethics, I certainly dallied with them over the last two days in efforts to find Victor and help Lucia.

Nick smiled at me when I reached the lobby. "Well?"

"Let's talk somewhere else."

As we walked outside I twirled Lucia's protection bracelet around my wrist—as if a spell would help save my reputation. I wasn't that desperate yet.

"So, did you find Cruz's application?" Nick said.

"Carmen wouldn't let me into Victor's office. In fact, as of right now, I'm persona non grata at the clinic." I closed his gaping mouth with the tip of my finger. "An angry client called in a complaint about me to Carmen. If she presses the matter, my license could be revoked. I can't tell you any more than that, Nick. I crossed too many professional boundaries today already."

He studied my face. "You don't have to explain. I think I can guess."

"Reading my mind?"

"Nope. Minds are your specialty. However, I recall a furious housewife you've 'seen around' who stomped on your aura this morning following your reluctance to visit her husband. I apologize for not listening when you told me you didn't want to see Bernie. I'm sorry."

"Very perceptive, but I should have stayed in the car. And I still can't give you details. Carmen doesn't know about Victor's call to Gates yet. Maybe we're chasing an illusion. Maybe Victor isn't missing after all. He could be home using a prepaid phone for all we know."

"We could drive to Victor's house and check, but Bailey just pulled in." Nick waved at the detective driving into the lot.

Matt Bailey parked his car and sauntered toward us in jeans, a sport coat, and pointed cowboy boots. "Sorry I'm late. I got hung up on a call. Where can we go to talk?"

"How about a cup of coffee?" Nick said. "I'll buy."

We crossed the lot to the Chinese-Mexican-American Deli at the top corner of the mini-mall and slid into an orange vinyl booth at the window inside. Nick and I sat together with Bailey facing us. Our waitress, a young woman in a white apron, hairnet, and nose ring, took our order for three coffees. She turned over the porcelain cups on saucers already on the table and poured in a brew that might have been coffee but smelled like burned rubber.

Nick stirred two packets of sugar into his cup. "Dr. Morales called Bernie Gates at Gates Realty this morning."

Bailey arched his brow. "So Morales is back?"

"No one has seen him," Nick said. "He's allegedly been calling Mrs. Rojas, too."

"Allegedly?" Bailey said.

"I took the phone while Lucia was talking to him," I said. "Victor, or whoever heard my voice, hung up on me."

"On other calls, Victor told her he was with Paco Rojas," Nick said.

"Her deceased husband?" Bailey stared at the cup in front of him. "Morales hasn't been home. The neighbor called, asking what to do about his mail. His phone records show no activity, either from his house or his cell, since last Wednesday. His last call came from the clinic."

"The call from the clinic could have come from any one of a number of people. Some of the staff stay past six, and Park Clinic doesn't have security cameras," I said.

"You've been doing your homework," Bailey said.

"I work there," I said. *Or used to.*

"It doesn't matter who called," he said. "If Morales is making phone calls, he's not missing. I received information this morning that made me think he took off on his own."

I tilted my head. "What kind of information?"

"The good doctor deposited a five-thousand-dollar cashier's check in his bank account Thursday morning."

"From who?" Nick said.

Bailey shrugged. "I contacted the issuing bank. The check was purchased with cash. Morales made the deposit at an ATM in Boyle Heights."

I pushed away my cup. Even with milk and two yellow

packets, the coffee tasted like something off my garage floor. "I don't understand."

"Not much to understand. Bottom line, the guy's not missing," Bailey said. "Meanwhile, I have two homicides to investigate. You said you have information on Morales and the Paco Rojas case. Talk to me about Rojas." He drained his cup and beckoned to the waitress for a refill.

"Victor and Paco paid protection money to a local gang," I said.

"No surprise." Bailey pointed through the window at Buzz Cut, Biceps Boy, and Tattoo Neck on the street. "There, at twelve o'clock. That trio identifies themselves as 'mall security.' My money says every shop on this street pays protection. So what's your point?"

"Paco Rojas paid protection, yet he was killed in a gang drive-by," Nick said. "Teresa Suarez ran the protection business for the gang, but she was shot in a local alley. Gangs are tribal. Tribal cultures usually don't attack their own. If they do, it's because of money or a woman."

"Money," Bailey said. "Saldivar was on the River Gang shit list for skimming off cash. The only thing I can't figure out is why he was shot in front of a rival gang member's wife. Teresa Suarez was killed the day after she visited her husband in prison. My guess is her husband told her why Saldivar was shot and she opened her mouth to the wrong person." Bailey looked at me. "When was the last time you saw her?"

"Outside the clinic on Saturday, talking to the guys out there." I cocked my head in the direction of Buzz Cut and his friends.

"What was she wearing that day?" he said.

I would guarantee that Bailey cared as much about fashion as I cared about locker room gossip. I eyed him cautiously. "A black jacket, slacks, and a tan sweater."

"I searched Teresa's apartment this morning." He reached into his sport coat, pulled out a piece of paper, and unfolded the photocopy of both sides of my business card with Bailey's number in my handwriting and Teresa's notations on the back. "This card was in the pocket of the only black jacket in her closet. The jacket, I assume, she was wearing on Saturday when you wrote out my number for her. Did you tell her to call me?"

I shook my head. "Sorry. I can't comment. Teresa became my client on Saturday. Our conversations are privileged."

"She's dead, Liz. Don't be like everyone on the street. Help me solve these murders."

Bailey's earnest plea almost swayed me. I wanted to help him. But, because Teresa didn't confess she committed a crime, and because she didn't name the person or people she feared, everything she told me had to stay confidential. Her revelation that Paco, not Saldivar, was targeted was hearsay, and not admissible in court. I was bound by privilege even after her death, and it sucked.

I shrugged in futility.

"You won't help? Do you know who killed her?" Bailey said.

I sipped my coffee, ignoring him.

He leaned across the table. "Did she tell you who killed Saldivar?"

Even if I revealed to him that Paco was the target, I had no proof. I peered through the window, avoiding his question. Carmen crossed the parking lot from the clinic to her car, probably to go home to dress for the fund-raiser.

"She can't tell you, Bailey," Nick said.

"Maybe you'd feel more open to talk at the station, Liz," Bailey said.

"It wouldn't make a difference. I'm sorry," I said.

Nick waited while the waitress topped his coffee then said, "Listen, maybe the reason Teresa took your phone number is right there in front of you. Read what she wrote. 'River.' You know Saldivar was in the River Gang. 'bh.' You know Saldivar lived in Boyle Heights."

"Big deal," Bailey said.

"Raymon Cansino works in Boyle Heights," I said.

"Thousands of people live and work in Boyle Heights," Bailey said. "I don't have time to play a game of Clue with you two. Tell me what you know, Liz."

"Raymon Cansino tried to convince Paco Rojas to sell his building," I said.

Bailey stretched his legs into the aisle and leaned back with his arms crossed. "Did Teresa tell you that?"

"Liz and I searched Victor's office Saturday night," Nick said. "One of his last computer searches was on C&C Properties. Cansino was pushing the Rojases to sell."

"How would Teresa know him?" Bailey said.

"Lucia or Paco could have mentioned him to her," Nick said. "She could have seen Cansino at the wake and recognized him. Or maybe she saw the letter in Victor's office. She did work at the clinic."

"It's a stretch, but I'll check Cansino out," Bailey said. "You searched Morales's office? You're a busy pair."

"He's a friend, and he's missing," I said.

"He *was* missing. Now he's collecting checks and working the phones." Bailey signaled the waitress. "I have to leave."

Nick slid out of the booth and waited for the waitress to bring the check. Bailey and I walked to the door together.

"We'll talk about this again. I want you to reconsider telling me about your conversation with Teresa," Bailey said. "Do the right thing, Liz."

"I am doing the right thing. By the way, Raymon Cansino will be at the Park Clinic fund-raiser at the Mayfair Hotel tonight. You might want to drop by."

"Will there be banquet chicken?" Bailey said. "I love banquet chicken."

Chapter Twenty-nine

Bailey left us in the parking lot. I had time before I had to get dressed for the fund-raiser, and I wanted to make a stop before I went back to the Valley. Nick fiddled in his pocket for his keys.

"Are you going home?" I said.

"Not yet. I offered Oscar an incentive to do some digging on the Saldivar/Rojas shooting for me yesterday. I'm going over there now to see if he came up with anything. Could be interesting. The River Gang is deep into the worship of Santa Muerte, and Oscar has a strong relationship with the followers." Nick unlocked his car and took a small velvet jewelry box from the glove compartment.

"What's that?"

He opened the box, revealing a weathered two-inch twist of frayed hemp on black velvet. It looked like something Erzulie would cough up.

"The incentive," Nick said. "His information in exchange for a piece of twine from the rope that hung his hero Jesús Malverde in nineteen hundred and nine. One of Malverde's devotees in Sinaloa gave it to me as a thank-you for a favor."

An artifact from the execution of the narco-saint? I didn't ask what kind of favor Nick performed to earn the bounty. "Is it authentic?"

"Might be. Might not. Oscar believes the rope holds the spirit of Malverde, so to him it's priceless." Nick dropped the box into his pocket and locked his car. "I'll pick you up at your place at five thirty."

I shook my head. "I'm going to Oscar's with you. I want to see this."

"No way, Liz. I have to go alone." Nick's phone rang. He answered and listened. "I don't understand. Let me talk to Syd." A pause, then, "Tell her to call me." He hung up without saying good-bye then stared at the pavement.

"Who was that?"

"Sydney Tenbrook's assistant at the *Times*. They can't run my article about Paco and Lucia. Her assistant gave me an excuse about fact-checking."

"I thought Sydney was enthused about your idea," I said.

"She was. I'm calling her private line and find out what changed her mind." Nick dialed then said, "Syd? Nick Garfield."

He cajoled, nodded, and made promises, then hung up and said to me, "A salesman got a 'friendly' call suggesting that the *Times* would look foolish promoting an article on a business about to go under. The salesman wouldn't tell Syd who made the call. The only people who knew about the article aside from us and Lucia were Carmen, Cruz, and Victor, or the alleged Victor."

"Not so. I'm sure my parents knew. Dave knew. And Erica Gates overheard me tell Tony Torrico on Saturday. Any one of them could have told a wider variety of people," I said. "If Bernie told Erica that Botanica Rojas was about to be sold, she could have made the call to spite you for embarrassing her this morning." *Or to spite me.*

"Or someone who wanted to divert public attention away from Lucia and her building until they convince or bully her to sell," Nick said.

"They won't hurt her, Nick. If Lucia died without a will or administrator, the property could be tied up in the court system for years."

"Unless Lucia signed over her legal power of attorney to Victor after the wake. Don't forget about the five-thousand-dollar deposit Victor made to his account Thursday morning. I'd hate to think he took the money as a bribe to secure the sale of her building," Nick said.

"Crazy. Impossible. How could all of us, especially Carmen, be that wrong about Victor Morales?"

"I suspect the answer lies over there." Nick pointed at Botanica Rojas on the other side of the street. "I have to go, Liz. I'll let you know if Oscar came up with anything when I pick you up tonight."

"Five thirty sharp. Don't forget, we have to pick up Robin, too." I cupped my hand along the side of his face before he left. "Be careful, Nick."

Instead of going to my car, I scanned the Park Clinic lot for Carmen's Volvo to make certain she hadn't returned.

Determined to make another attempt to locate Cruz's résumé, I went back into the clinic. Miguel looked up from his newspaper; Jackson glanced at me from her desk. Their welcoming smiles told me I hadn't made the Least-Wanted list yet.

Feigning ignorance, I said, "Is Carmen in the back?"

Miguel shook his head and went back to the paper.

"She left to get dressed for the fund-raiser, hon." Jackson wiggled her fingers in the air. "She's got to look special tonight."

"Darn." I snapped my fingers. "I can't believe I missed her. I think I left my phone on her desk this afternoon, and I'm expecting an important call. Do you mind if I run back to her office and get it? I'll only be a minute. No need to bother Miguel."

The forgotten phone ruse worked for me in the past, a broad enough deception to get me back to the offices and cover me if I got caught.

"Sure, hon." She opened her drawer and handed me the key ring. "Her key has her name on it. Just lock the door when you're done."

I slipped through the hall and rounded the corner to the offices in back. If Carmen told Tony and/or Helen about Erica's complaint and my unwelcome status, I would repeat my lost phone excuse. The techs, busy shuffling patient files, didn't pay attention as I passed them. The dispensary technician had her back turned. When I reached my destination I rifled through the ring until I found the key I wanted.

Victor's lock opened easily. I stole inside and closed the door. Opening his bottom desk drawer, I pushed through files until I found what I came for. I took out the folder and then flipped through the rest, looking for a Rojas file, Cruz's name, or any file with job applications. Nothing, nothing, nothing.

"Who's in there, Helen?" Tony Torrico's voice came from right outside the door.

I froze. The door didn't open. Inch by inch so not to make a sound, I crouched behind the desk. What the hell would I say if Tony came in? I lost a contact? Needed to use the phone? *On the floor?* I did what any sane, rational person would do—I gritted my teeth, waiting until I heard Helen's reply.

"Mrs. Sosso in room five. Her stitches look infected, Doctor. She's in pain."

"On my way."

After their voices faded, I shoved Victor's personal file under my sweater and pressed my ear to the door. Satisfied I was in the clear, I opened the door and left. I gave Jackson the keys, showed her my phone with a smile, and then got the hell out of there.

Thirty minutes later I was home at my desk with Victor's file. I searched through the papers for Cruz's application three times and came up blank. But an even stranger discovery prompted me to check again. I was right—the letters to Paco from Bernie Gates and Raymon Cansino were missing.

Chapter Thirty

"Jazzing Up," the headline on the glitzy silver and gold invitation to the fund-raiser, was the Cherries' creative attempt to tie their money-raising effort to "jazz up" the Park Clinic plumbing to the Jazz Age past of the Mayfair Hotel. The "Formal Attire" line centered in script at the bottom meant I had better plug in the hot rollers before I jumped in the shower.

While the rollers did their thing on my freshly shampooed and dried locks, I slathered on lotion and put on my makeup. Satisfied with the curls tumbling to my shoulders, I added an extra layer of mascara to my lashes, dabbed tinted gloss on my lips, and then slipped into my pale lavender knee-length dress. Tiers of delicate lace draped in inverted Vs over the chiffon skirt, reminiscent of a sultry 1920s flapper dress. I put on open-toed bone pumps then stood in front of the mirror, swishing the skirt and my curls.

Erzulie watched with her head on her paws from the top of the dresser. I modeled for her opinion. She didn't move. Not even a complimenting blink. Something was missing. The dress didn't need accessories other than my blue porcelain and pearl earrings. Erzulie lifted her head and pawed the trinket next to her—Lucia's protection bracelet. She sniffed at the bangle, and then swatted it across the dresser top.

I could take a hint. I slid the bracelet onto my left wrist and glanced over my shoulder into the mirror—it worked. I jammed lip gloss, my license, a house key, a twenty-dollar bill, and my phone into my beaded evening bag. As I twirled for Erzulie's final approval, the doorbell rang.

There was something so incredibly sexy about a man in evening clothes, and Nick carried the look with chic sophistication in a European-tailored black suit, pale blue shirt, and silver silk tie. His slim jacket accentuated his broad shoulders and cut to the waist in an invite to slip my arms around him and dance all night.

He stepped back on my front stoop and gave me a soft, appreciative whistle. "Amazing."

"Thank you, but aren't you supposed to touch me while you're complimenting? We don't want the evil eye to haunt us tonight, do we?"

His soft, slow kiss tasted like peppermint. He took my arm and escorted me down the steps to the car, where I attempted to climb into his SUV with grace—not an easy feat in a short dress and three-inch heels.

Before he shut the door he said, "Fasten your seat belt."

I chuckled, proud of my familiarity with at least one of his movie references. "I know. 'Bumpy night.' Quoting *All About Eve* again?"

He got into the driver's seat and started the engine. "I was going to say 'because it's rush hour and we're late,' but nice call on the quote, kid. You're learning."

"We still have to pick up Robin."

"Already taken care of. I got caught in traffic and thought I might be late, so I asked Dave to pick her up."

"You didn't." I covered my eyes to block visions of Robin slamming the door in Dave's face. "You *know* she hasn't forgiven him for the two nights she spent in jail. I have to call her." I fumbled for my phone. "She'll have a fit if he comes to her door unannounced, Nick."

"Have faith, Liz. They'll work it out," he said, turning right on the boulevard. "It's only a drive downtown, and we'll take her home. I have something more important to tell you."

"Oscar?"

"The draw of the mystical is amazing. Oscar delivered. He couldn't wait to get his hands on the Malverde twine. Two River Gang members were paid ten thousand dollars to murder Paco, then five thousand to murder Teresa. There's another five thousand on the table for the next hit."

"The next?" I caught my breath. "Did he tell you who?"

Nick shook his head.

"Did Cansino contract the murders?"

"Oscar didn't know. Or wouldn't tell me. When I asked him about Cansino, he told me to leave. I gave Dave everything when we talked."

"This information doesn't incriminate Cansino. We need something that will link him to the murders, Nick."

"If he's the guy. We can start with Cansino's letter to Paco and work from there."

"Can't," I said. "I went back to the clinic to search for Cruz's résumé in Victor's office, and guess what? Both Cansino's and Gates's letters to Paco were gone. I bet whoever called Victor from the clinic the night of the wake took them."

"Or Victor went back to the clinic on Sunday and took the letters himself."

"I still have a huge problem believing Victor would disappear on his own or defraud Lucia. It just doesn't make any sense. But I am convinced Lucia needs legal protection. If she's willing, maybe Kitty Kirkland could assume legal power of attorney over her affairs while Dave and Bailey investigate Cansino and Victor."

"I like it. I'll talk to Lucia with you."

As Nick drove onto the ramp for the 110 South, Mom called with the first of her series of updates from the hotel: Dad and Kitty were at the bar schooling the bartender on how to mix martinis. The orchestra had arrived. Dilly and her husband were stuck in traffic. Cherries Betsy Koch and Suzette Carlson were setting up the sign-in table.

Nick turned on the CD player, and Ella Fitzgerald sang in the background while I volleyed Mom's calls and estimated how close we were to champagne. When Ella started the second verse of "Something's Gotta Give," Mom called again.

"I need you here now." Her voice rose two octaves. "The guests are arriving. Carmen's not here yet. What if Carmen disappeared, too? Should I give everyone their money back?"

"Calm down and check the lobby," I said.

I heard her say to Dad, "Walter, go down to the lobby. Liz wants you to see if Carmen is there yet." She kept me on the line while she snapped instructions to the banquet staff. Dad's voice interrupted her in the background, and Mom said, "She is? Did you tell her to meet me in the ballroom? Liz—are you close?"

"Pulling off the freeway now, Mom. See you in a few minutes."

Nick exited at 8th Street, turned right on Garland, then left onto 7th Street, less than a half mile east of Park Clinic and Botanica Rojas, and two blocks south of Good Samaritan Hospital. He parked on a side street. We ambled hand in hand around the corner to the front entrance of the hotel.

Flags waved above the portal of the white and red brick Mayfair Hotel towering fifteen stories under the first stars in the early evening sky.

Blithely smoking a cigarette outside the iron-filigreed glass entrance was last person I wanted to see first—my ex-husband Jarret. He leaned against the wall with smoke circling his sandy brown hair and black dinner jacket. A pale redhead in a vanilla strapless sheath cuddled against him, cooing in his ear.

Jarret grinned. "Knew I'd meet you two here tonight. How are you, Lizzie Bear? Nick?"

Nick tilted his chin. Jarret tilted his chin. Their friendliest exchange in months.

I forced a smile. Had to. "Thank you for coming. It means a lot to Mom," I said. She surely extracted a large donation from Jarret to attend; there were no freebies at the Cherries' functions.

"I couldn't miss one of Viv's parties. She always asks so nice." He took another drag and then crushed the cigarette beneath the sole of his polished black shoe. The redhead brushed her bangs away from her eyes and fluttered thick lashes at Jarret as if waiting to be introduced. Jarret ignored her.

I tucked my hand under Nick's arm. "We'll see you inside, Jarret."

"Save me a dance, Lizzie Bear."

Tall white orchids on glass tables lined the hotel foyer. Ahead, four frieze pillars drew my eyes from the deep green and black deco carpet up to the skylight, two stories above the long, elegant lobby. Guests in evening attire mingled between the old paintings and brass light fixtures on the walls and gathered around faded coral velour club chairs and small tables topped with brass reading lamps.

"I feel like I'm stepping into the past," I said.

Nick put his arm around me. "This hotel has a great history. Raymond Chandler set his short story, 'I'll Be Waiting,' in this lobby. And the first post–Academy Awards party was held here."

I loved that Nick knew things like that.

My heart did a happy skip when a suave, older gent wove toward us through the crowd, carrying himself like a statesman in a black suit, white shirt, and black tie. His wide smile crinkled cheeks tanned from days on the golf course. His warm brown eyes matched mine. And his thinning salt-and-pepper hair looked freshly cut and tamed for the occasion.

He greeted Nick then wrapped his arms around me in a bear hug. "Hello baby girl."

"You look very handsome tonight, Daddy," I said.

"Under duress, but anything to please your mother," he said. "So Nick, is this your first Cherry Twist fund-raiser?"

"Yes, sir," Nick said, warmly shaking Dad's hand.

"Stick with me, or Vivian will put you to work," Dad said. "There are two reasons the Cherry Twists pull off their charity functions so successfully. First, it's a family operation and they recruit their free help from within. Suzette's husband and his quartet provide the music. The grown kids and grandkids are put to work at check-in or in the kitchen. The rest of us do as we're told."

"What's your job?" Nick said.

Dad straightened his shoulders. "Dave and I run security, of course."

"And is Liz the house psychologist?"

I laughed. "Hardly. Who could analyze that bunch? I play agent-at-large, but because you bought tickets, I'm relieved from duty tonight."

"Happy to oblige." Nick turned to Dad. "And the second reason the Cherries are so successful at fund-raising?"

He crooked his finger for Nick to come in close. "The Cherries kept blackmail photos from their days on the Sunset Strip. The college boys they partied with in the free-love sixties are now prominent elder businessmen with reputations to protect, and fat checkbooks."

"Dad." I checked over my shoulder to see if anyone heard his joke and took it for fact.

"What?" Dad said. "We were all too drunk or otherwise incapacitated back then to remember. The Cherries are altruistic. They know how to rally their friends around worthy causes." He checked his watch. "We should go up to the ballroom. Have you heard from Victor?"

I gave him a quick update on the phone calls and the bank deposit. "What do you think, Dad?"

"Ridiculous. I'll be surprised if Victor is even alive." Dad, the ex–homicide detective, was never subtle. "The phone calls smell like a scam to me."

"Liz and I thought scam, too," Nick said. "But we don't have proof."

"What do you think about the money he deposited?" I said.

"A distraction," Dad said. "The money could be a smoke screen to create the illusion that Victor is involved, while the scammer tries to control the Rojas woman. Bad news. Victor is a good man. This is a real shame. Now I know why Viv came up with plan B for tonight. Come on, kids. If we don't get on the next elevator to the ballroom, we're all in big trouble."

I tucked elbows with the two handsomest men in the room, and we made our way through the growing throng of black suits and sequined dresses to the elevator bank. We crowded together into the back of the middle car. The elevator doors opened to the third-floor vestibule. Betsy Koch, one of the six Cherries, drafted her niece to check off our names at the sign-in table, and then we strolled through double doors into the ballroom.

The Cherries brought the 1920s feel of the lobby into the ballroom, creating a Jazz Age nightclub atmosphere. The crystal chandeliers were dimmed to low; small brass lamps pooled light on each of the twenty white-draped tables of ten. The waitstaff, sporting short white jackets over black slacks, filled water glasses. Guests congregated in corners or near the tables. Lines formed at the two bars on opposite sides of the room. The Boomer Jazz Quartet—a bass player, drummer, and saxophone player, with Cherry Suzette Carlson's husband on vocals and piano—played a soft rendition of "Night and Day" from the stage.

"I like Sinatra's version of 'Night and Day' the best," Dad said, leading us to a table next to the dance floor.

"Great Cole Porter song," Nick said. "Fred Astaire sang it to Ginger Rogers in *The Gay Divorcee*, nineteen thirty-four. 'Can I offer you anything? Frosted chocolate? Cointreau? Benedictine? Marriage?'"

I did a double take. I knew I looked good, but that good? "What?"

"Dialogue from the movie, Liz. Fred Astaire to Ginger Rogers," Nick said.

Fred and Ginger. Right.

Mom, resplendent in a champagne lace gown, waited at our table with four glasses of champagne. Kitty Kirkland, sleek and statuesque in a black tuxedo suit and white tie, and her petite wife, Quinn, in blue silk, joined us with champagne in hand. We toasted to a successful turnout, and then Nick and I took Kitty aside. After a brief recap, we asked if she could help us stabilize Lucia's legal affairs.

"I'd be happy to," Kitty said. "I have court in the morning but I could meet with Mrs. Rojas tomorrow afternoon if she's willing. You're certain she didn't assign legal power of attorney to Victor already?"

"We're not certain," I said. "But he's not showing himself to represent her. Can Lucia override an existing document?"

Kitty nodded. "I can draw up a revocation for her to sign and have it notarized. Then we draw up a new POA naming me, or whomever Mrs. Rojas chooses to speak for her. All contingent on her wishes, you understand."

"We understand," I said. "Thank you."

After she left, Nick and I searched through the crowd for Bailey. Three tables away, Jarret and the redhead chatted with a local councilman. Across the dance floor, Erica and Bernie Gates laughed with their tablemates. Dilly and Dewey Silva sat at the front table with Tony Torrico and Carmen while the band played "Mood Indigo" onstage.

"Raymon Cansino just arrived," I said, pointing to the entrance.

Cansino threw back his shoulders and wove through the throng of people, stopping and shaking hands as he worked the room.

Dave and Robin arrived at our table together—neither visibly angry, bruised, or beaten. Nick pulled Dave aside and cocked his head in Cansino's direction.

I was more concerned about Robin. "I'm so sorry. Nick and Dave didn't tell me about the change of plans or I would have stopped them."

"Don't worry," she said, smiling.

"Girls, you both look deliciously sublime tonight." Mom beamed with approval and took Robin's hand. "Come and say hello to Walter. Liz, dear, would you bring us some champagne?"

Mom had begun issuing her children orders at her parties as soon as Dave and I were old enough to carry in a tray of canapés. I called it her "Queen-gene" and wrote a psychology paper on it in school. Got an A.

I acquiesced to her command, leaving to fight my way through the crowd at the bar. When my turn came I ordered two champagnes, left a tip for the bartender, and turned smack into Raymon Cansino.

"You're Liz Cooper. I remember you from Paco Rojas's wake," he said.

I was curious who told him my name. "And you're Mr. Cansino."

"Call me Ray." He blocked my path, asked the bartender for a whiskey on the rocks, then went on. "Lucia is very fond of you. Just this morning she told me how helpful you've been since Paco died. Tragedy." He shook his head with a show of regret as genuine as the smile on the runner-up in a beauty pageant.

What was he up to?

"Did she?" I said, doubtful. "I'm sorry. She hasn't mentioned you to me."

He winced. "I think I understand why. She hasn't been herself since—well, it doesn't need to be said again. I thought I'd introduce myself to you, and say hello. It looks like Park Clinic drew a successful turnout tonight. Victor and Carmen should be pleased."

I nodded in agreement as my brain scrambled for a comeback. Cansino waved at someone over my shoulder, excused himself, and left me standing alone.

The noise level increased as the drinks flowed and the music played. When Bailey came into the ballroom, I caught his eye and signaled him to our table. I took my chair just as Betsy Koch's granddaughter, our waitress for the evening, put a plate of lettuce with a slice of tomato and three croutons at the setting. Nick, on my right, was about to take a bite of salad when I nudged him.

"Move over a seat," I said.

"Why?"

"Bailey's here."

"Good. He can sit there." Nick pointed his fork of lettuce at the empty seat to his right.

"No. Move over. Please. I want him to sit between Robin and me," I said. Nick still wasn't following. I tapped his shoulder and said softly into his ear, "I want to introduce Robin to Bailey."

"Oh." He rolled his eyes. "But Dave—"

"Is sitting on her other side. I know. Dave knows Matt. See? It's perfect. Scoot over and make room."

We executed the double seat switch. Bailey took the now-empty chair to my left next to Robin. Introductions were made and chitchat continued through the banquet chicken accompanied by boiled potatoes and green beans. Nick, Dave, Dad, and Bailey entertained the table with jokes through dinner. Robin giggled. Mom and Kitty gushed about the large turnout. And I ate my first decent meal since Saturday night. Things were going well.

"Cansino is at the table back in the corner," I said to Bailey.

"I saw. By the way, great chicken. Thanks for the invite." He set his napkin on his empty plate and excused himself to walk the room.

After he left, I leaned over to Robin. "What do you think? Cute, right? Want to go out with him?"

"He's charming." Her blush spread from her face all the way down to the ruffled neck of her peach gown. "But he's way ahead of you. He invited me to dinner Saturday night. Can you believe it? Lucia's spell worked in one night."

"Huh?" I swore I heard Bailey and Robin's entire conversation, little more than cordial introductions and some teasing with the rest of us. "He asked you out?"

"I was tempted to say yes. After all, he came with flowers," Robin said.

"Flowers? What flowers?"

"And the apology. You should have heard him, Liz. You're right. You're brother is cute. Especially when he's humble."

"My brother?" I said. "Dave? Asked you out?"

"Shhh. Keep your voice down." She glanced over her shoulder at Dave, and then back at me. "Yes. Who did you think I was talking about?"

"Matt Bailey."

"The detective who just left? He's nice, but he's not my type. I swear I never noticed how sweet your brother is when he tries," Robin said. "He *is* kind of cute."

Dave? Sweet? Charming? Cute? Lucia's love spell on Robin had taken an absurd turn. But I couldn't argue with the twinkle in Robin's eyes.

Dinner plates were cleared away for dessert. Mom glided to the podium, brought the room to attention, and then asked Carmen to come up onstage.

"Thank you, everyone, for coming tonight," Carmen said into the microphone. "People who live on the streets lack the most basic necessities. Your generosity this evening will make it possible for Park Clinic to provide the homeless of our neighborhood with a safe place to take a hot shower—a simple, affirming task we take for granted. Dr. Morales and I are deeply grateful for the support you have given Park Clinic. We, and our staff, salute you." She paused as the audience applauded. "Tonight I'm honored to introduce a special guest, a local athlete who has donated so much of his time to city programs for the homeless. He has graciously agreed to say a few words. Ladies and gentlemen, please welcome Los Angeles's favorite baseball pitcher, Jarret Cooper."

Nick and I lunged for the bottle of red wine at the same time.

Dad shrugged sheepishly at me. "Plan B."

Chapter Thirty-one

One pitch can shift the momentum of a baseball game, just as an act of kindness has the potential to change a life." Jarret charmed the audience from the stage, mixing compassion with easy humor. He was comfortable in front of a crowd, showing flashes of the confident, boyish athlete I married before the drugs, booze, and cynicism took their toll.

Jarret gave a version of the spiel he'd been using in public for years, tailored to suit the occasion. Carmen nodded appreciation as he lauded Park Clinic's contributions to the community. Mom smiled proudly. Dad, who hated speeches of any kind, fidgeted. Nick ate his cake and then started on the piece I left untouched.

Our waitress cleared away the dessert plates, stopping to whisper in my ear, "The kitchen staff is leaving soon but there's cake left in the walk-in if you want another piece later."

After Jarret left the stage to appreciative applause, the band began to play "Blame It on the Bossa Nova." Nick pushed back his chair, offering his hand. "Dance?"

"Love to," I said.

Dave, Robin, and my parents followed us onto the already crowded dance floor. When the band segued into "Sway," Dad started a round of dance-partner swapping. He danced with Carmen, Dave with Mom, and Tony with Erica Gates. Nick twirled Robin. I did the cha-cha with Dewey until Jarret tapped his shoulder to cut in.

"Thank you, young man," Dewey said. "She has too much energy for me."

Jarret slipped his hand around my waist, and we danced together in an easy, familiar rhythm. Dancing with him was like putting on old slippers—once fuzzy and warm, now cracked and worn out.

"Heard you need a place to live, Lizzie Bear." He let go of my waist, turned me, and brought me back.

"I'm looking at houses to buy," I said.

"With the bookworm?"

"On my own."

"I knew you'd get tired of him." He turned me again.

I twirled and came back. "Wrong. Nick and I are very happy. I need an investment."

"Sure, Lizzie Bear. Whatever you say. Move back in with me. It'll be like old times."

"I wouldn't use old times as a selling point if I were you. Plus, think of how awkward it would be at the breakfast table when Nick sleeps over."

"Dump him. Come back to me," Jarret said.

I chortled. "You're dreaming. Wake up."

When the band began to play "Just One of Those Things," Nick tapped Jarret's shoulder to cut in.

Jarret gave Nick a mocking bow, swept his hand in the air, and stepped aside. "Of course. This must be your song."

"A rescue mission. Liz looks pained," Nick said.

"Why wouldn't she, considering who her date is?" Jarret said.

Nick thumbed over his shoulder. "Your rent-a-model is looking for you."

"Did you hit on her and get turned down, Nickster?"

"Don't take the cut-in so hard," Nick said. "You have to be used to getting benched by now."

Neither one noticed when I left them exchanging verbal jabs on the dance floor, a show I knew too well and lacked the patience for tonight. Their bickering was a dance that had only a little to do with me. I craved familiar comfort. Sugar comfort, like the cake I missed at dinner. Nick and Jarret were still arguing as I detoured through the crowd and dodged behind the partition separating the kitchen door from the ballroom.

I pushed open the leather-padded swinging door and spotted the walk-in refrigerator at the back of the empty room, beyond the length of stainless-steel counters, stoves, and sinks. Unsure if it would lock behind me, I used a small round bar tray to prop the heavy refrigerator door open then flicked on the light switch inside. Six plates of frosted white cake were lined up like toy blocks on a shelf in the back. I swiped a finger of frosting for a taste. Cream cheese—my favorite. I leaned my shoulder against the refrigerator door, tucked the tray under my arm, balanced my cake plate in my hand, and turned off the light to ease my way out.

A voice echoed off the steel equipment. "Everything set? You know what to do?"

"Set. Cruz gave Lucia the new medication at eight," a familiar male voice said. "She'll be disoriented for a few hours."

I stopped, rigid. The voice was Tony Torrico's.

The first voice again: "I'll be back in an hour. Stay visible out there. Tell people you just saw me in the lobby. Where's the cop?"

"Talking to Carmen," Tony said.

"Watch the Cooper woman and the boyfriend. Stall them if they start to leave. I don't want them showing up while I'm with Lucia. Got it?"

"Just make it fast, Ray. I'll call if they leave."

"Not if. Make sure they don't. An hour, Tony. You keep them here until you see me back in the ballroom. You hear me?"

My bare arm was going numb on the cold steel. If I let the door close, the handle click would make noise. It was too late to walk out and pretend I didn't hear them. My shoulders began to shiver. I tried to turn my back to the door and let my dress act as a buffer between the metal and my skin. My body went from shiver to shake. The tray under my right arm bumped the door and slipped, bouncing to the concrete floor with a clatter.

The voices stopped. The refrigerator door flew open, throwing me off balance. A hand caught my arm and Raymon Cansino pulled me into the kitchen. Tony swore under his breath.

I held up the cake plate in my hand. "Whew, thanks. All that for a piece of cake. Thought I'd be trapped in that damned refrigerator for the rest of the night." I took a step toward the door. Cansino held my arm in a vise grip.

He took the cake plate and gave it to Tony. "Here's your excuse for being in the kitchen. I'll see you in an hour."

Tony cocked his head at me. "What about her?"

"Oh. She can go back into the ballroom and tell her friends everything she heard. What do you think, you moron? I'm taking her with me."

"No." I tried to wrench my arm from his grip. He held tighter.

"Let her go. I can't be part of this anymore," Tony said.

"Bullshit. You're in too deep to stop," Cansino said.

"But they'll look for her. What if someone saw her come in here?" Tony said.

Cansino shrugged. "So? They won't find her. Just get out there and cover for me."

When Tony opened the kitchen door, I drew in a breath to scream. In a flash, Cansino had my back to his chest with his left hand clamped on my mouth. He knocked the air out of me with a kidney punch. My knees buckled. He half dragged me to the service elevator as I kicked and pulled at his hands. The elevator door opened. Cansino pushed me inside. I bent over, wrapping my arms to my waist to ease the pain. Lucia's protection bracelet rubbed against my ribs.

I pulled the bracelet off my wrist and tossed it into the kitchen as the elevator door closed, hoping Nick would find it and connect it to Lucia—unlikely, but it was all I had. Cansino slapped me so hard my teeth jarred.

"Not anymore." His words were flat, without expression, like he was disciplining a disobedient dog.

"What are you going to do to Lucia?" I said.

"If I were you, I'd be worrying about myself."

The service elevator opened onto an unlit side street. Cansino covered my mouth again and dragged me out onto the sidewalk. A black Escalade with tinted windows idled at the curb. The bald, barrel-chested driver got out of the car and opened the back passenger door. Cansino forced me inside.

Victor Morales sat hunched in the backseat, unshaven and haggard under the dim interior light. His jaw looked swollen and bruised. His veined hands gripped the tops of his thighs.

The door slammed shut. The light went out. The door locked automatically. Cansino and the driver got in, and we pulled away from the curb.

I touched Victor's hand. "What happened to you?"

He looked at me through hollow eyes. "They're going to kill me and commit Lucia."

"Correction, Vic," Cansino said from the front seat. "Both you and your friend here will be alive until Lucia signs over her power of attorney to you, so you can sell me her building and sign the papers to commit her. After I deduct the five thousand cut everyone will assume you demanded before you disappeared, there will be enough cash from the sale to pay for a nice psychiatric hospital for the few days she has left."

"You're crazy. You won't fool anyone." I leaned against the door, pulled the handle, and pushed to no avail.

"Correction. Everyone knows Lucia Rojas is crazy. Her ridiculous hex made it easy for me. Her neighbors, along with Tony, will confirm to Social Services that she's unsound. And the law can't dispute the sale her respected doctor made using her power of attorney before he left town. I think nervous breakdown for Lucia, don't you?"

"No. I'm thinking insane greed." I turned to Victor. "Are you all right? Did he hurt you?"

"Vic here was our guest at Cruz's apartment," Cansino said. "We kept him busy. It would have been a shorter stay if you and your boyfriend would have left Lucia alone for me to complete my business with her." He turned to me from the front seat. "I think I might enjoy having you killed. You cost me time and money, Liz."

"How do you know who I am? I know Lucia didn't tell you."

"Oh, Tony told me everything about you and your family," he said as the car sped west on 7th Street.

And we know all about you, Cansino.

"Cruz DeSoto works for you?" When Cansino didn't answer me, I turned to Victor. "How did they convince you to hire her?"

"Tony gave me her résumé with Father Nuncio's falsified recommendation. Like a fool, I trusted him instead of checking her out myself. I believed him."

I chastised myself for ignoring my original instincts about Cruz. But criticism or regret wouldn't save Victor or me. I needed a plan. I wanted to keep Cansino disengaged from thinking about what he was going to do with Victor and me.

"What were the papers you went over with Lucia after the wake?" I said to Victor.

The confusion on his face confirmed Cruz had lied. The driver stopped for a light. I pulled back the button to open the blackened window. Locked.

"Through the miracle of good drugs and Vic's selfless cooperation, Lucia will sign papers tonight," Cansino said.

Victor said to me, "Tony called me to the clinic the night of Paco's wake. He offered me a five-thousand-dollar bribe to sell her building. I flat out told him I wouldn't do anything so unethical. We argued. I asked for his resignation. He pushed me, and knocked me out. I woke up in ropes in an apartment."

"You should have said yes," Cansino said.

"Have you been calling Lucia? Was that you who hung up on me Saturday?"

"There was a gun to my back," Victor said. "They made me say things to keep her trust but make her seem delusional to you and Nick. They threatened to hurt Carmen if I didn't do what I was told." He knitted his brow. "How is she? How is Lucia?"

"Carmen's good. Lucia is tougher than she seems." I turned to Cansino. "Why tonight?"

"Thanks to the fund-raiser, I know where Lucia's friends are for a few hours. No one will be making another surprise visit."

Suddenly I understood his bizarre introduction to me earlier. *He was making sure Carmen, Nick, or I saw him there to use us for his alibi.*

"The power of attorney and transfer of deed are predated," Cansino said. "See, everyone will be told that Vic sold me the building the night of his buddy Paco's wake, deposited his finder's fee in his bank account the next morning, and then . . ." He spread his arms and shrugged. "Disappeared. The same way you're going to disappear, Liz."

Cansino didn't know his ruse wouldn't hold. I found the

building deed days after the alleged transfer. Nick would know the dates were falsified. Cansino's next real estate transaction would be a move to jail. I just had to stay alive to enjoy it.

"You murdered Paco and Teresa for a building?" I said.

"I don't murder people," Cansino said with his finger to his chest. "I present my men profitable opportunities to remove obstacles for me. Paco was stubborn and too old to live. The Suarez woman should have minded her own business instead of opening her mouth to you."

Tony. He must have been listening in the hall while Teresa and I talked. "Tony took your letter to Paco from Victor's office."

"Oversight that, thanks to you, Tony caught. He's a good man," Cansino said.

Good man my ass. "What's in this for him?"

"You're damned talkative for a dead woman," Cansino said. "Tony will get his cut."

The driver stopped the car in front of Botanica Rojas. I looked across the street for Tattoo Neck and his friends, supposedly watching the building for Nick. The sidewalks were empty. I couldn't see anything in the dark mini-mall lot past the cement wall. And the chance of Nick finding Lucia's protection bracelet, deciphering the clue, and then finding me was next to nil.

Cansino said to the driver, "Stay close and out of sight. I'll call you when we're done. Meet us in the back." He dialed his cell phone. "I'm outside, Cruz. Get ready to buzz us in."

Appealing to Cansino's conscience (he didn't have one) or his compassion (he lacked attachment) wouldn't save Victor, Lucia, or me. I climbed the steps to Lucia's apartment with Cansino's gun pressed to the small of my back.

Chapter Thirty-two

Cruz flashed Cansino a questioning look when she saw me behind Victor on the stairs.

"Get inside and do what you're told." Cansino pushed the gun barrel deeper into my back and we filed into the dark apartment.

The votives surrounding Paco's photo, his ash-filled urn, and a massive porcelain bowl on the altar shed the only light in the room. The flames flickered when Cruz shut the door behind us. Lucia slumped in a chair at the dining table. Her head lolled as she tried to look up. Victor rushed in, kneeling at her side. Cansino pushed me into the armchair.

"Why is it so dark in here? Turn on a light and get me the deed before she passes out," Cansino said.

Cruz flipped the switch on the wall next to the desk, flooding the room with overhead light. She opened the desk drawer and handed Cansino the yellowed paper.

Cansino removed another packet of papers from his inside jacket pocket and sat next to Lucia, touching her sleeve for attention. "Hello, Lucia. It's Ray. Paco's friend. This won't take long then you can go to bed. Victor is here. He's going to take care of you now. You do what Victor tells you, and everything is going to be okay."

Lucia seemed bewildered, her face sallow under the glare of the overhead light.

The phone was footsteps from me on the desk, but Cruz stood sentry in the middle of the room. I had ten pounds on that wiry thing with a smug smile. I knew I could get her out of the way to make a leap for the phone. But the gun hidden at Cansino's side was the big fat neutralizer.

"Who are you? Who's here?" Lucia slurred her words, squinting at Victor, Cansino, and then at me.

Cansino pressed the gun to Victor's back.

"It's Victor, Lucia. I'm here." He brushed a strawberry curl off her forehead.

She gave him a loopy grin, then glanced over his shoulder at me. "Is that Teresa?"

Paco's photo on the altar behind her gave me an idea. Manipulative, but I was desperate. "Yep, it's me, Teresa," I said. "Paco brought me up for dessert."

The hopeful light in her eyes and the sweetness in her smile choked my lying heart with guilt.

"Paco?" Lucia pressed her hands to the table and tried to stand. "Where? I can't see him. Paco?"

With my heart breaking and my nerves shot, I said, "He doesn't want you to sign any papers."

Cansino bolted out of his chair. He pulled me up and squeezed my chin between his thumb and forefinger, his face so close I felt the spittle of his hiss. "Shut up or you're out the window with a bullet in your head."

Odd thing, knowing he would kill me anyway: defiance overshadowed fear.

"How messy, Ray. Who do you think would get to the front door first? Your driver or the police?" I said.

He pushed me into the bathroom and held the door closed until I heard something shoved under the doorknob.

I flipped on the bathroom light and leaned against the door, shaken. I couldn't just stand there, cowering. Cansino needed Victor and Lucia to sign the POA and deed. I was an unnecessary and inconvenient liability.

I wasn't going to wait for Cansino to come in and shoot me. My only hope was to rile Lucia enough to delay his plan until, or if, Nick and Dave figured out where I was. Fat chance. Nick was probably still arguing with Jarret. If I made enough noise, maybe I could prevent Cansino from getting what he came for—signed papers. Then what? Didn't know. Didn't have time to think about it.

No window. Damned old bathroom had no window. The medicine chest. I rifled through bandages, toothpaste, mouthwash, Paco's shaving cream, plastic razors, and came out with Lucia's long metal nail file. In the cabinet under the sink I found Epsom salts, boxes of soap, a heating pad, and an aerosol can of men's extra-strength deodorant. I tried the spray nozzle. A failed drizzle. Back to the medicine chest for a safety pin. I scraped the nozzle hole with the pin, rinsed the nozzle, then tried again. A hearty spray.

A metal pole rested between the walls in C-shaped slots and held the shower curtain over the tub. I took off my shoes, stood in the tub, lifted the pole out of the slots, and removed the curtain. The pole was too long to use as a weapon, but I had the curtain to work with. They don't teach this stuff at scout camp.

With deodorant in one hand and the file in the other, I started talking through the door. "Lucia, remember the hex. The hex brought Paco's killer here. Don't trust anyone, Lucia. Don't listen to them."

I heard Cansino. "Cruz, shut her up. Now!"

A chair scraped across the floor. Footsteps. I held the deodorant can and braced the door so it wouldn't push open. I didn't want skinny Cruz. I wanted Cansino.

She pushed against the door. I pushed back, shouting, "Get help, Lucia. Don't trust them."

I heard a rustle, another chair scraping, and footsteps crossing the room. Cansino came closer, swearing. I moved to the side and flattened myself against the wall in case he shot through the door. The door flew open. I hit the deodorant nozzle, releasing a stream of extra-strength in Cansino's face.

He groped at his eyes. I jabbed the nail file into the hand holding the gun. I grabbed the loose shower curtain off the sink. I threw the open curtain on him and shoved him into the hall with all the strength I had. He lost his balance and fell. I darted for the desk phone, three steps away. Cansino tore off the curtain and lunged for my ankle. I pitched flat to my stomach, kicking at his head and shoulders with my free leg.

The gun skidded across the floor. Victor went for it. Cruz got there first. She pointed the gun at Victor, and he froze.

"I said no more." Cansino yanked me by my hair to my feet.

Lucia slowly pushed herself up from the table. She reached for the porcelain dish on the altar. I struggled against Cansino to distract him and the others. With hands shaking, Lucia swung the dish against the back of Cruz's skull. Cruz stumbled forward. Victor wrenched the gun from her hand. He aimed the weapon at Cruz and Cansino.

Cansino whipped me around and locked his forearm against my throat. Using me as a shield, he stepped toward Victor. "Put the gun down."

Victor didn't move. Cansino pressed tighter against my throat, edging me forward. I couldn't breathe. The room began to swirl.

The front door flew open. Dave and Bailey stood at the threshold, firearms drawn.

"LAPD. Put down the gun," Dave said to Victor. Then to Cansino, "Let her go."

Victor set Cansino's gun on the table and raised his hands in surrender. Cansino released me and backed away. Nick rushed into the apartment, catching me in his arms as I wobbled, woozy.

I looked up at him. "Fashionably late."

Chapter Thirty-three

As Lucia's apartment filled with men in LAPD blue, I assured Bailey, Dave, and Nick that despite the gun he aimed at me earlier, Victor was a victim. Bailey took our statements. Patrolmen handcuffed Cansino and Cruz.

Cansino tossed his head in insolence as he and Cruz were led away for transport to the Rampart Community Police Station to be booked for Assault and Battery, Kidnapping, and Conspiracy to Defraud. Dave phoned in an order to pick up Tony Torrico for questioning, and he requested an ambulance to take Lucia to the hospital for observation.

Lucia was curled up in the armchair, still disoriented from the unknown drug Cruz administered via Tony. I crouched next to her and said, "You did good, Lucia. I don't know how you found the energy, but you stopped Cruz."

She managed a wan smile. "Paco told me to. We didn't like her. You saw him, didn't you? He was here."

I took her hand, nodding as I glanced at Paco's photo on the altar.

The EMTs arrived and carried Lucia out on a stretcher with Victor by her side.

I collected my shoes out of the bathtub and checked my reflection in the mirror. *What a piece of work.* My left cheek and throat were red; my arm, ribs, and both legs ached. Soon parts of me would become as lavender as my ruined chiffon and lace dress.

Nick came into the bathroom and grinned at me in the mirror. "You're still beautiful."

"You're looking through the eyes of—"

"Love." He kissed my neck gently. "Let's get you home."

I flushed, bruised cheek and all. "Nick, how did you find the bracelet so fast? And figure out my clue? You're amazing."

"I know." He straightened his tie in mock pride then squinted. "What clue?"

"The protection bracelet. I threw it into the kitchen when Cansino pulled me in the service elevator. Isn't that how you knew where I was?"

"No. That would be a little obscure, even for me."

"Then how did you all know to come here? I didn't see anyone watching the building."

"You weren't supposed to see them—no one was. I didn't trust Oscar to keep his mouth shut after he told me there'd be another hit. I paid Teresa's pals to stay out of sight. When I got the call on the dance floor saying my *chica* got out of a black Escalade and went upstairs with two men, I grabbed Dave and Bailey, and we came to join your party. You didn't save us refreshments, I see."

"We had punch," I said. "So the protection bracelet was meaningless, as predicted."

"Or Lucia's spell ensured that the boys outside saw you," Nick said.

"You didn't notice when I disappeared from the fundraiser? Some date you are."

He winced. "Sorry. Not right away. Your mother asked me to dance after you left the floor. When the music ended I thought you were in the restroom or went down to the lobby."

"My mother wanted to dance with you?"

Nick laughed. "Instead of Jarret. I call that progress."

"I call it a miracle. Congratulations."

The next night Victor, Carmen, Robin, Dave, Nick, and I gathered in my parents' living room with wine and hors d'oeuvres to celebrate.

Victor, rested and dapper again, sat on the couch with Carmen and described his five days of captivity. "I was tied to the bed every night. First, my captors wouldn't talk to me. Cansino came the second night to force me to call Lucia. By Friday, the gang members were drinking and bragging about how they killed Paco. They paid José Saldivar to befriend Teresa and walk her home for a week. Then they broke the lock on the Rojases' downstairs door and lay in wait for Paco to step out on the sidewalk with José and Teresa. They counted on the police to view the drive-by shooting as revenge on Teresa and her lover. Paco would be collateral damage."

"A lot of *ifs* in the plan," Nick said. "What if Paco had the lock fixed right away and gave Teresa a key?"

"They weren't in a hurry. Cansino paid them to watch until the opportunity presented itself," Victor said.

"Cansino assumed the grieving widow would sell?" Dad said.

"Tony assured him she'd be vulnerable. Neither of them knew I would have power of attorney over her affairs," Victor said.

"Until Tony heard you talk about it at the wake," I said. "That must have changed their plan and triggered them into action against you. But what about Cruz? Who is she?"

"I can answer that," Dave said. "She's the only one who didn't lawyer up before questioning. Cruz DeSoto is an illegal from Guatemala. She was a nurse down there and came here to earn money to send home. She ended up as Torrico's housekeeper. They paid her a thousand dollars above her caretaker salary to stay with Lucia and report to Torrico every day."

"I realized Tony tricked me into hiring her the first night Cansino made me call Lucia. Cruz answered the phone and told Lucia I was on the line with Paco." Victor closed his eyes. "I believed Tony. I trusted him."

Carmen took his hand. "We both did, Victor. He was a good doctor."

"How could someone like Tony Torrico fall in with someone like Raymon Cansino?" Mom said.

"They go back a long time. They were in the same high school class, and they belong to the same golf club for starters," Dave said. "I'm still digging."

"Was the developer in on this with Cansino, too?" I said.

Dave shook his head. "We talked to Wright this morning. He offered full cooperation in Cansino's investigation, including the circumstances of the sale of both buildings next door to the Rojases'. If there was intimidation involved on either side, we'll uncover it. The LAPD Real Estate Fraud Unit has been eyeing Cansino for a while. For now, he and Torrico will sit in jail for kidnapping."

"And for elder abuse," Nick said.

"I'm alive because Liz and Nick cared so much about Lucia," Victor said. "Their daily unannounced visits ruined Cansino's plan to pressure Lucia. Cansino didn't know when you two would show up. He made the move last night because he knew where you would be for a few hours. The fund-raiser gave both Cansino and Torrico an alibi while she signed the papers. Then Lucia was supposed to be admitted to a psychiatric hospital, using my signature on the commitment papers. I'm afraid to think about what they were going to do with me."

"What will happen to Lucia now?" Robin said.

"When she gets out of the hospital, she'll have a professional nurse with her—a real one—until Lucia decides what she wants to do." Carmen turned to me. "Kitty told me what you and Nick suggested. Victor and I talked with Lucia this afternoon. We agreed it made more sense to have Kitty assume Lucia's legal POA while Victor maintains her medical POA."

"And if the stream of women visitors who visited Lucia at the hospital today is any indication, the neighborhood will forgive and forget the hex," Victor said. "She won't be alone."

Nick and I exchanged knowing grins. Father Nuncio rallied his people.

Carmen squeezed Victor's hand. "And we can get back

to making our clinic better than ever. I think you'll like Dr. Ashworth. She reminds me of Liz."

I glanced away, downhearted. My career remained in jeopardy.

"I think we need more wine." Carmen got up and started to the kitchen. "Liz, come help me."

I followed her, knowing Carmen didn't need my help to uncork a bottle. And she was as familiar with Mom's kitchen as I was. She opened the pantry door, took out two bottles, and lowered her voice. "I had a conversation with Bernie and Erica Gates last night."

My shoulders sank.

Carmen took my hand. "You want to hear this, sweetie. When Bernie and I were dancing he asked if I knew you or your husband. He called you Mrs. Garfield. Bernie had no idea who you were, or that you worked at the clinic. When I left the dance floor, I asked to speak to Erica in private. She admitted Bernie didn't know she was in therapy or that you were a therapist."

"That doesn't excuse my actions, Carmen. I never should have gone to Bernie's office with Nick. Erica has a right to be angry," I said.

"I mentioned a complaint to the California Board of Psychology would require time and statements from her. I gently suggested that her privacy is more precious than retribution," Carmen said. "She relented, and rescinded her complaint, Liz."

All my tension drained. I sighed, relieved. "Thank you, Carmen. I'm very grateful, but I'm so sorry I put you in a position to defend me. Maybe the Park Clinic Wellness Group should make a new start with a different counselor."

"I'll miss you," Carmen said.

"I'll help you find someone wonderful," I said.

After dinner and Mom's strawberry shortcake, Robin stood to leave. "I love being here with you all, but I have to be at the office early."

Dave, Nick, and I followed suit with apologies. As the four of us ambled to the street, Dave stopped Robin. "So? Will you have dinner with me Saturday night?"

"I don't know," Robin said with a teasing grin.

"C'mon. Give me a chance," Dave said. "A nice restaurant, a little wine—"

"Go *out*? I'll never drive anywhere with you again, Dave Gordon. When I got in your car last October, I wound up in jail. Last night you left me stranded to find my own ride home from a hotel in the middle of who-knows-where-ville. There is no way I'm getting in a car with you."

"I left to help Liz." Dave turned around. "Nick?"

"You're on your own. She has a point," Nick said.

"You're a big help. What if I bring dinner to your house, Robin?" Dave spread his hands. "You have to admit, I can't desert you at home."

"I refuse to eat takeout for dinner." Robin kept walking. "Maybe I'll cook."

Wednesday afternoon Nick parked behind Dilly Silva's car across the street from the empty house in Studio City. Dilly waited in front of the mass of overgrown trees and shrubs blocking the two-story bungalow. I took Nick's hand and led him across the street.

"Is there a house in there?" he said, shielding his eyes from the sun as he peered through the thicket.

"Give it a chance," I said.

We crunched over dead leaves and dirt to the front porch. A big bay window blocked by torn drapes was to the left of the door. The sash windows on the right were covered with newspaper.

Dilly unlocked the heavy wooden door. "The owner died a year ago, intestate—no will. Ownership was awarded to an out-of-state relative, and the property literally just went on the market. Despite the way it looks, the listing agent told me that the roof, plumbing, and electricity were upgraded in the past five years. She claims the place just needs some cosmetics like paint and a gardener. I recommend a plastic surgeon."

Afternoon sun filtered throughout the vacant rooms. We wandered into the living room with its depressing beige and green damask wallpaper. The brick fireplace on the far wall showed flecks of white paint under soot. I meandered from room to room. The dining room was covered in sad brown wallpaper with a peach and beige dogwood pattern. The old-fashioned kitchen had original 1940s tile but no appliances. The downstairs half bath was an uncompleted home-improvement disaster of cheap fixtures and silver vinyl wall covering. Upstairs were two small bedrooms plus the master with a fireplace and two windows. The adjoining bathroom had a linoleum floor, an ancient sink, and a rusted tub.

Nick studied each nook, inspected every corner, checked

the view from every window, and opened each door and built-in cabinet. Dilly brushed dirt off her pink tweed suit and tsk-ed from room to room. I saw walls coming down, new paint and fixtures, a fire in both fireplaces, and polished floors.

Alone on the back porch, I watched a hummingbird pass the lemon tree in the corner of the overgrown and deserted backyard. I imagined squeezing lemons for lemonade in the big kitchen and laughed. *Me? Make lemonade from scratch?* I was still smiling when Nick came out.

"I like it here," I said.

"I think it has good bones, but it needs a lot of work," he said.

I looked up at Nick. "So do I. Maybe that's why I feel at home."